**PRAISE FOR**
*AN UNSEEMLY WIFE*

"Moore writes with lyrical beauty about a marriage that is at once bound by love and the customs of their faith and times, and challenged by opposing dreams for the future. I fell in love with Ruth and her family, was gripped by her fortitude through dark days, and held my breath to the heart-stopping end!"

—Juliette Fay, author of *Shelter Me* and *Deep Down True*

"Moore has created a breathtaking epic of an Amish family venturing forth in a most un-Amish way to pursue the American dream, gaining and losing much in the process. A transporting, dramatic, and thoughtful read—just the way I like them."

—Nichole Bernier, author of *The Unfinished Work of Elizabeth D.*

"E. B. Moore's *An Unseemly Wife* is absolutely top-notch historical fiction, illuminating as if with rays of sun an American landscape as cruel as it is lush, as harsh as it is hopeful. This story of Ruth and her Amish family's westward migration is an emigrant tale with a twist that will wring your heart—you'll never, ever forget it. I couldn't look away from this novel, and its characters will live with me always. An absolutely beautiful, harrowing book."

—Jenna Blum, author of *The Stormchasers* and *Those Who Save Us*

*continued . . .*

"In *An Unseemly Wife*, E. B. Moore takes us on what at first seems a familiar journey by covered wagon toward the American West. But Ruth Holtz is no ordinary heroine. She and her husband and young children are Amish who have broken with their Order, yet strive to remain separate from their 'English' fellow travelers. In that cleft lies Ruth's darkest challenge. Navigating the wagon trail toward Idaho turns out to be easier than navigating the shifting loyalties of family and fellow travelers. Ruth's ordeal is delivered in language so attentive, sensuous, and unflinching that its brutality catches the reader unaware. *An Unseemly Wife* is a disquieting tale of dreams and delusions, community and separation, loyalty and betrayal. Ultimately, Ruth is a survivor among survivors: a woman who, despite the seismic shifts in her world, stands tenaciously at her own center."

—Kathy Leonard Czepiel, author of *A Violet Season*

"*An Unseemly Wife* is one of those rare novels of beauty and darkness, transfixing us with a place few can imagine and a narrator as fierce as she is true. Ruth's journey may emerge from another century, but her failures in faith and love are our own—as are her triumphs. E. B. Moore creates a world with the slightest strokes of a pen, and the story's ghosts will remain with you long after you close the book."

—Michelle Hoover, author of *The Quickening*

"In *An Unseemly Wife*, E. B. Moore walks the rare tightrope of artistry, writing this harrowing and gripping novel with exquisite care and detail, putting into sharp relief the story of an Amish family crossing the country by wagon."

—Randy Susan Meyers, bestselling author of *The Murderer's Daughters* and *The Comfort of Lies*

# AN
# UNSEEMLY
# WIFE

*E. B. Moore*

NEW AMERICAN LIBRARY

New American Library
Published by the Penguin Group
Penguin Group (USA) LLC, 375 Hudson Street,
New York, New York 10014

USA | Canada | UK | Ireland | Australia | New Zealand | India | South Africa | China
penguin.com
A Penguin Random House Company

First published by New American Library,
a division of Penguin Group (USA) LLC

First Printing, October 2014

[N̲A̲L̲] REGISTERED TRADEMARK—MARCA REGISTRADA

LIBRARY OF CONGRESS CATALOGING-IN-PUBLICATION DATA:
Moore, E. B. (Elizabeth B.)
An unseemly wife/E. B. Moore.
p. cm.
ISBN 978-0-451-46998-4
1. Amish—History—19th century—Fiction. 2. Wagon trains—Idaho—History—19th century—Fiction. 3. Wagon train—West—Fiction. 4. Frontier and pioneer life—Idaho—Fiction. 5. Idaho History 19th century—Fiction. I. Title.
PS3613.O5553U58 2014
813'.6—dc23      2014000348

Printed in the United States of America
1  3  5  7  9  10  8  6  4  2

Set in Stemple Garamond
Designed by Elke Sigal

*For*
*my mother,*
*who told me the Plain stories;*
*and when she lost her memory,*
*I retold them to her*

## ACKNOWLEDGMENTS

My many thanks to Alice Tasman at the Jean V. Naggar Literary Agency for her unflagging belief in my story and to Tracy Bernstein at New American Library, who picked up the novel with equal enthusiasm.

To my constant first reader, Priscilla Fales, and my children, Brad, Cally, and Sarah Moriarty, who listened to the telling and retelling of the "wagon of death" until they wanted to scream.

To Philip Gambone, who encouraged me to go back to school in my advancing years, as well as to Yaddo and the Vermont Studio Center for months of uninterrupted writing.

To the many people at the Joiner Center, especially those in my long-term poetry group: Susan Nisenbaum Becker, Ann Killough, Frannie Lindsay, and Christine Tierney.

To the many at Grub Street Writers, starting with Jenna Blum, who lured me into attempting a novel; the Novel Incubator creators and inspirational teachers Michelle Hoover and Lisa Borders; and my Incubator classmates, who helped me focus as never before: Belle Brett, Amber Elias, Jack Ferris,

## Acknowledgments

Kelly Ford, Marc Foster, Rebecca Taylor, Emily Ross, Rob Wilstein, and Jennie Wood.

To my weekly Cambridge Writers, who continue to hold my feet to the fire, seven pages at a time: Sheila Finn, Lallie Lloyd, Frances McQueeney-Jones Mascolo, Louise Olson, and Sandra Shuman.

And to my Grub offshoot group, who have the knowledge, devotion to craft, and the fortitude to read on demand a whole novel start to finish: Nichole Bernier, Kathy Crowley, Juliette Fay, and Randy Susan Meyers.

There is in every true woman,
a fire, dormant
in the light of prosperity,
which blazes the dark hour.

—*A found poem taken from
the writings of Washington Irving*

# An Unseemly Wife

# PART I

By Land Possessed

## CHAPTER 1

Fall 1867

A shadow on the sun should have marked the day the way God marked Cain, a warning to Ruth her quiet world would soon be cast asunder. But that September morning, sunlight flooded the orchard ripe with peaches, pears, and apples, their scent carried on a breeze through Ruth's kitchen window. She savored the smell, and, black sleeves pushed above her elbows, she worked a ball of dough in steady rhythm.

A wisp of hair strayed from her white prayer cap and dangled in her face. With a flour-smeared wrist she brushed the brown strands aside. Her glance happened out the window to the dooryard, past the white barn, to the spread of gently rolling fields cut by the lane, and there they were on horseback, man and boy. Not Plain, not any sort of Amish—*English*, in their sorrel-colored pants and shirts, the man with red-veined cheeks, his hairless chin smooth as his son's, the two of them on the road. They paused at the end of her lane.

Blood surged within her, and she swelled, protective as a she-bear. "*Mein Gott.*" Ruth dropped the dough. She moved fast to the door of their fieldstone house, made herself flat against the frame, and peered out. "Not a peep," she said to Esther. Her three-year-old sat cross-legged on the kitchen floor, a doll in her lap, the doll in black dress, apron, and shawl.

Ruth pursed full lips, her rounded cheeks flattening. The tip of her nose felt cold. Her Opa had warned her against English. He'd told stories of hooded men in the Old Country, their torture rooms and his escape across the ocean.

Here, the dreaded *Them* rode hatless, fancy collars and buttons down the front of their shirts. These two, the first English ever to step on their land, hers and Aaron's, pristine Lancaster farmland.

Granted, these English came without hoods and thumb-screws; nevertheless, having them at her door gave Ruth a chill.

She put a finger to her lips. "*Shhh.*" She wished Aaron in from the barn, where he'd been all morning. The boys were safe in the woods, Daniel, responsible at eleven, sent to watch Joseph and Matthew collecting nuts.

"Stay away from Gropa's oak," she'd told them. Who'd have thought the ancient tree climbed high would be a lesser danger than those close to home?

The English guided their horses into the lane. Ruth leaned toward Esther, her voice urgent. "Stay in the house." The strings of her white cap flying, she left the child working on the doll's bonnet, latched the door, and, unmindful of floured hands, clutched her skirts as she rushed to the barn. She'd head the English off, but she needed Aaron.

Ruth stopped in the tack room doorway, one eye on *Them*, and hissed toward the stalls. "Aaron."

Thank God Joseph and Matthew weren't in the yard. Too curious by half, what would they do faced with hatless English? They might talk to them.

Hallooing, the English reined in. Aaron came from deep in the barn, handed Ruth his pitchfork, and ducked under the lintel. He smoothed his beard and brushed straw from his black clothes.

Ruth gripped the fork's handle and stood behind the door, her nose pressed to the cool hinge. She watched through the gap. If the English made a move toward the house, she'd . . . she'd what? Stab them with the pitchfork?

She set the long handle against the wall. Aaron would deal with this intrusion. She listened to pigs snuffling in the barn and felt their restlessness, a change in the air to match the change in her body. Aaron, too, had been off his feed for months now, as if *he* were the one blessed with new life in his innards.

From his horse, the English looked down at Aaron and said, "People say you raise the best horses."

So it was voiced throughout the Plain community, but it was something Aaron never claimed. On his tongue, the words would be prideful. A sin. He took pleasure in the raising and training as Ruth did, their work blessed with accomplishment.

"Do they?" Aaron said. He waited, square beard below his collarbones, no smile softening the line of his smooth upper lip.

Uninvited, the English slid from his saddle. "We're going west," he said, with a satisfied air. "Lock, stock, the wife, and three boys." He spread his arms. "I've a big wagon, and nothing to pull it."

Aaron, hat in hand, passed the flat brim through his fingers.

"Uncle's out there," the boy offered from his horse. He was maybe nine, like Joseph. "Got a thousand acres. Idaho land, beats Pennsylvania hollow."

"Free land, stake it and it's yours," the man said. "A government promise."

Aaron's shoulders twitched, his usual answer to something laughable. Government. Aaron and Ruth's people had nothing to do with government, never would.

The man nattered on. "Apples, peaches, and apricots"—whatever those were—"all big as the boy's head."

Aaron eyed the boy and grunted. "Did you see?" Aaron said. "Your own eyes?"

"Sure. Couldn't risk the family on hearsay."

Behind the door, Ruth kept her hand to her mouth. Oh, those English.

"What's your land?" With a swing of his arm, the man took in Aaron's fields. "Seventy-five, a hundred acres? Nothing to what's out there." He swaggered toward Aaron. "Got to get moving 'fore it's gone."

"Won't be gone." The boy slouched in his saddle. "There's lots."

"So they said in '49." The English gave Aaron a knowing look. "And where's the gold now?" He took Aaron's sleeve. "I need horses."

Aaron withdrew his arm and started toward the pasture. Still talking, the English followed, spreading his hands bigger and bigger to illustrate whatever his mouth announced. Aaron nodded, a matter of politeness, Ruth assumed.

She nipped to the house and hovered by the door, an eye on Esther and one on the field where Aaron showed horse after horse, smoothing his hand down a haunch, rubbing tendons, exposing the frog on a hoof of each horse.

The men came back to the dooryard, the English all a-chatter, leaning close to Aaron. Aaron shifted away and inclined his hat as a buffer. Finally the man mounted his mare. He and the boy turned toward the road.

At that moment, Ruth's three littles in black pants, jackets, and low-crowned hats broke from the woods. They ran across the stubble field toward Aaron. Joseph in the lead, always in the lead despite his short leg. His built-up boot clumped the ground.

Out of breath, Matthew lagged behind. He worked his stocky five-year-old legs. Behind him, Daniel, the eldest, walked with the bag of nuts. Joseph raced into the dooryard. "Papa, who's that?"

The English looked back.

"Hurry," Ruth said. She calmed her voice. "In the house." She pushed Joseph along. "It's near dinner. Esther's waiting."

Joseph balked. He shaded his eyes at the sky. "Not by the sun," he said. Nine, and he questioned most everything.

"*Verrückt*," Aaron said. "The man's crazed—you should've heard him."

Ruth checked the lane once more. The English, their backs to her, gained the road and set off at a trot. To her left, the noon

7

sun fell on the orchard where branches burdened with ripe fruit bent toward the ground. This abundance, Ruth and Aaron's reward for loving care, had been a blessing, but today the blessing weighed on her, as if their overflowing cup might exact a toll.

❧

A week passed, and Aaron's sister Anna bore her eleventh child, a son. Ruth dropped all thoughts of English.

Anna couldn't hide her disappointment. She'd made no bones of wanting a girl, and, oddly, Aaron seemed to share her distress.

His nights grew fitful.

By day, he walked the farthest hedgerows of the farm and scratched his head. He ignored weeds flourishing around the dooryard fence posts. Paint peeling on the barn went unscraped until Ruth did it herself and brushed on whitewash.

He counted his sheep, then ignored them as they overgrazed the field. He traveled the county talking to whom, she didn't quite know. He held his own bubbling council.

"Aaron," she'd start. "Shouldn't we . . . ?" And he'd walk away midsentence as if he hadn't heard. At moments he seemed a different person.

Ruth moved the sheep to their upper forty, where alfalfa grew knee high. What could these unknown people be telling him?

One restless bedtime with Ruth beside him, he lay on his back, arms folded across his chest. "Another child," he said. "What will they do?"

"Your sister has a son—aren't you happy? Wouldn't you want one?"

"Yes," Aaron said. "But when he's grown, he'll need a farm of his own. What then?"

He worried about Anna the way Ruth's brother Dan'l worried about her. Family. She knew the pull, the sweet ache, love wrapping them warm and safe.

"Acreage," Aaron said. "They need acreage." He rolled on his side and tapped her hand.

"I'm listening," she said and bent her head, her long braid falling between them.

"They've a scant seventy." He twined work-worn fingers in hers. "A farm for each son—they'll sit cheek by jowl. They best think ahead."

"How?" Ruth said. "Stop babies?"

"No." Aaron laughed. "Only old age does that." He stretched and pulled her against his body. "English would say go west."

"*Verrückt*," Ruth said. "They're crazed—you said so yourself."

Aaron nuzzled Ruth's neck. "I'm crazed for you," he said and kissed behind her ear. Pink surged from lobe to crest. She couldn't hide her feelings if she wanted to. This man, the Aaron she knew and loved.

"Ahh," he said.

A warm shiver took her, and she curled into the scent of him, myrrh and aloes. How she treasured the touch of his fingers at the back of her neck, his nuzzle, his heated breath as he whispered loving words. Words she'd be embarrassed to repeat.

Where would she be without him, his guiding hand at her back, the strength of his arms around her, their devotion like a stone bridge built rock by rock. Without him her world would be rubble. But why think it? She arched against him, losing herself in the surge of their bodies.

⁂

Two evenings later, the English returned with money. Aaron gave horses in trade; they had little use for money.

Ruth stayed in the shadows of the barn milking Bathsheba, the smell of hay and warm milk rising around her. The man didn't leave. He and Aaron lingered by the stalls, where she heard the talk talk talk he stuffed in Aaron's ear.

As the cow chewed her cud, the man made the westward trek sound simple, over the river and through the woods to Pittsburgh, as if Oma lived there. But instead of Oma, there'd be a gathering, hundreds of English from all over the east. Leave it to them. Ruth would stay snug where she was, on the farm. She milked faster as she listened, her head pressed to the cow's side.

The man said, "Forty, maybe fifty wagons in a line, protection against highwaymen and Indians." They'd live in the wagon for half a year, more if they wintered over short of the mountains, the wagon their home.

What home? A box on wheels with a canvas bonnet, its tongue sticking out for horses to pull? A box made of beams and planks and slats in an order so exact the box had a name, not a useful name like corn crib or coffin, but a proper name: Conestoga. Still, just a box on wheels, so big it demanded a six-horse team. Ruth's hay wagon used but two. So conspicuous, one could say fancy. Fine for English, but not for Plain like Ruth and Aaron.

The man's voice rose. ". . . river, that's the Mississippi," he was saying. Over plains and mountains and deserts, and there it would be, free land. "The heaven of it." He gave a triumphant laugh. "Sitting there waiting."

How could anyone be so daft? Idaho wasn't heaven.

Without realizing, Ruth squeezed hard on Bathsheba's teat. The cow kicked. Her hoof hit the pail and with a clang it tipped into the straw. The evening's milk flowed to the gutter. Bathsheba lifted her tail and let loose a yellow arc.

"Amen," said Ruth to the cow.

❧

One early November evening, after supper, the littles in bed, Ruth and Aaron sat warming by the stone hearth. In her armchair, Ruth sewed in the light of a candle, the flame playing shadows on the whitewashed walls. The dark wood windows and doorframes glowed. Red coals sank in the ash. She couldn't have been more content.

"West," Aaron said. "Where the land is. That's where they should go."

"Your sister?" Ruth laughed. A separation like that? No. Their lives were too entwined, the same as Ruth and her family. When Ruth married and moved to the other side of New Eden, the distance, only a few hours by buggy, felt enormous. She'd missed her parents and Dan'l most of all.

"Yes," Aaron said. "With all those littles, they'll have to. They can't stay here."

"Leave the Fold?" Ruth wasn't laughing now. "They'd never—it's against the Ordnung." They all lived by the Ordnung, and the Elders held them to its rule.

Ruth flicked her hand as if green-heads buzzed in her ear.

Aaron sat forward in his chair. He took off his boots and scooped tallow from a tin. With a cloth, he rubbed first one boot, then the other. "There's no better place." He didn't raise his head.

"Not better than here," she said. "I know what happens." Ruth rested the needlework in her lap. "People die, if not from hunger, then worse." She held up a hand and counted off on her fingers. "Tainted water, no water at all, frozen dead in the mountains." She pushed her sewing into a basket on the floor. "Delia says Indians take people's hair and skin to the bone." Delia, her friend and constant visitor, had a gruesome story on every subject, from root rot to childbirth, and now Indians. "You wouldn't wish that on your sister."

"Wild tales. What does Delia know?"

"Horst told her."

"He's her brother—she has to believe him, but he doesn't know everything." Aaron worked the rag on his boot and scowled. "You can't believe every wagging tongue."

"You seem to." Ruth shifted forward, hands on the wood arms of her chair. "Free land indeed!"

He lifted his head. "It's true."

"Land or no," she said. "They couldn't live among English."

"Don't be a goose." Aaron dropped his boots on the hearth. "English don't bite."

"They have teeth," she teased. "Great spiky teeth."

"Nonsense." He banged his stocking feet on the floor and stood.

"Why so angry?" Ruth said. "This is nonsense. We're not the ones with eleven children."

"Not yet," he said and stomped from the room.

Ruth blanched. He couldn't think they themselves would go west. No.

She wouldn't worry. Their eleventh child was a long way off. Aaron always said, Tomorrow's sorrow is not for today. His habit of rhyming away her fears made her smile.

They couldn't leave. God and community the structure of their life, Aaron the bread of hers, together her existence made whole. He wouldn't ask her.

## CHAPTER 2

❧

# *Spring—A Snake's Tongue*

The wagon lumbered ever farther from home, the six-horse team straining on the steep terrain, Bathsheba tethered by a long rope to the tailgate. The trail west weighed on Ruth, shriveled her as she hunched on the Conestoga's bench. The April wind with a whiff of decay shifted, bringing her a solid stench. She recrossed her black shawl tight over tender breasts and held one corner to her nose.

A carcass lay in trailside weeds, a great beast, bones disjointed, flesh devoured beyond any notion of a living shape. The family rolled slowly past, ample time to know whatever brought the creature down had been bigger yet, and eaten its fill, maybe wolves, a pack of them, followed by foxes, the bones scattered, and scattered further by birds and rats and winter-starved creatures unused to eating meat. And there, pale in the black remains of a rib cage, maggots thrived.

Ruth wished Aaron had obeyed the Ordnung. *Stay separate*, its rule, but Aaron had to have that free Idaho land. "Other Amish will follow," he'd promised. "Until then . . ."

Until then, they would be on their own, no Fold to turn to, out of grace and alone.

⁊

In New Eden, Ruth had squelched her objections, her temper in check. She knew the submissive woman her mother taught her to be, the woman she never quite managed. Such a woman was God's will, the Elders said, and her husband wished at least a semblance, so she'd held *No* in her mouth. She held it writhing until her lips betrayed her and "No" leapt out sharp as a snake's tongue, and she didn't stop there.

"The Elders will have your head on a platter, a gift to the crows." Louder and louder, how good it felt, having it all out, a collywobble of words. And soon as the sickness ran its course, mortification set in.

So unseemly. Head low, folding her skirts close, she'd edged toward the hearth of their fieldstone house and bit her offending lips.

Yet she couldn't squelch her thoughts. She and Aaron should have worried the bone together, but he had said nothing. Tall and sure, he'd turned on his heel and strode to the barn, where his near-finished wagon awaited the final topping, canvas he would spread over the arc of wood ribs.

And all too soon she had found herself stopped on the ridge, their farm still in sight nestled at the heart of the valley.

Ruth had climbed from the wagon. Loosening kinks in her hips, she'd stretched and walked a bowlegged circle of the family's campsite. A bell sounded, muffled in the distance. She knew the timbre, the easy tone—her own bell calling cousin Ely to dinner.

She thought she saw him moving from barn to house. Transfixed, Ruth tasted bile, covetous of him and his bride, covetous of their new life on her land, tending her animals, sleeping in her bed. This, Aaron's doing.

She'd wished she could talk to her brother.

That night she wrote:

*Dearest Dan'l,*

 *Dark is on us yet I see the farm as it was at sunset. The barn door stands open. The fence Joseph helped whitewash glows with sun. He still has the white in his boot seams.*

 *I see every beam Aaron's Gropa cut from the woods, every piece of fence you helped us hammer in place. This leaving weighs my heart more than you can imagine.*

 *Aaron's excitement infects the littles and for this I am grateful. I wish the same excitement infected me. Instead I am gnawed with foreboding.*

 *Much as I love Aaron, and I do down to my very toes, I find myself resentful of being stampeded. This unwifely resentment so hard to admit even to myself I put in a letter for your eyes and no one else. If I were to write in the beautiful book you gave me these words would burn my eyes upon every opening. So I pray my feelings will disappear along with this letter.*

*The good news—under way Aaron is again the
man I married. We will be as one soon.
After writing I feel better already.
Your Loving Sister,
Ruth*

Nausea took her, and pain. Was it the trailside carcass, or Ruth's
time finally come, the unborn child compressing her innards. She
held her distended belly, one arm under, the other over the top,
feeling the prod of an elbow, maybe a knee, as her belly tightened.

She reminded herself, this timing wasn't Aaron's fault.
They'd had deadlines dictated by snow and swollen rivers, by
mountains many hundreds of miles distant, by people they
didn't know and didn't trust.

For the last week, she'd squirmed with twinges as the
horses hauled the white-topped wagon into the Appalachians,
the start of two thousand miles overland, and their fifth child
way overdue.

She waited for the tightness to ebb, and as her muscles
loosened, the wagon broke from bare trees. Below, three to
four miles off, a sudden valley spread. So reminiscent of home.

Here, fields gave way to gardens tilled in straight rows
where green shoots testified to spring and the attention of loving hands. Mustard bloomed in the hedgerows, dogwood scattered white in the edges, and at the heart of the valley houses
nested beside a narrow river.

"Aaron." Ruth's call a whisper. His name couldn't carry
through Esther's chatter and the boys raucous as blackbirds,
all of them ahead of the horses.

Esther's high voice rose with excitement. "Let's live here!" Three and a half now, she rode on Aaron's shoulders, Daniel, Matthew, Joseph, clambering beside them, their black clothes speckled with dried mud.

"We can't live here," Aaron said.

"Why?" Esther's fists full of his dark hair, she twisted Aaron's head. She leaned sideways, her cheek close to his.

He gripped her knees. "It belongs to someone else," he said.

"I'll hammer a stake." She clapped her hands. "Then it's ours."

Aaron swung her to the ground. "When we get to Idaho, you will hammer the first stake."

"When?" Esther skipped beside him, a hand in his. "Tomorrow?"

Ruth clutched the bench. Aaron wouldn't want to stop. They might miss the line of wagons leaving Pittsburgh, lose the safety of numbers, the guidance they needed threading wilderness, the greater mountains, the desert.

If they missed the gathering in Pittsburgh, the wagon train would leave, and sure enough they'd be separate—not the separate God intended, close within their Old Order; they'd be alone at the mercy of . . . of who knew what. Ruth could imagine what Delia had called a Thomas-hawk embedded in Aaron's head. She shouldn't have confided her fears to Delia, yet she always did. Best friend or no, Delia loved to tease. Who names a hatchet anyway?

Ruth knew of Gabriel's nameless sword and David's slingshot, Saint Sebastian's arrow-filled body. Any such could cut them down, clubs, lances, daggers. In the Bible, nary an Indian showed himself.

She believed she could guard against English, keep her soul safe and her littles, close her eyes, cover their ears, but the body? She couldn't protect against attackers, and strong as he was, Aaron could only prolong the inevitable, so in this case contact with English would be a blessing. She hoped she was right, and God would understand the difference.

Ruth's pains bit harder and closer together, sapping the strength it took to hold to the seat. In full labor, she called louder this time.

"Aaron." His name rasped from her throat, squeezed as she clenched. They'd make up time later. She had to stop.

Aaron looked over his shoulder, his hand on the lead's bridle. "No stopping," he called. "We'll eat under way."

"But . . ."

He turned and walked backward. "What's the—?"

"The baby," she said.

He blinked. "Are you sure?"

She gave him a withering look.

Above his beard, his face lost its robust color. He pulled the team from the trail, across the verge, and into a field. With a crack, their wheel crushed a stray bone deep in the winter-killed grass.

Spring kept to the valley. The ridges, still waiting, smelled of melted snow.

"Daniel," Aaron shouted. "Set the picket." Daniel hurried to anchor the line and tie their horses.

"Matthew, Joseph, collect wood."

"Now?" Joseph banged skinny arms on his sides. "It's midday." He kicked the grass with his built-up boot and headed off with a hop-skip. Matthew, half his height, followed, sausage arms out soaring like a hawk.

Aaron leapt onto the bench beside Ruth, his long legs folded. "Lots of wood," he bellowed at the boys. "And take Esther." He straddled the bench, his footing unsteady as he bent over and inched a hand under Ruth's knees. Despite his great reach, her belly blocked him.

"What are you doing?"

"Helping," he said.

"Helping what?"

"I'm picking you up?"

"No, you're n—"

Her mouth opened, lips stretched across her teeth. Aaron extracted his hand, raised his arms in retreat, and just short of falling, he caught the wagon top.

When she regained her breath, Ruth said, "You are *not* picking me up."

A *thock-thock* sounded as Daniel's mallet drove the picket into the ground. Minutes later, deeper thunks announced Joseph dropping an armful of deadfall.

"Papa?" At the side of the wagon, Esther's little voice. "More wood?"

"Lots more." Aaron, his words fast. "Lots and lots. Go."

"Don't shout—you'll frighten her."

"I'm not shouting," he shouted.

With a frantic look in the wagon, then down at houses in the valley, he flexed his fingers. Sweat beaded his smooth upper lip and slid into his beard.

Aaron in a dither, she wouldn't have thought it possible.

Wasn't he the one, in the comfort of their own home, the one who'd discounted birth on the trail?

One evening in their bedroom, Aaron had said, "We go when the mountains clear." Slipping into bed, he'd pulled the quilt over his chest.

"But the baby." Was he funning? She held her belly as if warding him off.

Give birth in a wagon? No, not even a Conestoga. A wagon took people places, took goods and chattels, the labor of one's living. A wagon wasn't meant for the labor before birth.

Aaron had settled into the thick mattress. "We go," he said, "when the trail's right."

Ruth had one knee on the bed about to crawl in. She stopped and stared at Aaron. "And the birthing?"

"Can't be worse than birthing a foal." He put his hands behind his head. "I've done plenty."

Ruth, now on her feet, hands on her hips, white nightdress hanging off her growing bulge. "And the mare stood by?"

"Well . . ."

Ruth snatched her braids loose. "You could ask Esther for help. She'll be there watching me bleed."

A hint of worry crept into his face. He turned away. "I pray it won't come to that," Aaron said. "But why argue? It'll come when it comes—that's what your mother always said."

Ruth sat in the chair. She wouldn't get in the bed.

Ruth's mother had been there for all the birthings, her practiced touch and reassurance a godsend. If only her mother were still alive—two years, and Ruth still missed her. She wanted to ask her, Do all men behave this way?

Delia would have said, Yes, men do, Horst being Horst.

Ruth missed her too, Delia, as beyond reach as her mother.

Ruth had to remember, Aaron had always loved her, and she him.

Though he'd made light of birth on the trail, and she'd been angry, Ruth knew, if he could, Aaron would have postponed their leaving.

❧

In a lull between spasms, Ruth spoke slowly. "Spread canvas in the wagon," she said. "Birth in the grass, that's fine for you and the mares, not me."

"Of course not." Into the wagon, he stretched a long leg, froglike; then his hands and the other leg followed, swimming over their possessions.

She listened to Aaron dig through baskets, shift mattresses, heard the *whoosh* as he threw the stiff cloth over them. She dreaded rearranging the mess his haste created.

Back home, Ruth didn't mind field dirt on her capable square hands, or the mess of the day building through the house, but before bed she took no rest till she'd set it right, scoured the cauldron, scrubbed and oiled the table, the sideboard, swept the floor, cleaned and pared her fingernails.

Delia could leave a pan full of dishes for morning and sit by the fire, her plump fingers tickling a cat in her lap. It was a talent Ruth didn't have. Delia often said Horst should have married Ruth. He hated a rumpled bed, the dusty lintels over the door where he'd run his fingers. He had driven his wife to distraction all her short life, showing her the dust.

With eight near-grown boys to help, Delia said Horst

could dust lintels himself. She had enough, alone all day at her cooking.

Ruth wouldn't have traded Aaron for the world. She laughed, but Ruth knew if Horst acted that way to her, she'd have gotten her back up. Being an Elder didn't make him God. He was already a little too nearer-my-God-than-thee-could-ever-be.

She didn't know how Delia put up with him.

It didn't matter that Aaron dropped his underdrawers at the foot of the bed, his socks on the floor, and sometimes forgot, tromping through the kitchen in muddy boots. He had been everything she could have wanted, tender, protective; he'd sweep a floor as readily as Ruth would put her hand to the plow or the pitchfork. They were a team wrapped in the Plain Fold, united in their vision of farm and family.

On the wagon seat, Ruth loosened her clothes. "My nightdress, can you find it?" A rush of liquid warmed her skirts. "It broke," she said.

"Broke?" Aaron scrambled forward. "What broke?" He handed her the nightdress, eyes darting away from her face as it twisted, another contraction strengthening.

At Daniel's birth, her first, Ruth's water had broken, and she'd thought the baby would come right then, but nothing came, only a big pool of pink liquid. Five hours of hard labor kept her terrified, waiting for her mother's arrival.

Ruth had been at the birthing of kittens, sheep, horses, cows, pigs. But she'd never seen the first liquid. Later she figured their water broke in the field.

Inching off the seat, Ruth's muscles unclenched, and she slid backward into the wagon's center. She panted.

Aaron panted.

His eyes followed her halting progress and final collapse on the sheet he'd spread without direction. He folded a blanket and wedged it below the bedding at the small of her back, and she bent her head in gratitude. In his own frantic way he wanted to help, and this time, bless him, he did the exact right thing.

Another spasm built. She closed her throat on squirrelish noises, and Aaron cried out as if pain sprang in his own body. "We need a midwife," he said.

"Yes," Ruth answered between breaths, "I think you do." Like Ruth, he'd been at lots of birthings, but not hers. Her mother or Delia or a helpful neighbor, all experienced midwives, had shooed him out, much to his relief. To Ruth's relief too. His suffering at the sight of her suffering made everything worse.

Aaron hopped over the seat to the ground, heading down valley at a run. He stopped, said, "Holy heaven," and spun around. "Daniel, halter Jehu." Aaron ran for the horse, haltered by the time he swung onto the animal's bare back. "Water, heat water," he yelled. Rope in hand, he made off at a gallop.

All those miles to the village, who knew when he'd return. Could he even find a midwife? And oh—she'd be an English.

What would God think?

Never mind God—what did Ruth think? She hadn't imagined the English near so soon, nor this oh-so-personal nearness. She'd never considered touch.

❧

When birthing Daniel, she'd lain in the comfort of her own bed, but the pains had seemed a harbinger of death, not life. She thought something had gone woefully wrong. Ruth pushed with all her might, and nothing but a mightier pain had come as her reward. She'd screamed.

When the clench faded, she levered herself from the bed. Aaron had gone to fetch her mother, but she needed help now. She would walk to her neighbor if she must.

Bowlegged, she'd staggered out the door. Another contraction locked on. Her knees let go, and, falling, her fingers closed on the bell rope. A clang filled the crannies of her head as she sank to the ground. She arched and dug her fingernails into the earth, just as now she tore at the cloth beneath her.

Lying on the ground, she'd opened her eyes, staring into the maw of the iron bell. The bell seemed to wait for a command. She could see inside the lip, past the sound bowl to the tuning chips hacked in a circle.

Trying to stand, she'd clasped the rope again. A great bong sizzled through her body along with another contraction. She became a child again. She wanted her mother, the gentle hand on her brow, the sound of her voice telling Ruth all would be well.

Ruth had tugged the rope, the sound deafening. Seven of a Tuesday morning, no time for a bell to ring, and her neighbor Marta, with eleven children of her own, knew Ruth's first time was near. But it seemed like hours before she arrived, the woman with her arms under Ruth's shoulders, helping her up from the pool of blood and into the house.

In her pain and fear, the smell of dirt, of blood, Ruth didn't care about anything, least of all opening her legs for Marta to look.

Ruth barely heard her own distracted cry and Marta saying, "You've a ways yet." For all her neighbor's concern, Ruth might've been baking her first loaf of bread. Marta sat hour after hour knitting while Ruth tried not to scream.

Her mother arrived in time to hold Daniel's head as he finally came out, waxy and white all over his angry pink body, a full cap of dark hair. He wailed.

"Just like his mama," Marta said, and picked up her knitting. "Another ten and she'll think nothing of it."

Each child came shorter thereafter, Joseph five hours, Matthew three and a half—Esther practically fell out after two. Never did Ruth think nothing of it, but then, Esther was her fourth, not her eleventh.

❧

Ruth lay on the canvas, trying not to hold her breath. Time after time, spasms clenched her lower back, not her usual labor. They came closer, lasted longer, and no advancement.

In minutes between the crush, Ruth listened to their horses as they made the most of an early halt. Languid tails slapped at flies. She heard the rip of grass, their slow chewing, the shake of a mane. She'd be glad to trade places, eat grass and nicker, or join the littles collecting wood.

She tried to let her muscles rest in the in-between, but alone in the wagon, Ruth's fears took her back to the barn, to the birth of Bathsheba's latest calf. A bloody business.

The calf had presented one front hoof, gelatinous yellow at the tip.

Aaron had pushed the hoof back, his hand, then his arm to the armpit disappearing inside Bathsheba. He closed his eyes and groped for the head, straining, his feet slipping on the wet straw. "She's breech," he'd said and twisted his arm, the cow's tail hitting him in the face. If he couldn't turn the calf, it would die, and so would Bathsheba.

The cow's mighty contractions crushed his arm. "Needles in my fingers," he said. "I can't feel anything." He withdrew his arm, blood running down and staining his clothes, and, greasing the other arm, he dove for the head again.

After much grunting, he finally lined the calf right, and at the next spasm, his knee braced on her haunch, he pulled, and both groaning like the end of the world, he and Bathsheba delivered the calf.

The thought made Ruth tear at the sheet by her side as her own contractions came closer, lasted longer.

If Aaron remained down valley, and the baby lay breech, what then?

And yet, if Aaron were kneeling beside her, she wouldn't want him in her innards, not to his wrist, much less his armpit; he'd be realigning her tonsils.

She rolled on her side, knees tucked, not yet ready to squat. It should be time, and yet it wasn't. Pain took her and she drifted from her body.

# CHAPTER 3

### ❧

## *Of Blood and Birth*

Drifting, Ruth heard nothing of her littles' voices, saw nothing but long-ago years. What a time they'd had, Ruth eighteen, Aaron twenty. Her gift from God, he smelled of rosemary bread, his mother's, and something all his own. He came smooth shaven, and dressed in black stovepipe pants, suspenders, jacket, and hat. All his clothes conformed to the Ordnung, as did the cut of his hair just below his ears. The beard had come after they married, upper lip smooth, also according to rule. And Ruth would have had it no other way.

Sitting next to Delia, Ruth had seen him stride into church. With a shy smile, he nodded to the Elders, his eyes deep set and brown. He crossed the room to the men's benches and sat, knees together, his head bowed. She found nothing disparaging about him, not even the unruly cowlick tossing a lock of brown hair in his face.

Ruth's head should have been bowed too. He'd raised his eyes and caught hers. Had he been looking at Delia? All the boys did, not that she cared. Men too, though they'd look quickly away.

Had he hoped to catch *Delia's* eye? Ruth's embarrassment surged as his eyebrows came together, his mouth down in disapproval. But his eyes held a smile, or so she'd told herself. A smile for her, and she'd been right.

Ruth elbowed her friend. "Who *is* that?" she'd whispered. A thrill ran through her, something new, making her feel soft and uncomfortable, about to split her skin like a ripe tomato. Church no place for ripening thoughts.

"He's a Holtz," Delia said. "The other side of New Eden." She inclined her head at Ruth and lifted both eyebrows at once.

Ruth looked away, the ridge of her ears heated. She didn't stop to wonder how his prayer-closed eyes could have stumbled on hers. It didn't matter; she liked the look of him. She didn't dare look a second time, at least not then.

After months of furtive glances, Aaron offered a few words, and finally he walked Ruth home from church. Shorter than he by a head, she hurried beside him, two steps to his one long stride. He said almost nothing, his eyes on the road, but he took her hand in his right as they came in the dooryard. When they stopped at the steps, he looked at her sideways, as if head-on would blind him, and said good-bye at the door. She savored the touch of his fingers.

"What's wrong with your hand?" her mother asked when Ruth wouldn't wet it in the dishpan after supper. "Did you burn yourself?"

"You could say that." Ruth plunged both hands in the water. She couldn't tell her mother, not that she had anything to tell, only the feeling that she might soon have something to keep to herself.

The next afternoon Aaron came to help her father. A two-month calf fetched up lame, and with Ruth's father too busy with lambs, Aaron carried the calf to their barn. He wore the animal about his neck, great and brown, a leggy muffler he laid in the straw, easy as he would a wounded bird. Ruth sat cross-legged beside him and kneaded the calf's leg until her fingers cramped. The animal recovered itself enough to dash off.

"Ungrateful beast," he said. "In his hooves, I'd have stayed." He touched her cheek, two fingers slipping over the smooth skin. His eyes, the ones that wouldn't look before, wouldn't stop. She didn't breathe. She could have been underwater. And then surfacing, she gave the slightest gasp and a fearful glance at her father over by the lamb pen. He didn't seem to notice, his attention taken with cropping lambs' tails and binding off testicles. Aaron followed her look. He returned his hands to his lap.

Her body blocking her father's view, she reached over and one by one unfolded the fingers of his left hand. When she came to the littlest, she found it stunted. The finger twisted against his palm, helpless as a newborn mouse. It wrung her heart, made her want to take him in her arms and hold him. Keep him safe.

"What happened?" Ruth asked.

He curled the finger in a fist and leaned on his elbows. "I'm parched," he said. "Aren't you?"

Ruth brought him grape juice she'd mashed that morning,

and she watched him coax a feral cat from the hay, his voice smooth as cream. He tickled the cat till it purred. Her brother Dan'l had tried it once; the creature bit his thumb to the bone. Everyone knew, you don't play with feral animals. But Aaron had a knack.

❧

In the wagon, another spasm laid Ruth out. Knees up, soles of her feet flat on the bed, her breath came faster.

*Now*, she hoped. *Now?* She hauled herself to a squat, arms clasped around her bent knees.

Outside, the littles' voices rose above the crackle of their fire.

"Daniel, how much water?" Joseph's question.

"I don't know."

"Ask Esther," Matthew said, most likely flapping his arms. "Girls know that stuff."

Esther answered without hesitation, "Till a fish floats."

"We're not cooking it, are we?"

"No, Matthew, don't be a goat." Daniel this time. "Papa says boil water. Idle hands are the Devil's workshop."

In the silence, Ruth knew they looked at their dirty palms.

"My hands?" Esther's words edged with worry. "The Devil's?"

"Not with Mama in the wagon," Daniel said. "Joseph, stir the ashes. I'll get more wood."

Ruth shifted her weight as her muscles tightened. So daunting, that in the face of the Devil, she must be their fortress. She couldn't abandon them now. They needed their mother as she had needed hers. She had to birth this baby.

Her arms gripping tight, breasts squashed to her thighs, Ruth squeezed hard enough to surely skid the infant across the canvas, yet only a surge of blood flowed along valleys in the cloth between her feet.

Ruth's legs trembled. She abandoned the squat and rested on her side. This child should have come faster than Esther.

Ruth rolled on her back. Her eyes traveled the waves of white where it drooped arc to arc above her head. She rose on an elbow, looked out the curved opening, and over the top-board at the tongue slanting to the ground. Doubletrees, harness, and chains waited on the grass. When she held the baby, they'd get under way. If she—

No, *when* she gave birth.

The pains consuming, she receded from the wagon. She sped with poor Aaron galloping house to house in the valley explaining how he'd taken his too, too pregnant wife into the mountains and, lying in a Conestoga, she needed help. What woman would accompany him? English weren't *verrückt* as all that.

At least he had a mission. Better than standing green and helpless at her bedside.

❧

Sweat poured off Ruth's face as she came to herself lying on the sheet-covered canvas.

"Water's on." She could hear Matthew jumping up and down. "Daniel, what do we do now?"

"Papa always walked in circles."

"Does that help?"

"I don't know, Esther."

The littles' shoes crunched the brittle grass.

"It's not helping me," Joseph said.

"I'll ask Mama." Matthew's heavy footsteps started toward the wagon.

Oh, God no. Ruth's back went tight. Clenching bands swarmed around her sides and engulfed her whole body. Don't come; he mustn't. She held her breath and bit back the words warding him off. They'd be screaming words, and what kind of fortress would she be then? She pushed with all her strength.

He mustn't see her, but there came his hands, the heels prying at the canvas, lifting it from the topboard, there at the level of her feet. It was one thing for Marta to look—she knew what to expect, the roil of bloody sheets, legs increasingly red-streaked from her knees into the junction of dark hair.

She pulled at the canvas beneath her, feeling for the blanket Aaron had wedged. If only she could cover the worst of her. Feeling for a grip, she worked her hand into the folds. She found a corner, twisted it in her fingers, and yanked. Her weight on the remaining blanket, it wouldn't budge.

She rolled and, her arm awkward behind her back, yanked again. A small corner loosened, not enough to reach across one leg. She could see sky through the hole Matthew had opened.

"No, Matthew," Daniel commanded. "Papa says no one goes to the wagon."

Matthew withdrew one hand. Ruth squelched a hiss.

"What if . . . ?"

More hesitant steps.

The top of Esther's head, yellow hair askew, popped above the frontboard as she crawled up the tongue. This would be worse than Matthew. He would never give birth, but Esther would.

She needn't know the lurid truth so soon, coloring a vision of her future, making her fearful of an ultimate blessing.

Esther latched one set of chubby fingers over the board. Her forehead rose, eyebrows next, then eyes, thank God, cast at her footing.

"Esther, no." Daniel again.

Her head jerked sideways, hands slipping off the topboard. Flying feet appeared and disappeared. "Daniel, put me down— Mama needs me."

A scuffle followed.

"Mama needs you right here. You too, Matthew. Even papas don't go in a birthing room."

The pain lessened only to start again. Breech—what other reason?

She turned her ear to the littles. Thinking the worst would bring no good.

"It's a wagon," Esther said. "That's where we sleep."

"Today it's a birthing room."

"I want to see."

Ruth crushed the rucked-up bedding in her fists.

"This *is* the Devil's workshop," said Daniel. "Everyone, more wood. We've Mama's chores and our own. We'll need dinner. Let's see what's in the woods—fiddleheads, mushrooms. Joseph, check the field for dandelions."

Bless Daniel. Ruth let out her breath only to suck it back as another contraction struck. With much in this world to fear, for her littles, let birth be a happy event.

Ruth wouldn't dwell on what they'd find if the baby truly lay breech, and Aaron continued his down-valley search.

She tried to pray, but she'd prayed before, prayed Aaron

would change his mind and stay on the farm, prayed the Elders would stop them, prayed the baby would come before they left. These perhaps the wrong prayers.

As evening light slanted in, she kept her mind on the task at hand, no more fleeing, no leaving her body to fend for itself in the wagon. She prayed for strength.

Dark would come soon, and where were Daniel and the others? Daniel would gather them, wouldn't he? Keep them close.

And listen to her die? No. No, she wouldn't. Ruth heaved herself to a squat, weight on her heels, an arm around one knee, and steadied herself, the fingers of one hand hooked over the wagon sideboard only to have a foot slip on the blood-slick sheet. She pitched onto her side and yelped, the impact dizzy-ing. Did they hear?

There'd be no squatting.

She shifted on her back, knees in the air, her breath in bursts. Arms above her head, she gripped the topboard. Prayer and her littles, these gave her strength.

She ground her teeth. Her bare feet slid without purchase, and she threw the small corner of blanket beneath one foot. She widened the reach of the other past the wet.

Her feet anchored, she arched, straining her arms, pushing with every muscle from her scalp to her shoulders, down through her chest, her belly, thighs, calves, and toes. With a high keening, she felt her nethers tear as the infant finally crowned.

Fluids gushed, and her newest son, head without hair, lay on the bed. He squalled. In the cold, his tiny fists and long feet shook. *Thank you, Lord.*

Bloated with effort, her face throbbed. "Poor boy," she said, and drew him on her belly. She cleared his mouth, his nose, and the cord tethering him to her stretched. She reached one arm for her sewing basket tucked next to the mattress, there on top of the unused book Dan'l had given her. A book for thoughts she didn't dare say.

Lifting the lid, she took yarn and scissors, cut two short lengths, knotted one near his belly, one farther out, and snipped between them.

"You're free," she said.

She'd have liked to lie quiet, but dusk hurried her. She dried the infant, swaddled him in a blanket, and laid him beside her before massaging her spongy belly. She pushed with the heels of her hands, expelling the afterbirth onto the sheet. Any piece left behind could prove deadly.

She worked the mound of her belly where white stretch marks testified to her five children. Belly and breasts, each child had marked her as surely as she'd marked heights of her brood on her bedroom doorframe. She'd start again in the Idaho house.

The afterbirth hopefully out, she rolled the mass, her nightdress, sheet, and canvas together, and stowed the bundle out of sight. She'd attend it later.

Dark nearing, she lit a candle. Settled and ready to call the littles, she heard a horse gallop to a stop, its breath heaving. Aaron leapt onto the bench. Hands gripping the first arc, he leaned in the opening.

"I couldn't find—" His lined face turned joyous when he saw her in fresh nightdress, lying on clean linen, the baby swaddled asleep in her arms.

"Papa's back." Daniel's distant call.

"Papa, what's happening?" Esther's head bobbed into view as she balanced on the wagon tongue.

"Come, see our Little Aaron."

They all climbed into the wagon, Esther over the front-board. The boys swarmed over the tailgate and wormed in beside Ruth.

"This *is* a wagon." Kneeling, Esther planted her hands on her hips. "I was right."

"But now there's a baby." Daniel opened the baby's blanket. "See."

Esther wrinkled her nose. "He has a tail." She pointed at his belly.

"He used it to breathe inside Mama," Daniel said.

"That's nonsense." Joseph pushed Daniel's shoulder. "He has a nose."

"Not for breathing underwater." Aaron lifted his newest son.

"Then he *is* a fish?" Esther poked the infant's leg.

"Not a fish." Daniel and Esther inched closer. "And we're not going to cook him."

"Who suggested that?" asked Aaron.

Wagging her head side to side, Esther touched the tail with her finger. "He's not a tiny Papa." She put her nose to Little Aaron's. "He's a mouse." And thus they named him Maus.

❧

Through the night, Maus woke with little mewling cries. The fifth time, like the others, Ruth took him from his hammock and put him to her breast. He nursed, his eagerness so intense he raised a blister on the point of his upper lip. She changed him, returned him to his hammock, and slept until gray seeped into the sky.

Before the sun came full, Aaron and Daniel saw to the horses and cooked breakfast. Ruth scrubbed sheets and canvas and, with Matthew and Joseph's help, hung them in the wagon opposite the hammock.

After breakfast, their baskets and chests repacked, the horses harnessed, Aaron called to Esther, "Hurry now, we've lost a day." She ran from the woods adjusting her drawers and straightening her skirts.

Finally under way, they followed the mountain ridge. The trail wended through black stick trees, and Ruth with Maus in the crook of her arm held to the bench, one leg cocked beneath. The wagon top slung side to side. Jolts tore at her swollen flesh. Maus whimpered.

She'd cut his cord without thought, and now he hunkered close, his crinkled brow strangely old. He rooted her shawl, and she bared her breast. Nipple at his cheek, he latched hold and wouldn't let go as if he saw the snip of a greater cord.

He drifted into sleep, her nipple in his mouth, arms and legs folded as they were in the womb. From time to time his lips trembled.

Ruth straightened her spine. She wrapped herself around him, his shield, fierce into the coming dust. She'd weathered birth alone, and together she and Aaron would weather this westward trek, Delia's stories of Appalachian animals, four legged or two legged, be damned.

*I will lift up mine eyes,* and she did. Above her in high canopies, buds released a greening wash.

## CHAPTER 4

May—Seven Peas in a Pod

I n the mountains, Maus now five days old, Ruth woke to the coldest dawn. Outside, the trees gleamed silver in a glaze of ice. The branches groaned. A freshening wind snapped their jackets and shards fell on the Conestoga's top with the tinkle of broken glass.

Maus, nattering in his hammock, must be cold. Ruth crawled from under her quilt, folded the patchwork, and laid it over him before donning her underdrawers. As she pulled her dress over her head, a limb crashed.

Aaron leapt from bed, snatched the quilt and Maus from his hammock, and hopped from the wagon. "Everyone under," he called. "Bring your mattress."

Out and sitting on the frozen ground, Ruth fought her

skirts as she slid backward on the side of her rump. She worked slowly beneath the wagon, and the others crowded in beside her. Aaron passed Maus, now screaming, to Ruth, and Aaron himself crawled under.

While wind laid waste to the woods, they huddled safe beneath the heavy oak. "Solid as a house," Aaron said. "And slow as one." He thumped his fist on the ground. "We're later every minute."

"What about Bathsheba?" Esther asked. The cow lowed, her tail turned to the wind.

"She can't fit under," Joseph said.

"Poor Sheba. She can have my apple."

"Poor horses," Matthew said. "Noah can have my sausage."

"Your favorite may not be Noah's." Daniel's shoulders twitched like his father's, too kind to laugh aloud.

After the wind eased, they crawled from their lair.

"Another morning wasted," Aaron said. "We can't afford this."

"When's spring?" Esther said. "I don't like winter."

"This isn't real winter," Ruth told her. "Just a quick revisit." Nothing to what wintering over in Idaho would be, snow and ice for months without a house.

"Summer's very soon," Ruth said. "Months of it." She repacked the ticking, and Aaron harnessed the horses with Daniel.

"What happens if we miss the train?" Daniel asked across Noah's back.

"We can't miss it." Aaron tightened buckles on his side of the horse. "We'll make up the time."

Ruth, hurrying the mattresses into the wagon, felt a drop

on the back of her neck. She looked up. Daylight shone through a slice in the canvas, and, below, a chunk of ice pooled on a barrel top.

"We can't go yet," she called.

Aaron, his mouth drawn down, wrenched at ties holding the canvas to the topboard. Rushing made him all thumbs, and he hissed as he struggled.

The lines finally pulled free, he climbed on the outside, his boot toes under the loose cloth. Inside the wagon, Ruth cut a square from a roll of extra canvas and waxed a length of thread. She slipped the patch through the hole to Aaron, then ran the needle inside to out and through the patch. Aaron passed it back in a small, tight stitch. "Come on, come on," he growled as he pushed the needle in Ruth's direction. "Hurry."

Ruth blew on her fingers and, fast as she could, pulled the thread and sent the needle through to the outside. Each stitch so small it felt like the hole would never close. No sense making bigger stitches only to resew when the patch leaked.

The hole finally closed, Aaron mounted Noah the wheelhorse, the only one with a saddle. Sleet mixed with rain as he rode round-shouldered under a cape falling over his knees and the back of his saddle. Head out the top, his hat brim dripped. Ruth lowered Esther's bonnet and her own against the wet, glad of the brim. She settled a waxed cape on their laps, and one over their shoulders, the canvas overhang too little protection against inclemency.

Their wagon alone on the rain-swept road, Ruth prayed God had chosen Aaron as He chose Noah, and once over the mountains they'd find an olive leaf. All would be well, by God's will, and she put her trust in Him.

The boys took off their hats and hung their heads over the tailgate, hair slicked dark as team and wagon snaked the switchbacks, oak planks groaning. The sound almost as if the oak talked.

For them the tree had been like a person, talking to each in their time.

⊰৵৹

Ruth had loved Gropa's tree from the first spring of Aaron's courting. One Sunday he'd picked her up in a one-horse cart. At a rattling trot, he drove to the far edge of his father's woods and helped her out as if she couldn't do it herself. She tried not to laugh.

Once among the trees, he took her arm, tentative at first, then tight against his body as they veered this way, that way, to the biggest tree in the forest. The branches embraced a large clearing, the low ones offering an easy ladder into the canopy. He climbed high, and from his perch he called, "Come see— nothing's more magnificent."

Arms high, she worked her way hand over hand to Aaron's branch. He folded his knees for her to get by. The land stretched before them, the quilted fields spread over some sleeping giant, but much as she treasured the land, that day his pant legs caught her eye. They rose, showing an intimate glimpse of skin above his socks, his legs hairy as Esau. Freckles lurked beneath the reddish hair, boyish and manly at the same time. So inviting, she wanted to touch, to know if the hair felt soft or coarse. He shifted and the glimpse disappeared.

His eyes took in her every move and looked out over the valley. He sat quiet, a distance about him. She wondered where his mind had drifted.

"I used to sit here with Gropa," he said. She could see how much he missed the old man, dead these many years. Aaron ran his hand up the trunk of the tree his grandfather had planted.

Ruth did the same. She wanted to know everything he touched, everything that touched him.

Aaron pressed his shoulder to hers. "Our littles will climb this oak and their littles after them." He'd kissed her cheek. "I wish Gropa could see us now."

Had anyone asked, Could this man cut down this tree?, she'd have said of course not. Not Aaron. Yet thirteen years later it came to pass.

Ruth had bedded the garden for winter, the harvest long since jarred and stored, the beets, beans, peas, tomatoes, and cucumbers lined on shelves down cellar. She'd spread a covering of hay on her treasured asparagus, the ground double dug years before, the patch weeded and ready for next year's resurrection.

That's when Aaron had had another resurrection in mind. Ruth wanted no part of it.

Before breakfast, and after they'd fed and watered the stock, Aaron took the two-man saw from pegs in the tool shed. The biggest saw for the biggest tree.

"Not the oak," Ruth had said. "I trust you wouldn't cut the oak."

"Yes, there's no better, not for a Conestoga."

White oak best for a Conestoga, and a Conestoga the sturdiest wagon for crossing the country, and crossing the country . . . Why would anyone want to cross the country? Ruth had yet to cross Lancaster County. Trading vegetables in New Eden was foreign enough to last a lifetime.

With a basket over one arm and a long-handled shovel in the crook of the other, Ruth followed her family across a field to the woods. At the edge she stopped, head bent, listening. A thrush. The bird should have been long gone, yet she heard one. He unspooled his lilting song as if he sang for her alone.

Ruth strayed from the path, the song pulling her deeper into the maze of trunks. Shy hermit, the bird showed only a distant flick of his wing, and left her among trees and trees, all looking down, all shaking winter-black fingers.

"This way," Aaron called.

She closed her eyes against him. She wanted to say no, but a dutiful wife didn't. Yet there it was poised between tongue and teeth, puckering her mouth, plucking at her lips like an unripe persimmon.

Ruth walked bundled in the black of her faith, heavy shawl drawn close. The white prayer cap held her knotted braids. The basket, full of their midday meal, bumped her hip.

"Mama, the tree," her littles jabbered.

They all pressed on toward the base of the great trunk—Aaron in the lead, the three boys in black like their father, then Esther, a miniature of Ruth, except her prayer cap was black. Ruth caught up with Matthew, arms outstretched as he winged through the trees, a hatchet in one hand. He chirped at birds only he saw, but Ruth knew them by his wing beats: the speed of a hummingbird, the languid buzzard, arms back, a swallow's long dive.

"What's wrong with that boy?" Aaron asked. "You shouldn't fill his head with birds."

"He does his chores," Ruth said. "Why not fly one to the next?"

Matthew, now a gliding hawk, spied a chipmunk, its cheeks stuffed bigger than its body. Matthew dashed after, paying no mind to the hatchet he carried.

"Watch the blade." Aaron's bark overflowed on the boy. Ruth felt the bite, knowing it was meant for her.

"I'll take it," Joseph said. He puffed his skinny chest. "Matthew's too young."

Aaron took the hatchet and gave it to Joseph. Daniel carried the ax. He was the wheelhorse in Ruth's team of boys, steady and patient, soon as strong as Aaron. They all pulled together according to their strength.

Esther carried a small basket over one arm. In her other hand, her well-loved doll dangled by its leg.

Ruth had made the doll. A black bonnet over its white prayer cap shadowed the blank face, no features, as was the custom. Ruth set her mouth in a hard line, lips clamped on silence, a lesson from the speechless doll.

High of the oak's fall line, Ruth laid down the shovel and basket. She surveyed the tree. She hated to see the leaves, how they curled brown on their stems and clung, unwilling to give over life. The leaves rattled.

Ruth's family had circled the base of the tree, their look funereal as English would see it. Ruth's grandfather had told her as a child, "English wear black for the dead, not every day."

Ruth had worked at seeing through their eyes. She squirmed at the thought of Them shoulder to her shoulder, Them watching her as they would all too soon, if Aaron had his way. An impulse she couldn't trust.

She'd tromped the shovel into the ground, handle straight up. She would use it to dig the tree's curved roots, roots Aaron would shape into hames, these the collars for their four mares, for Noah, and Jehu the stallion. Twelve roots, collars for six horses. Their muscle would haul the wagon west unless Ruth could prevail.

Aaron assigned tools. "Now, my woodsmen." His eyes glittered. He and Daniel hefted the two-man. They adjusted their hands on the wood handles, one at each end of the long-toothed blade, the blade longer than Aaron was tall, and Aaron in his hat well over six feet.

They shifted their weight foot to foot and flexed their knees. Matthew, again with the hatchet, stood close to the trunk, the blade poised to cut bark where the saw would start. On the other side, Joseph took position, legs spread, his longer leg taking the weight behind the short one, ax ready. They'd cut smaller trees before, but this—this was different.

Joseph readjusted his grip. He swung the ax above his head, and, high on the toes of his good leg, his might gathered into a slant stroke, he'd brought the blade down. The honed edge sank into the oak. Joseph pried at the yellow flesh. A chunk big as his hand popped from the bark, and with each stroke the yellow notch grew.

Ruth turned away. She heard Matthew's little chips, heard the uneven rasp as the saw started. With every pull of the blade, the kerf deepened, Aaron and Daniel working to a rhythm of unhurried slaughter.

Ruth couldn't bear to watch. The smell of hot oak made her sick, too much like yellow blood as it dribbled on the ground. *It's only a tree*, she told herself. She wouldn't think on Gropa, or the generations—the baby inside her among them—that would never survey their land from its branches.

Esther had tugged at her skirts. "I'm hungry."

Ruth pulled the child over to the basket, safe from the flying chips, and picked up a walnut. She cracked it between the heels of her hands, their home forest always ready to feed them. "Is Dolly hungry too?"

"Yes," Esther said. "But Dolly has no mouth."

Aaron and Daniel stripped off hats and jackets, the air ringing with silence after the saw's drone stopped. Sweat marked their shirts and flattened their hair. Ruth gathered their clothes. One jacket on the ground, Esther curled herself on top. Ruth covered her. "Dolly needs a quilt," Esther said.

"Come winter, we'll make one." A time when their hands might have had extra minutes, what with the harvest in and stored, the slaughtering done, meat salted and dried or pickled. Winter, when Gropa's tree would be drying in the woodshed. Ruth had a year and more before departure, or so she'd thought.

The saw resumed, stopping only for short breathers and a chance for Daniel and Aaron to wipe sweat from their eyes. The sun climbed, glinting through brown leaves.

Late in the day Aaron finally shouted, "Back." The trunk sawn near through, he and Daniel yanked their blade from the kerf and ran.

The oak stood motionless.

Aaron waited at a distance, his head cocked.

He took a step toward the tree.

Ruth whispered the warning, "Aaron." They both knew the way of trees, how they sometimes twisted on the unsawn hinge, fell off-line, and crushed the sawyer.

Aaron took another step. He stopped. Then three long

strides, thoughtless as a bachelor, and in twelve more, he touched the trunk with his fingers, his eyes on the canopy. He gave a tentative push.

Nothing.

Palms flat on the bark, he pushed harder, David against the oak's Goliath. A faint ticking came from within the tree.

"Daniel, the saw," he'd said. He extended an arm.

"No." Ruth caught Daniel's sleeve.

He twisted free and picked up the long blade. The top leaves of the tree quivered.

"Aaron!" This time, Ruth shouted. The limbs trembled, and a loud report echoed through the woods.

Aaron jumped. A clamor of late birds burst from the woods, their alarm heard in Ruth's every bone. Daniel, halfway to his father, dropped the saw and ran. The hinge had broken, the trunk slamming the kerf shut.

The great oak growled, low at first; then, listing, the growl turned screech as it tipped toward Joseph's notch. Aaron fled before an avalanche of limbs thick as a man's body crashed to the earth.

The weight of the giant trunk crushed the first branches. More came after, branch on jagged branch shattering, their great leafy swats in a tangle.

Under a rain of leaves, the littles rushed in, pups at the kill. Ruth's shoulders sagged. She pressed her temples between thumb and fingers.

"Don't shilly-shally." Aaron waded through the downed canopy. He chopped his way to the trunk. Ruth set to with Matthew and Joseph, hauling slash into piles at the edge of the clearing. Daniel and Aaron ripped limb after limb from the trunk. They piled larger branches, the straight for boards, the rest firewood, while Esther, out from under her father's jacket, dropped fists full of twigs on the slash.

By the following evening, the dismembered tree stretched at their feet. Aaron fetched the horses, Jehu, Noah, and two mares. He chained their harness to the trunk.

They waited while he wiped the crosscut, reset the saw's teeth, and filed the bevels sharp. A man never careless of his tools. Never careless of anything.

He finished sharpening, propped one end of the saw on the ground, and stood looking at the severed stump, sap beads sweating from its myriad rings. He heaved a full-chested sigh. "Well," he'd said, his face downcast. "It's done." Aaron ran his fingers through his hair. The boys brushed at their yellowed pants and flicked bits of dead leaves from their shoulders.

Ruth's eyes swam as she pulled at twigs lodged in her prayer cap. She shook Esther's arm. Curled asleep, Esther held the empty food basket, her face pillowed on the doll. "Time to go?" she'd said.

Aaron shouldered the long saw. "Hup now," he called to the horses. The trunk jerked. The horses strained against their harness and tore the tree from the earth's grip. The ends of severed limbs gouged the ground as if they could stop this final separation from the woods.

"At least his tree will be reborn," Aaron had said. He walked slowly ahead of the horses, the saw blade flexing over his shoulder. The farther from the woods he went, the more the handles bounced. Too pleased he was with the start of his Conestoga.

Ruth stayed behind, work a cure for what ailed her. She'd stomped her shovel toward the outermost root and flung rich earth over her shoulder.

At the end of a week, Ruth had pulled the last root, the hole big enough to bury the entire family.

❧

Rocking on the wagon's bench, Ruth folded her hands in her shawl, away from the pricking rain. She dredged up a psalm, but thoughts of missing the westward English crowded out the soothing words. In crept highwaymen and the Indians they'd have to face alone, these thoughts a kind of groundwater pressing on her chest, rising to her neck and over her mouth. The wagon lurched. She grabbed for the wet seat, the backs of her hands bared to the rain.

Beside her, Esther touched her cheek. "You're gray." Her forehead creased. "When Dolly gets gray, I wash her."

"You're a good mother," Ruth said. "Dolly's fortunate to have you."

Ruth started another psalm. *In the Lord I put my trust—*

Aaron, walking beside the wagon, put a hand on Ruth's knee. "You are gray."

"Just tired. I'll be my old self soon; the flow will stop."

Aaron came up beside her, worry filling his eyes. He held her hand. He could make her mad, but underneath it all, she trusted his heart. She always had, to a fault perhaps.

❧

By the midday rest, clouds held their breath. Ruth took comfort as she milked Bathsheba and set out bread and cheese, the milk dipped warm from the bucket. Bathsheba nuzzled Esther and gave her a lick in thanks for the apple.

"Cow slobber," Aaron said. He wiped Esther's face, kissed the top of her head, and glanced at the sky. "Looks to be clearing. We'll make time now."

Aaron sat close to Ruth on the bench, an arm around her shoulders, leg against leg. She leaned into him, drew in the rich scent of his labor, lanolin in the fibers of his wool jacket, wood smoke, and at his neck the scent all Aaron, warm and rich and comforting. "That's the last of the ice," Aaron said. Ruth peeked up at his face. Yes, he believed it and so did she.

❧

That night they all slept warm under canvas, seven peas in a pod on wheels. This too should have been a comfort, all of them snuggled together, but her thoughts of peas and pods led Ruth to those heavy summer evenings listening to frogs inflate their throats.

Cicadas had trilled across overheated fields while she shelled peas on the porch. She had broken the stems and pulled the string edging the pods, pried them open and stripped out the plump green rounds. Her mother had put them in a pot, hot water at a rolling boil.

Those evenings on the porch had been blissful, yet now she twisted them in fearful images. She wouldn't tolerate it. She'd managed birth on the trail; surely she couldn't let the night play tricks on her. She and the family would stay in their pod; no one would pluck them out.

Come daylight, they traveled the downward pitch, and, true to their nature, the unclenched buds blossomed, a reminder to Ruth: *Keep faith.* By next winter, they'd be on new land, the house started, and between then and now the glories of summer and more summer would be theirs.

The after-pains of birth lessened. The blood flow lightened, healing already begun as cramps gathered her innards together. She ignored the click of sleet on canvas, winter's final attempt at dominion. No matter how it blackened the woods, winter could not prevail. And sure enough, the sleet softened to the thrum of rain.

At home they would have set out tomatoes started in the kitchen window, tender seedlings given sun in the day, and brought in if nights proved cold. When the pampered seedlings toughened, Ruth would plant them. This they would do in Idaho.

Ruth bundled Maus in her lap, asleep in the sway of the wagon. She awaited his cry and the bare-breasted moment before he suckled. Esther wiggled beside her.

Matthew and Joseph, by the tailgate, wrestled like foxes. Joseph's heavy boot hit the sideboard with a resounding *clunk.*

Daniel, on foot, leaned into the wind. He scouted ahead with Aaron. Intrepid, they checked for bog in the trail, watched for rockslides. What was a little inclement weather?

❧

Strange, how at home they prayed for spring rain. It tempted green from its sleep, a good start to squash, carrots, to corn in the fields, and wheat. Rain a cause for celebration. But on the move, wet seeped into clothes, dampened bedding even in the wagon. The mired road brought progress to a crawl. Every slow day brought them later to the staging field and the possibility of missing the train. Her brother Dan'l had hammered her with the possibility, had scared her to death, their last Easter at home.

She thought she'd stopped him with her message, every word considered. She'd agonized, each letter of her angular cursive scratched from nib to paper.

*Late March, 1868*

*Dan'l, My Dear One,*

*Your letter warms my heart. Nothing would please me more than to see you and Rebecca and your littles come for Easter, though I know this is a mission cloaked as visit. You come to talk family, to remind us of commitments to our land and the Fold. You want to remind me, I now have the life you and I wished for when we were littles fishing the creek.*

*Believe me when I tell you I have said all this and more. I have clashed with Aaron and he with me, rigid as swords neither of us want to be. You will see no blood, but it is there, in the barnyard, in the haymow, the kitchen. In the bed.*

Yes, she'd written "bed," hoping to shock him into silence.

*I must attend this strife and sew the wounds as best I can. You MAY NOT wade in this mess. That being said, I look forward to a visit.*

*Your Most Loving Sister,*

*Ruth*

Easter had come early in April that year. Dan'l due any minute, and Ruth had prayed the Elders wouldn't choose to visit as well.

If they said, No, you can't leave, they would start a cataclysmic struggle. But Aaron would leave anyway, unless they convinced him of a greater obligation, Aaron's obligation to his neighbors and the Ordnung.

Dan'l had ridden up the drive on horseback, his black jacket loose in the wind. Ruth's big brother, so much like Aaron, tall but heavier set, and his beard seemed grayer, his eyebrows bushier, a man of thought and careful action. He took off his hat.

"Rebecca and the littles took a late start," he'd said as he came through the door, a worried wrinkle above his thick brows.

What a relief to see him, to have him here, a comfort in the tumult, even if silent on the subject Ruth didn't want discussed. Dan'l's eyes traversed the kitchen. He took Ruth's hands in his and kissed her on both cheeks. "Where's Aaron?" he said.

"In the barn getting cider with the littles."

Dan'l's lips close to her ear, he said, "You should have told me sooner."

"You two would have pulled me apart." She stepped back.

"It's madness," Dan'l said.

"Yes," Ruth said. "Well, it is and it isn't."

Aaron came in the door and set a jug on the table. Dan'l spun around.

"Is and isn't what?" Aaron asked, eyeing Ruth.

"Madness," Dan'l said. "What about Indians?" With a face

full of disbelief, he stared at Aaron. Aaron's eyes didn't shift from Ruth.

She shook Dan'l's arm. "You weren't supposed to do this."

"Yes, but you don't know," he said as the kitchen door opened. "They take the hair off your head, skin and all."

"Hush." Ruth put a finger to Dan'l's lips.

Matthew and Joseph brought in cups and put them on the table.

Aaron wiped his mouth and tugged at his beard as if to rid himself of anger. "You should come," he said. "Hundreds of acres, put them to the plow, and they're yours." He uncorked the jug and poured a cider for Dan'l. "You have to work it, and you know work—you've grit like your sister." He cut uneasy eyes toward Ruth. "Never an idle hand."

"Onkel Dan'l." Esther hopped into the kitchen and threw her arms around his knees. "We'll sleep under the stars, did you hear?" She leaned back, looking up. He bent, and tickling her face with his beard, he kissed the top of her black-capped head.

"We each made a mattress." Matthew pointed in the corner. "That's mine."

"But, Aaron . . ." Dan'l started.

"Boys," their father said. "Chores in the barn, go."

Dan'l waited until the boys shut the door. "Aaron, listen." He rested an arm over Aaron's shoulder, a hand on his forearm. "What of your land, your faith?"

"In Idaho"—Aaron sidestepped Dan'l's grip—"they call the land God's country." He corked the jug.

"That's as may be, but English—they'll turn on you." Dan'l paced around the room. He ground his palms together, his face pinched. "Friend against friend, family against family. They eat each other."

"Don't tease," said Ruth.

"I'm serious."

"You sound like Opa."

"You think the Old Country was bad?" Dan'l turned on Ruth. At arm's length, he took her shoulders in hand, the swell of the baby between them. "In the mountains, a stranded family *ate* their dead."

"Enough." She pulled away. "You'll say anything."

"It's true." Joseph had stumped in from the barn earlier than expected. "The Donners," he said, his face alight. "We learned them in school." He looked from Dan'l to Aaron. "Trapped in the snow, they ran out of food. They ate—"

"What a thing to teach." Aaron rubbed his chin. "It's good we leave."

"If you were starving," Joseph said, "could you eat human flesh?" He lifted Ruth's hand and sniffed it.

Esther, Daniel, and Matthew tromped in the door.

"Eat flesh?" said Esther. "Who does?"

"Papa and Mama do," Matthew said. "We get sent to the barn."

"That's communion." Daniel gave Matthew a push. "Not real flesh."

"No?" Joseph seemed disappointed.

"No," said Ruth.

Dan'l sank in a chair. "I'm glad that's cleared up." He rested his elbows on the kitchen table, head in his hands. Behind him, Joseph scuffed the floor, dooryard dirt under his soles. Ruth swept it away with the hearth broom. Too bad her brother's objections didn't sweep away so easily.

He leaned forward, sliding his hands toward her on the table. "Aren't you afraid?"

Aaron watched Ruth from under his brows. She sat across from Dan'l and, reaching out, rested her hands on his. "No," she said, her voice gentle. "I'm not afraid." She'd never lied before, not to anyone and certainly not to Dan'l.

She hadn't yet left New Eden, and she felt untethered; the ground had shifted under her feet, a sensation of falling. Infected already, and she hadn't so much as spoken to an English.

Aaron dragged a chair from the table and sat. He leaned back, his legs straight out resting on his boot heels, arms crossed on his chest.

Dan'l stood. "Please," he said and planted himself in front of Aaron. "Why is New Eden not enough? Think of Ruth, think of your littles, even if she won't." Aaron sat up and tucked his legs close to the chair.

"Daniel!" Ruth flamed. "We go for them." She'd hauled herself upright and stood beside Aaron. "The land is boundless, not like here where English crowd our farms. Soon every breath will smell of English."

"Now who sounds like Opa?"

"Well, look what he did. He came here for us. Can we do less for our littles?"

"I still think it madness." Dan'l shoved his chair into the table.

"Then we are mad," Ruth said. "May it please God."

Aaron stood and took Ruth's hand.

Dan'l strode to the door. He looked back. "Wide is the gate, and broad is the way, that leadeth to destruction . . ." He bowed his head, quietly opened the door, and stepped out.

Ruth ran after him. "Don't go," she said. "Let's say no more. We'll have Easter at Delia's. Meet us there." He and Horst might team against Aaron, but at least she wouldn't be caught in the middle.

The littles ran out the door after him, waving him down the lane.

Aaron closed the door. "Ruth." He hugged her. "Thank you," he said, "for taking my part. You don't neglect us."

"Of course I don't." She took the dirty cups to the dishpan. "I had to stop Dan'l." She sloshed cups in the water. "I couldn't bear the quarrel."

"But you agree." He rested a hand on her shoulder.

"With Dan'l, yes." She faced him. "Our life is here in the Fold. If others came, we could—"

"Others have gone already, a Plain family near Harrisburg."

"Not our kind."

"The Old Order." He huffed. "They're shortsighted as you." He paced to the table. "We begat and begat, and our land's overrun." Hands above his head, his fingers splayed. "Why can't you see?" He bared his teeth. "If Noah had a wife like you . . ."

Fingers into fists, he slammed the table. "This isn't a choice—we have to go."

"You may be right about the land, but it is a choice. Your choice."

"My God, woman." Aaron's face grew blotchy; his eyes crackled. "You know I'm right and yet—" He swung his arm wide. The flat of his hand hit the jug. It tipped off the table and smashed on the floor, the liquid fizzing in a pool. The kitchen filled with the sharp scent of hardening cider.

"See what you made me do." Aaron kicked the broken jug and slammed out to the barn.

Ruth threw rags on the spill, and down on one knee, the baby pushing at her innards, she picked up the shards.

Violence, and she had caused it. No wonder the Ordnung demanded she be submissive. Without it, she'd spoiled the very thing she struggled to save.

❦

With the trek well under way, Ruth thought she'd put anger behind her, yet thinking on Easter brought it fizzing through her. She chafed her arms.

The forest, with its lack of distracting vistas, closed in as heavy as a headache. Every joint ached with inaction. She longed to do something productive.

At home, she washed blue worry away on rivers of sweat, while here the nightly rush, maintaining the simplest necessities, brought little sweat and no real feeling of accomplishment. She wished she could sit comely like Delia.

On further consideration, no, she didn't see a benefit. *Comely is as comely does*—her Oma's words. Her beloved Jehu managed hard work and fine looks. But not being comely, she just wanted to use her talents, and sitting wasn't one of them. These meanderings of idleness added to her irritation.

Esther reached across Ruth and poked Maus. "He's stinky." She dug her face into Ruth's side. "I make in the woods," she said, and poked him again.

"Esther, keep your hands to yourself." Ruth hoped she kept the growl out of her voice. She couldn't blame Esther—everyone's patience was running thin.

"He'll use the woods in good time."

"Before forever?"

Ruth opened his swaddling. "Yes, well before that."

❧

After a steaming dinner, Ruth lit a candle on the bench and wrapped hot stones in blankets at the foot of her littles' covers. They snuggled down in the half-light, inside the wagon too dark to see the tailgate. Maus in his hammock swung from the bows.

Ruth laid herself beside Esther for prayers, starting with, "God bless Oma." She pictured her in the little house in the same valley as Ely's—yes, *Ely's* farm; their land and house and barn were his now. And the animals. His.

Would Ely take his boots off in the kitchen? His bride, would she spoil the seasoning on the iron pans? And the floors, would she scrub them and oil them the way they deserved? Would their dog sleep on the bed? Ruth could see their dog's muddy feet, clear as if she stood in the room. Did they even have a dog?

What came clear was her lack of charity. It nettled her heart, and she disliked this unaccustomed self. Dog in a manger, Ruth was, as she started her own new life.

When would it stop, the sensation that her arm had been ripped away?

"God bless Uncle Dan'l," and on down the family and Fold to the last lamb.

"When is forever over?" Esther kicked a leg in the air.

"It's only been three weeks." Ruth rearranged her blanket.

"Tell about Idaho."

"Papa's told you."

"You tell." Esther burrowed in close. "Tell how we'll eat nothing but bacon and cake." Bacon, Ruth's favorite, Esther's too; Aaron and the boys crazed for cake, the story of its combination told endlessly.

On Ruth and Aaron's second married night, wanting to show him how sweet their life would be, she'd risen in the smallest hours. In secret she'd made his favorite, a cake full of carrots, cream, cinnamon, nutmeg, along with a full cup of dark honey. She'd slipped back beside him in bed and woken before dawn, the bed empty. The smell of bacon wafted up the stairs.

At table that morning, they'd feasted.

Shaking his head, Aaron laughed. "Who eats bacon and cake for breakfast?"

"We do," Ruth had said and cut another slice, crisp pork laid across the top.

Ruth blew a bubbling tickle on the soft skin of Esther's neck. Giggling, the child scrunched her shoulders.

"Sweet and savory," Ruth said. "And your room will be so big Dolly can have her own cradle."

"She's too old," Esther said. "She wants a bed with rope, like mine, and a kitten to sleep with." She wiped the back of her hand across her neck.

"And sheep?" said Joseph from his bed.

"Herds of sheep." Daniel hunkered near. "And Bathsheba will calf and soon we'll have a herd."

"We could use a dog." Matthew's voice hopeful from near the tailgate.

"Yes, a dog." Joseph marched his fingers over Ruth's shoulder and nipped at her neck. "He'd herd sheep."

"Cats catch mice," said Esther.

"I can't wait for Idaho." Joseph shuffled his legs as if running.

"Can I take cats home?" Esther leaned her head up.

"Come Idaho"—Ruth smoothed Esther's cheek—"we *will* be home."

And it would be everything Aaron promised. How much easier it was to see this in the warmth of her quilt.

CHAPTER 5

## Under a Stone Sky

They rode under leaking clouds. Spatters came, then downpours. Mud sucked at the hooves of their six horses, rising to their fetlocks with every step. The wheels churned ruts and kicked up clumps of muck. Another endless day under a stone sky.

An odor of damp horse eddied past Ruth and into the wagon's hint of mildew. Aaron took turns with Daniel on Noah, Ruth always on the bench, every jolt tearing at parts newly healed. Joseph, Matthew, and Esther rocked inside the wagon.

"Joseph, don't kick," said Matthew.

"I'm not." His boot hit the topboard.

Esther held the Bible in front of her face. "Be quiet—I'm trying to read."

"You don't know how."

"Yes, I do." Esther started out loud, "The Lord is my shepherd, I . . ."

"It doesn't say that—you aren't even on Psalms." Joseph flicked the page. "That's Luke."

"I'm going to school in Idaho," Esther said.

"No, you're not. There's no school."

"Mama . . ."

Itchy with continued inaction, they pressed Ruth till she came near ripping her hair. Thank God, the day dried and she shooed them out to run beside the wagon. She wished she could do the same with Maus. His nose stuffed with cold, he woke often, and at the breast he couldn't breathe and suckle at the same time. How could she get him well in this pervasive wet?

At nightfall they made camp, a hole in the Appalachian woods. In the vast dark after bedtime, their fire gave off no more light than a candle.

The later the hour, the more giant trees stalked the night, pillared legs coming closer as twig fingers played shadows on the wagon's cover. Ruth wished she spoke beyond the tongues of men. If she spoke the language of trees, she'd ask them: Please, stand down.

While the others slept, Ruth sat wrapped in damp wool by the fire and watched the orange light push against the dark. Her shoulders steamed as she held her hands to the flame. Each flicker lit a glimpse of movement in the woods. Leaves? Or worse?

When the flickers wilted, she piled on more sticks. *"That our light might shine before men,"* she said aloud. There were no men but Aaron, and he slept undisturbed.

Ruth drew a bag of quilt squares from under the seat and took them to the fire. She flattened the pale brown square Esther had started, and smiled at Dolly's black silhouette, the stitches big and uneven. She'd sewn one arm shorter than the other, the white oval face with an unintended cleft to the chin and a round smudge of a mouth.

Ruth's square had a line of white fence posts. She planned to run them square to square, showing the ripple of Idaho fields. The quilt so much the image of Lancaster—Maus would know New Eden after all. She could only hope Aaron wouldn't think this sewn memory counted as a graven image. She skirted the brink of sin, and she knew it.

Ruth folded the edges of each tiny post. She basted them in place, three to a square; then, with stitches too small to see clearly by the fire, she let her fingers feel the way. Each little stitch, set firmly in place, calmed her as did the vision of what was to come:

Idaho, land of plenty, pastures stretching to the horizon, and the house, Aaron's promise, with a bedroom for every child. In the house, he said, there'd be a fireplace in every room. In the barn there'd be fat cockerels, short-horned sheep, and long-horned cattle. There'd be plum trees in the orchard, quince, and hazelnut by the hundreds. Theirs a fruitful life. He'd brought Ruth to it as she'd brought Jehu to tolerate a saddle.

※

The stallion had been a yearling, resistant, and, having no choice, she'd used the snubbing post. She'd winched him to her will.

Snapping a long lead to his halter, she'd walked him from his stall to the dooryard, where a post stood four feet in the ground, the top above her head. The saddle lay in the dirt. Jehu shied from the tangle of stirrups and girth.

Giving him plenty of rope, Ruth wrapped the end twice around the post. She pulled the rope taut, and Jehu rose on his hind legs. He rolled his eyes, wrenching his head side to side.

At every toss of his head he gave a little slack, and she yanked the rope, bringing him to her inch by inch. Almost at the post, eye to eye, he stiffened his front legs, hooves set. She waited. He tossed his head again, and she had him, his nose snubbed tight to the post.

Repeated days of nowhere to go, he calmed enough, and she threw a blanket on his back, eventually the saddle, then cinched the girth, and after a struggle she mounted.

She loved Jehu, thought herself kind. No whip, she hadn't broken him; she'd bent him to their shared work.

With every jerk of Aaron's invisible rope, Ruth had to keep in mind it didn't mean he loved her less.

❧

In the great sea of dark, she clung to the firelight. She counted her known surroundings. The beaten earth, the half-charred sticks, the undersides of leaves on the nearest tree, a front wheel of the wagon, its spokes thick with dust, the metal rim nicked at the edges, its rock-pitted center. The back wheel was lost to the night.

Ruth stroked her shawl and put a finger to the hard sole of her shoe, so much to be thankful for. A distant coyote yipped.

If only she could see a moon, the soulful eyes, its mouth open as if howling, yet silent as herself. Anything to dispel the dark.

What foolishness. Wasn't what waited beyond the fire's light the same as she'd seen in the day, unrecognizable for now, a joy tomorrow, just as Idaho would be? All in God's hand, a hand she knew but couldn't see. This faith, her constant companion.

❧

At home, Aaron had faced down insidious whispers when he first skipped church. They traveled tongue to ear through the Fold.

By mid-March, still much to do, Aaron had worked into the nights. Sunday came, the day of rest, and there could be no rest.

"Aaron." Ruth had waited in the two-seater buggy, Daniel at the reins. Joseph, Matthew, and Esther in the back, freshly scrubbed in the bucket and sewn into their newest clothes. "Time for church."

Aaron stood over the forge, heat wavering the cold air. He slipped the first of four iron rims into the coals. A section at a time glowed cherry red, and he pounded with his hammer till it turned black.

"Can't stop now." Aaron, in his leather apron and heavy boots, shifted the iron back and forth, enlarging the length of red while keeping the first part hot.

"You shouldn't have started. It's Sunday."

"I know what day it is."

"You can't miss church. Horst will wonder." Her belly foremost, Ruth climbed out of the buggy and marched over to the forge.

He stopped hammering.

Her voice low, she said, "What will I tell him?"

"The truth—what else?"

"You'll come to dinner, then." She returned to the buggy, hiked her skirts, and hauled her great belly through the opening and into the front seat beside Daniel. He flicked the reins and they started for the road.

"Time's short," Aaron called after them.

How could he? The whole Sabbath unkept, and leaving her to say what truth? She couldn't say, *Aaron's in such a rush to get west, he's ignoring the Ordnung, he's ignoring our land, he's ignoring God.* Ruth squirmed as if midges crawled under her clothes.

That Sunday, Horst and his sister Delia's turn to host service, their bell sounded across the fields, the truest sound in the valley. Noah trotted in the lane, joining a line of black buggies, their drivers waiting to tie up in the long shed.

As she waited, Ruth thought she could hear the *plink, plink* of Aaron's hammer. She looked to see if anyone cocked an ear.

Delia greeted her at the door, held her to her full bosom, then hugged Esther. "Where's Aaron?" she asked.

"Brrr, it's cold." Ruth kissed Delia. "Let's get everyone inside."

Other neighbors whispered as she and Esther wended their way to the women's benches. Daniel took Matthew and Joseph to the men's side.

Three hours later at dinner she told them, "A touch of fever." In all honesty, Aaron had a feverish need, what with spring approaching. Any minute a hint of red would come to the tips of winter branches. Fear of it fluttered under her ribs, or was it the baby pushing for more room?

Though the littles knew of the wagon, leaving still smacked of a secret. They'd helped in the build, cutting patterns, shaping the tongue, running gear, axles, wheels, and springs. Aaron had cut the hounds, bars keeping the wagon rigid. Daniel helped dish the wheels, the hubs set like keystones, the spokes brought vertical. They all had a hand in mounting the box and bows. A great endeavor for all, but the end destination made Aaron seem woolyminded, even greedy in light of the plenty they possessed.

Ruth had watched him the way she'd watch a fox-bit dog. Only his familiar body remained, square hands, worn nails, his angular beard and smooth upper lip. His black clothes looked too small as he worked, his head and neck unbinding his shoulders, despite Ruth's having cut his shirts and jackets full, sewn them loose enough to swing a scythe or raise an ax above his head.

Ruth worked at hiding the hairline rift widening between them. If the rift frightened her, what would it do to the littles?

In their eyes, Ruth wanted to keep him untarnished, but the secret came out one morning at breakfast. Ruth had passed a platter of scrapple. Aaron, at the head of the table, planted his hands flat beside his plate. He stood leaning forward and chanted, "We're westing." His voice deepened. "A quest we can't refuse."

Ruth couldn't laugh as she might have, had he been rhyming about anything else.

*West.* The word flapped in the kitchen, like the grackle she'd caught in their milkhouse, wings beating the stone walls, feathers broken and floating in their milk.

Ruth tugged at the strings of her prayer cap. White and brittle, the fabric crinkled on the lump of her braids. She sighed, pressing a hand at the base of her spine where the ache caught fire. The other hand smoothed her apron and rounded under her belly.

The one to come had rested on her spine more than the others she'd carried. It kicked. Another boy, she supposed. Another reason Aaron would cite for going west.

"Who will we visit?" Daniel had looked up from slicing bread in thick slabs.

"Do they have littles?" Matthew asked around a mouthful of pigs' feet.

"Swallow before talk," Ruth said.

"How far is west?" Joseph's eyes gleamed above sharp cheekbones. "Do we spend the night?"

"It's far," Aaron told them. "Months of nights just to get there."

Joseph looked at Ruth. Curious, he'd go anywhere at a dead run.

"This is no visit." Ruth hadn't meant to say it. Aaron needed to explain; it was his idea.

"Live there?" Joseph asked, eyebrows up. "Forever?"

The three boys had stopped slathering butter on bread.

"Forever." Esther thumped the table with a spoon. "And then we'll come home." She smiled and scooped corn pudding onto her plate.

The boys stared at their father.

"We go after snow melt," he said.

"How many wagons?" Daniel, the practical.

"One. Ours."

"We go alone?"

"We go with God."

"And the Ordnung?" Ruth had said. A simple question, not a harridan's accusation, but that's how it must have sounded.

"Idaho," Aaron said. "Just think." He turned to the window with its view of their valley's western ridge. "Land for you and all the boys to come. A farm of your own."

Matthew dropped his fork. "I don't want to live alone." His eyes had filled.

Daniel leaned an arm around his shoulder, his dark head against Matthew's lighter brown. "When you're big, Matthew."

"I'll never be that big."

Esther tapped the table. "What about me? I want to be a farmer."

"Esther." Ruth pressed a hand on hers. The tapping stopped. "We are farmers, fine ones at that."

The discussion should have ended there. How she wished it had.

Aaron brought his eyes from the window and spoke low as if to the bread on his plate. "I'd rather a fine wife."

Ruth's hand slid off Esther's. She touched her lips with trembling fingers, then took up her water glass. Water overflowed the corners of her mouth, ran down her cheeks into the neck of her dress, and trickled between her swollen breasts.

The littles shifted in their chairs. They watched Aaron as

he traced the grain in his grandmother's table, the wood alive with oils from her hands and the hands of her children and grandchildren. The first gray flecks in his beard moved as he mumbled, ". . . uneasy in her grave if we don't take the—"

"Table!" Ruth had jumped to her feet. She shouldn't have. "Never mind the table!" Her words rushed out, a horde of dogs yapping high and hysterical. "She'll rise right out of her coffin before we pack."

All this time later, Ruth's ears burned at the thought.

She'd cleared her plate from the table, scraped breakfast into the slop bucket, and ran out behind the house, her stomach heaving.

And the littles had seen it all, a chasm, she feared, opening beneath her feet and theirs.

Chill had taken her as if the fires of a larger hearth had died, cold echoing the house. Frost rolled through the barn and across fields gone stark as moonscape, home as she knew it no longer familiar. Yet their days had continued apace, Ruth lonely in the midst of Fold and family.

The following Sunday, she had waited for the clop of hooves announcing Delia and Horst's arrival for an evening visit. Aaron dared work in the shed, leaving Ruth to take the brunt of the visitors' comments. To explain the unexplainable.

Their buggy at the front entrance, Delia and Horst stepped out, his overgrown littles left at home. Ruth's brood clamored 'round, Delia a favorite of theirs as well as hers.

She stood at the open door. "Hurry, hurry—it's cold." The hubbub dying down, she knew Aaron's mallet would ring in their ears. Delia didn't seem to notice, the sound blocked by her bonnet, but Horst did. He rolled his eyes at Ruth. "Tsk-

tsk," he said. *Tsk-tsk*, and he didn't know the half of it. Being their head Elder, he would figure it out.

Three other families arrived and filled the house, distracting one another, she hoped. They milled around platters of food on the long table and talked. Ruth offered milk.

She tried to ignore their heads pressed together, the furtive looks in her direction, the comments said too loud and with too much innocence. "You're thinning your stock?"

"Yes." She didn't tell them Aaron had taken lambs to Harrisburg; he'd exchanged them for money. "Aaron thinks our fields are overgrazed." His truth, even if it wasn't hers.

"I saw a wagon through the shed window—is he a farmer or a hauler?"

"Farming's our life," Ruth said.

"Ours too, but who needs a wagon so big?"

Ruth arranged molasses cookies on a plate and passed them with the apologetic smile of a hostess interrupted by her duty.

Where one neighbor left off, another continued the needling. Herr Yoder stopped her circuit with a hand on her arm. "Is Aaron sick? He missed dinner after church, an especially good one—but then, you know, you were there." Did he blame her?

"Yes," she said, tossing it off with an uneasy laugh. "I was there—I—"

"Ruth," Delia interrupted, her body cutting off the inquisition. Dear Delia, Ruth's rescuer when she needed it most.

"Esther says you're making Dolly a quilt." Delia took Ruth's elbow and dragged her to the stairs. "Show me."

"I have to go—"

"No, you don't." Delia's soft arm folded on Ruth's, escape to the kitchen impossible.

Upstairs Delia pushed her into the bedroom and closed the door. They sat on the edge of the bed facing each other. "Enough," Delia said and took Ruth's hands. "This is me you're talking to." Her eyes, full of loving concern, invited the truth. "What's happened to Aaron?"

Ruth couldn't hold out against the lure of their friendship. She was tired. She needed an understanding ear, and none was more so than Delia's. She'd need her as this mess unfolded.

Aaron should have been her confidant, but his ear had turned deaf. Or perhaps her skill at words failed her. Either way loneliness had echoed around her.

Ruth hung her head. "Aaron wants to go west."

"Stop funning." Delia's breast shook with merriment. She flicked Ruth's knee. "Now, tell."

Ruth looked her in the eye. "He'd go without me." Ruth had known it in her heart, yet saying the fact aloud made the admission fill the room like a smoldering fire.

Delia covered her mouth. "No. You have to stop him."

Ruth shook her head. From downstairs, she heard the clink of forks on plates and the shuffle of boots mixed with companionable voices ebbing and flowing as their friends shared a week of stories and ate their way through Ruth's pies, cakes, and cookies.

Delia wrapped her arm around Ruth's shoulders, and in a rush Ruth told all to the last truth. "I promised to love, honor, and obey, but . . ."

"Oh, Ruth—" Delia hugged her, so warm and soft and

reassuring, Ruth struggled to hold her tears. "Whatever you do," Delia said, "my hands are yours—our house is yours."

Horst might have other notions, yet for Ruth the smolder in the room thinned. Delia gripped Ruth by the shoulders. "*You* can't stop him, but Horst can." Her voice high with excitement, she said, "I'll ask him."

"Please don't," Ruth had said. "Leaving will be hard enough. I couldn't bear a shunning, and you know that's what would happen." All those backs turned like they'd done to Herr Booker.

His boy found him drunk as death, pissing in the horse trough. He'd lost his balance and would've drowned if his wife hadn't yanked him out. He too had skipped church, blaspheming when the Elders confronted him.

Then everyone turned their backs, every minute of every day. His wife and children too.

❧

Rain on the trail, days and days of it, and just when Ruth thought she'd never see the sun again, it slanted through the clouds and hatched a spangle of rainbows. Drops, clinging to every twig and weed, splashed glory through the land. Joy ignited beneath a bluing sky.

The trail dried and hardened. The pace picked up. Trees went by in a blur.

Out in the open, they were warmed by the sun, heated inside the wagon, and as the days passed an odor grew more pervasive. Though not the deadly stench of a carcass, this interior stench, destructive in its own way, couldn't be left untended.

"We have to stop," Ruth said. A furry green had bloomed on their belongings.

"No." Aaron urged the horses on. "We're making time."

"We're mildewed. All will be spoiled by Pittsburgh."

At a clearing in the wood, Aaron and Daniel let down the tailgate and unloaded the heavier baskets and bureaus, opening them to the sun. Ruth wiped every surface with a water and vinegar mix. Esther spread her blankets on the ground, Dolly beside them. Daniel threw mattresses over the frontboard to Joseph, who kicked the straw loose with his heavy boot.

Matthew, arms extended, wheeled like a swallow through the mist. Ruth snagged his collar as he passed. "See to your bedding," she said, and laid out pants and jackets and dresses. The center of the clearing took on the look of their dooryard before departure, only more so, every container dumped, the contents scattered.

By late afternoon Aaron wielded his ax, chopping wood for the evening fire. Ruth folded the shirts that had dried and stacked them ready to go back into drawers.

In the empty wagon Maus slept in his dried hammock. To the right of the wagon the horses grazed on picket, the woods beyond them. Ruth checked the bureau drawers, most unstuck in the sun. Over bushes, their down quilts flapped like preening geese.

The horses lifted their heads. Grass hung from their mouths; their chewing stopped. Heads shaken high, they nickered, one to the other.

Noah fidgeted. He sidestepped to the width of his picket line and stamped his front hooves. Ruth shook out a blanket and watched the horses. Jehu reared, his attention on the woods.

The mares pulled at their tethers, their hind legs bunched low, eyes rolling.

"What a fuss." Aaron headed for the horses. He wended through his drying possessions, an eye on the trees.

"Aaron, what . . . ?" Ruth followed his look.

He raised a hand. "Hush," he said. "Don't move." With an outstretched arm, he pointed at the woods.

Ruth squinted. A barn-width away, she saw movement in the trees, a spot between the horses and the wagon. At the edge of the woods, an animal the size of a calf glided through the trunks, its spotted hide blending in the shadows. Ruth shifted her head and, peering, made out the biggest cat she'd ever seen. It came closer, wide head, tawny, its long ears tufted black. The magnificent creature watched the horses.

Even big as a calf, the mountain cat wouldn't take on a horse, surely. But the littles?

Matthew, Joseph, and Esther worked safe behind Ruth as they spread their clothes. Daniel patted his way among the horses. He cooed and rubbed Jehu's ears.

They settled, and in the silence a cry came from Maus, out of sight in his hammock. The cat turned from the horses. He crouched, lifted a large front paw, and stalked, one slow deliberate step after the next, toward the wagon.

Maus would be just that, a mouse to this giant cat. Panic swept through Ruth, the wagon being between her and the cat. She pictured its easy leap to the bench, the pounce, Maus's cry silenced. Then from the wagon, the cat's long body would stretch, front feet hitting the ground, Maus caught in its maw and carried into the woods.

"Aaron!"

The animal swiveled its ears and, crouching lower, took liquid steps toward Maus's cry. Aaron bolted, the ax above his head. His long strides ate the distance between himself and the cat. Ruth leapt forward, her short legs no match for Aaron's.

The cat balked. Its body twisting, the head snapped around at Aaron. Rocking on its haunches, the animal gathered itself ready to spring. Aaron surged forward. With a raging yowl, he bore down on the cat, ax descending, and, seemingly without effort, the cat spun low on its hind legs and slipped to the woods, where shadow swallowed him.

"What was that?" Matthew said.

"Just a cat." Aaron hung the ax on its hook. "Nothing to worry about."

"Papa." Daniel laughed. "You sounded like a cat in heat."

Ruth watched the edge of the woods. "I hope he doesn't think so." She whirled around. "Esther? Oh, there you are."

"If he comes back, may I keep him?" Esther said.

Aaron scowled. "No, he's not a pet."

The back of Ruth's neck prickled. She scanned the woods again. She had to be more vigilant. Maus put a whole new twist on dangers.

"Please," Esther said. "I won't let him eat Maus."

Ruth admired Esther's certainty, but then, she hadn't seen the cat.

❧

Half a day to reload, and the afternoon started gray, too early to know what would come. The cat didn't.

Ruth walked beside the wagon, the littles ranging ahead with Aaron while she kept an ear out for Maus. Free of the wagon's confinement, they walked, stretching hamstrings. So many days cooped in the wagon had sapped strength from their bodies.

Sun filtered through the overcast. Sun and more sun, recompense for the stone ceiling they'd carried on their backs those last slow weeks.

Their clothes, hardened dry, softened with use, the whiff of mildew grown faint. They felt the sun on their shoulders and reveled in its increasing warmth. Buds in the trees relaxed and, ripening, burst pink and white and the palest green. All over the woods the soft green wash grew leafy.

They pressed on through the day, making good time. The sun crested overhead, guiding them west with its red orb sliding down the sky, and when it disappeared Aaron said, "It's in Idaho before us. All we have to do is follow. Our land awaits."

Maus fussed less. A rash from the damp dried along with everything else. Ruth's bottom, fussy as Maus's, recovered from blisters raised by the wet bench. The trip started to feel like a courting picnic, all of one mind, the future gleaming. More sun streamed from God's blue heaven, and yes, He was in it, all come right with the world.

Ruth slept most nights. Her bleeding turned spotty. Esther no longer touched Ruth's face, with eyes full of worry. The child's brow smoothed.

Lulled by the motion, Ruth rode the bench, the sky a consistent bluer than blue, Aaron her fortress.

❧

During the months before departure, those days waiting, wondering if the Elders would appear, she'd missed that all-encompassing fortress. It was hard to know what Delia had told Horst, but shortly after Ruth's confession, the Elders did appear.

At her bread, Ruth had seen them through her kitchen window. Intent as crows, the five in black hats, cut across Yoder's field, clearly knowing they'd find Aaron building his wagon in the shed. They skirted where he'd plowed, the earth lumpy and sprouted with last fall's withered cornstalks. Harrowing to come would smooth the field for planting.

The Elders crossed the road and came up the lane between the barn and woodshed. Their boots crunched gravel, Horst in the lead, all faces in shadow.

Ruth wiped her hands on a towel. She smoothed her apron over the baby and patted her prayer cap before heading out the door. The wind caught strings of the white cap and scourged her shoulders.

"Welcome," she'd said. Cold blew across the plowed field, smelling of turned earth with its sweet promise of summer harvest to come.

The men nodded as they continued toward the shed's smallest door, no usual smile above their beards. Horst set his knuckles to the door, and, lifting the latch, he entered. Ruth followed the Elders inside. They didn't remove their hats; how could it be other? This wouldn't take long. After all, how long could it take to say, *This is forbidden*?

Inside, Aaron and the boys stopped work. Esther, quiet for once, stood beside Daniel and looked from Ruth to Aaron. Ruth moved over to the stove, her hands clasped on top of her belly. At the workbench the boys laid down their smoothing blades, their mouths in open awe.

Aaron swallowed, the sound loud in the quiet of stopped work. He straightened and pushed the forelock out of his face. A curl of planed wood stuck to his sleeve. He plucked it and, with his hand at his side, crumbled the shaving in little pieces, dropping them by his boot.

Grouped near the door, the Elders stood dwarfed by the wagon, its bows arched just shy of the rafters. The construction finished but for a final scraping and laying the canvas over top.

"A fine piece of work," Horst said, his eyes laced with suspicion.

Aaron swallowed again. "Long in the making," he said. His voice cracked.

Did Noah's neighbors admire the ark, or think him mad as he gathered the animals? Were they desperate when the clouds gathered, banging on the hull with their fists and begging for help?

"A wagon that big could take a lot to market," Horst said.

"More than I'll ever raise." The toe of Aaron's boot cut a line in the broken shavings. Esther scooped them with her hands, dumped them in the kindling, and stood next to Ruth.

"You'd be a help to your neighbors, wouldn't you?" Horst said.

"As long as I'm around."

"And how long is that?" Horst fingered his beard.

"Till snow melt," Matthew volunteered. Ruth nudged him.

"Soon as that?" Horst crossed his arms. The others did the same.

"Yes," Joseph said. "Everything's ready."

"And where are you going?"

"Idaho," Aaron said. He looked directly at Horst.

"I'm guessing that's not in Lancaster County."

"No. It's not." The news was out, and Aaron's shoulders relaxed.

"It's away forever," Esther said. "Then we come home."

Ruth glared at her.

"How does that fit with staying separate?" Horst said.

"Poorly at first."

"And at second?"

"We'll be separate unto ourselves until you join us."

"Me?" Horst's eyebrows shot up. He glanced at the others.

"Yes, you."

Isaiah, the smallest Elder, lowered his brows.

"Tell me," Aaron said. He moved closer to Horst. "How many sons do you have?"

"Eight, and you know it."

"Yes, and how much land?" Aaron stood square, steady hands spread, palms up without a tremor.

"A hundred and twenty acres. You know that too."

"Yes, the same as your brothers, your father's land divided. And when you die each of your sons will get how much?"

No one spoke. The Elders looked at one another.

Long moments stretched longer.

"Fifteen," Horst said, so soft it was hard to hear.

"What will your sons raise on fifteen acres?"

Again the Elders looked at one another in silence, except Isaiah. Was he listening?

"Not much more than a kitchen garden," Aaron said.

The Elders looked at their boots, shiny black against the

sawdust-covered floor. One of Isaiah's had dust on the toe. His face crinkled with distaste, he dragged the toe down the back of his pant leg. Ruth could see *No* written all over him, his mind made up before Aaron spoke. Aaron, at the least, deserved their full attention.

Horst took off his hat. He dented the crown and let out a long breath. He turned the hat over and popped the crown flat again. He looked at the other Elders.

"There's merit in your words. Already, Mennonites are migrating." Horst flicked sawdust from his hat. "But land alone isn't the answer. *Together—*" He flapped his hat against his palm. "We meet tribulation *together . . .* We make life right for all. Breaking with us puts body and soul at risk, yours and Ruth's and your littles'. Is this your intention?"

Aaron slammed his palm on the workbench. "I'm not breaking."

Ruth's whole body jerked. Esther ducked behind her skirts.

"I'm expanding." In his vehemence a fine spray flew from his lips.

The boys hung on to the table as if blown by a gusting wind.

Aaron pointed at Horst. "I do this for the Fold, for you and your sons, so don't accuse me of breaking." Breathing hard, Aaron swept the workbench clean of shavings.

Horst backed toward the door. "We don't question your faith, only your methods." He nodded at Ruth's belly. "And your timing." Unlatching the door, he clapped his hat on his head. The others touched the brims of their hats with a forefinger and filed out, leaving the door open.

Aaron shut it, his breath beginning to slow. "I'm glad that's over."

"Is it?" The baby kicked.

"But they didn't say no."

Ruth brushed her forehead with her fingers as if to banish a headache.

"Idaho, here we come," said Joseph with a big smile.

"But what did they mean by timing?" said Daniel. "What's wrong with snow melt?"

"Time for chores," Aaron said. "Go tell Bathsheba. She's waiting."

Heading for the barn, Ruth had heard Bathsheba's bell and the other cows lowing, their udders full. She let all five in, each going to the proper slot without being prodded. She haltered them and moved her three-legged stool next to Bathsheba, the leader, their biggest and best milker. The cow tipped her big head, bending one round eye on Ruth.

Bathsheba had stamped a hoof and thrown her horns side to side. "Sorry, old girl," Ruth said. "I know I'm late." The Ordnung wasn't the only rule of law on the farm.

Finished milking, Ruth kissed the cow's nose. Her bell swung from the strap on her neck. The clank would guide searchers if she were ever lost. Ruth stroked the cow's ears.

"If Aaron walks with English," she said, "will God still kiss him?" She whispered the question in the soft hair of Bathsheba's ear and unbuckled the halter. The cow, possibly closer to God than all of them, gave Ruth a look, licked her face, and ambled to pasture.

## CHAPTER 6

## Mid-May—Generosity Eaten

On and on, they rode alone through the woods, between the branches, a flaming sun setting thin clouds aglow, until one night the sky cleared to a deep black studded with uncountable white points.

Camping in a field open to the sky, the littles clamored at bedtime, "You said we'd sleep under the stars."

"Please?" Esther said. "Tonight."

"I'm ready now." Matthew threw a peeled stick on the fire. "I scraped my teeth."

"Get your bedding."

They lined up mattresses like wheel spokes around the fire's hub, Aaron between Matthew and Joseph. Ruth, with Maus tucked against her, lay next to Esther.

Matthew rolled close to Aaron, one leg off the other side touching Daniel. "Are there bears?" he asked.

"They're more afraid of us than we are of them," Ruth said. She hoped she was right. Esther kicked off her quilt and sat up. She turned her palms to the sky.

"Does God hang stars when it's cloudy?" she asked.

"Where does He store clouds?" Matthew wanted to know. "Where?"

"By the sea," Daniel said. "He fills them with water, then wrings them out."

"I'm glad He's taking a rest." Aaron tweaked Daniel's arm.

"Does He get lonely out there all by himself?" Esther folded Ruth's hand in hers.

"He's too busy." Daniel pushed Matthew's leg under his quilt.

"Besides, He has us to talk to." Matthew tucked his arms under.

"Keep your prayers short," Aaron said. "He's heard enough for tonight and so have I."

❧

Maus turned fourteen days old as they lurched their way valley to ridge, the land desolate, the Appalachian road mean with shale sliding under the horses' hooves. From time to time, smoother trails forked into the woods, these narrow and less travel-torn than the wider one leading west. The last tight buds cracked, green poking out like chicks from a shell.

Joseph ranged ahead. "Is that a house?" he said. He rushed down a lesser path.

"Stick to the way." Aaron waved him to the main route.

"Who would live there?" It's hard to know how a body could survive on such inhospitable land. For every step forward the horses slipped back a half, and conditions grew worse as rain began again. Dust between slithering stones turned to mud. Then washout.

The trail ahead grew steeper. Jagged rills carried water down the road in ever-deepening cuts. The wagon pitched slowly as one wheel sank, then rose and fell into another cut.

Aaron reined in the horses. "Too deep to pass."

"What do we do?" Daniel asked.

Ruth looked through the rear of the wagon. The road dropped behind them, steep and curving from sight.

Aaron dismounted and stood at Jehu's head. "Turn back."

The thought of home jolted Ruth.

"Back to the last side path," he said.

Daniel, at Jehu's head, guided the horses backward step by hesitant step. The wagon rolled under its own weight to a widening in the trail.

"Hold it, Daniel." Aaron nudged Noah's chest as the first two pairs of horses sidestepped. The tongue turned, and they backed and filled until full around, the wagon headed east to a side road where they would hopefully swing west.

Returning couldn't be. Between them, Ruth and Aaron had blighted any chance.

Ruth had thought nothing could be worse than Aaron's words about wanting a decent wife. She'd been wrong.

The night before leaving, he'd showed her the other side of his tongue. He spread silence thick through their bedroom. The candle blown, Ruth lay awake, Aaron stick-straight on his side of the bed.

Unapproachable, he'd withheld his touch so long, they wouldn't need more land, the coming child their last.

Despite the dark, Ruth knew the set of his face, eyes staring at the ceiling, his jaw tight. She heard the stampede of his thoughts breaching the silence. Their thudding hooves trampled her.

Aaron had rolled, his back to Ruth. The cover lifted from her part of the bed and a cold draft slid in. The straw mattress hissed.

Staying close to her edge, Ruth curled on her side, clutching the quilt to her bosom. Behind her, the winter-white sheets stretched, a prairie between them.

If they stayed on the farm, what home would it be with words cutting wounds too deep to heal? Or equally bad, they could live in their own private shun, he a captive and she a harridan looking for forgiveness. Would he forgive her, and if he did, would life be as complete as if there had been nothing to forgive?

Ruth had mulled these things as she buckled Jehu and Noah to the plow. Leaving on his mind, Aaron had refused to turn the earth.

If he wouldn't till the fields, she would, heavy work an inducement to the other sort of labor. It should have worked.

As the spring afternoon warmed, her work grew heavier. She pushed on, two horses moving fast, her team agile enough to ride, thick of flank, and muscled to the heaviest pull. Perfect for the Conestoga—yes, equally perfect for the farm.

Aaron and Daniel worked in the barn, docking lambs' tails and tying off testicles as her father had done that blessed courting day. From that day when she'd first seen Aaron's pathetic little finger, she'd wanted to protect him. She never thought protecting him from himself would be the hardest.

Strapping the harness on Jehu, she'd snagged his ear and yanked the strap into position. He shook his head and kicked Noah. Noah rolled his rump into Jehu, who bit him smartly on the withers. "Whoa, now, none of that," she said.

Usually the horses guided themselves, the way they did when haying, Matthew and Joseph packing the hay that Ruth threw rhythmic and high on the wagon's growing pile. But that day, Ruth was at the plow while Matthew and Joseph fished the creek and Esther waited, ready with water and a cup in the shade of the hedgerow.

Ruth set the blade of the plow and called *"Hup"* to the horses. She pushed down on wood handles as the horses forged ahead, and the earth opened, curling over in a smooth, even row. Her land, the earth she loved—how could she leave it?

Though she'd been childbearer, cook, housekeeper, milker, horse trainer, sheep shearer, gardener, plowman, field hand, without Aaron she would have no land, no standing, and, worst of all, no love to share joy or leaven her cares.

Love. Where was it? She'd doubted she'd see it again, Aaron no longer the man she'd married. It hadn't occurred to her he could change as quickly back to the man she knew, that this change lay within her grasp.

In the meantime, she finished plowing the last acre, all the while fretting over the way forward. Every direction held disaster.

With the horses still nipping and kicking, she and Esther had returned to the barnyard. Ruth stroked Noah's blaze and thumbed the hair in Jehu's ears. She knew her mood had lit their sniping. She washed them down and left them fed and bedded in their stalls.

As dusk came on, she collected the water bucket and Esther before heading for the creek. Ruth forced a cheery lilt. "What do you suppose they've caught?"

"Dolly doesn't like fish." Esther held the doll high by one arm.

"She won't have to eat it, but you will."

On the rock bank the boys sat bareheaded, hats held down by stones. Three glass-eyed trout lay in their creel.

"Too small," Matthew said.

"We'll starve." Joseph held his stomach. Ruth set the water bucket aside and sat behind him, both hands on his slumped shoulders. She felt the strings of growing muscle, the coarseness of his hair. He could eat three fish and still be hungry. His ankles showed at the end of his pant legs. He needed a new boot with a higher sole.

"In Idaho, the rivers overflow with fish," he said. She heard accusation: *You, my own mother—how can you stand between me and the future your parents gave you?*

Matthew's line gave a jerk. He jumped, grinning as he hauled hand over hand. The taut line ripped the water's surface. Droplets sprayed and fell back in overlapping circles. But the line went slack. His face sagged. "I lost it."

He leaned over and reached for his spool. The line jerked, tipping him toward the creek. His shoes slapped the stone ledge as Joseph grabbed his arm and jammed a heavy boot against the rock. Together they pulled on the line.

A shadow flicked in the dark water, and they knelt, each on one knee, the other foot braced at the water's edge. Joseph shielded his eyes.

Flick and fade.

Again flick, closer this time, and the shadow rose with a rush, cut the surface, and bolted high, water showering down on them all. Joseph caught the line. He whipped it, flinging their catch on the rocks behind them.

Matthew screamed, "Snake!" Both boys leapt for high ground as three feet of glistening black muscle whipped the rocks. Esther's bucket clunked into the creek.

She clutched her mother's skirts, the cloth bunched around her face. Ruth shifted the child behind her. "Not a snake," she said, "an eel."

The creature launched into the air, flexed, and fell farther from the creek. All that fight with no hope of gaining the water. Again and again, it leapt, mouth open, the hook firmly embedded behind bared teeth. Ruth felt every twist as if she herself writhed on the bank.

Gashes opened in the eel's graying skin, the meat near ruin.

"Mama," Matthew whimpered. "Mama, make it stop."

Ruth stood on the bank, hands raised, looking from child to tearful child, to the eel, to the bucket floating peacefully downstream.

"What a ruckus." Daniel came out of the field, picking his way onto the ledge.

Ruth handed Esther to him and lifted her chin toward the top of the bank. "Take her," she said. "And stay there." She took a knife from the basket. Along with it came the smell of fish.

Her legs spread beneath her skirts, she faced the eel. She rocked with its motion. Teeth flashed as it writhed at her, then away, and she darted, snatching behind the eel's head, and with one stroke of the knife down its pale belly she spilled innards on the rocks.

Avoiding the roiled intestines, the littles clambered to her. Esther sniffed and ground her nose with a fist. They circled Ruth, eyeing the eel as it hung from her grasp.

"You saved it," Joseph said.

"Not to the eel's way of thinking." Ruth washed the eel's organs into the creek.

"Father will be pleased." Daniel grinned.

Ruth knelt at the water. She ran the limp body through her hands and sluiced it. So close to ruin. She should have stopped its thrashing sooner. She should have stopped her own.

"May God forgive me," she whispered.

Daniel retrieved the bucket and Ruth curled the eel in the bottom. She washed her hands and straightened her prayer cap. "Yes," she said. "Your father *will* be pleased."

Evening encroached. Hatchling insects rose above the creek. They wheeled and disappeared as shadow flooded the valley.

The baby low in the spread of her hips, Ruth toiled across the field toward the stone house. Halfway there, the littles swung their arms, spinning and leaping and chirping. Her cheerful swarm of crickets.

Ruth struggled for breath, the air too sweet to breathe. This land, this life, already distant as a memory.

❧

By late afternoon they dipped into an Appalachian valley. "Sun's in our face," Aaron said. "God be praised."

More houses appeared. Ruth wouldn't consider them houses, more like chicken sheds, only worse, with weathered slats nailed crooked, ridgepoles collapsing, windows without mullions or glass. She wouldn't condemn a chicken to such a structure. The spreading pox infected the trees.

One shack, a dooryard from the trail, sat in a scratched-out clearing, the building slumped beside a could-be garden sprung with weeds. A stunted family littered the porch, thirteen, maybe more of them, pale as maggots, dirt streaked, their faces sharp with want. The elders slouched in broken chairs. A descending gaggle of littles hung off the porch. Some lay on the steps, feet kicking in the air. They laughed, open mouths showing rotted teeth in swollen gums. One child drooled from a slack mouth. A small girl held an infant covered with fly-bitten sores.

"What have they done," Ruth said, "to deserve this?"

Leaning in the crooked doorframe, the biggest man-child wore torn pants and a coating of dirt like the rest, his bent-stick ribs above a protruding belly. He scratched under his arm while his hooded eyes followed the course of Ruth's Conestoga, seeming to take in her succulent littles, the glow of their cheeks.

One by one, the pale rabble came to attention. They raised their chins as if catching a scent. All eyes on Ruth, she felt the wealth of flesh on her bones, how stout the cloth that covered her.

Beside these barefoot specters she stood out, a temptress in fancy clothes, luring them to some ungodly purpose. She should flee for their sake.

She wanted to snatch the infant and make off with it. Or

for her own soul's sake, she ought to reach out, give them food from her carefully allotted stores.

She knew the better thing to do, yet buried her face next to Maus. An unthinkable thing if she'd lived at home. Fear had its teeth in her throat. Their food allotted day to day, her family came before all else. What would this say to her children, watching her turn from these people's need? And yet again the risk nailed her to the bench.

This was not who she wanted to be. She believed the tenets of giving and receiving.

The wagon rolled on. Aaron with his eye on the trail, and those people out of sight, Ruth's muscles unwound. Shame bloomed.

Those wretched had taken her generosity and eaten it as surely as if they had eaten her flesh. Would she be forever stripped? Who would she be when they arrived in Idaho?

By the campfire that night, Ruth, fully dressed, bent her ear to what her eyes couldn't see. The trees ticked. Her heart lurched.

"Aaron," she whispered.

"I'm asleep," he said.

"Those people on the porch, are they the people of the west?"

Aaron didn't answer.

It shouldn't matter. In Idaho she and her family would be separate.

But what kind of separate?

A new kind, alone, nothing safe about it, and these specters would hover, pale on the fringes of her existence, accosting her if she dared venture from their land for horseshoes, for nails, for finding a flour mill. At least in New Eden the English looked like people.

❧

The days repeated themselves, Ruth braced on the seat. With an arm around Esther, she let her hold Maus while Aaron rode Noah by turns with the boys. The ones not riding clambered in and out of the wagon.

They passed what looked like the same crumbling shack, as if they were driving in circles. On the porches people seemingly delivered of the same worn-out womb lingered in the dirt, pale, their bones bent, a few more, a few less, all staring, their eyes intent and cold as snakes. Ruth couldn't shake their chill.

She watched the crest in the road behind. Watched for a cart, a lone mule, horses that might follow. She swiveled on her rump and looked ahead, staring into the woods, twitchy as a rabbit's nose. Would she be a rabbit and freeze in the path of danger?

The constant peering twisted a crink in Ruth's neck. She was being a goose, frightening herself. None of *Them* had threatened her, had they?

Every bite of food seemed fancy, yet tasted like tree bark. Ruth busied herself changing Maus's swaddling. She glanced forward. There was nothing to see, and she looked back through the wagon over the barrels, chests, and bedding, out the open circle of canvas to the road stretching empty in the distance.

So busy watching what wasn't behind her, she missed the approach of a cart in front until she heard a mule bray. A hard-working team of two plodded on dainty hooves, closer and closer. The open cart rocked on out-of-round wheels. Three men in dirt-colored clothes crowded the seat, the driver in the middle, an old man hunched on one side chewing a stick, on the other a thin fellow in a crumpled hat. A fourth, young and skinnier, his greasy hair long, stood behind the bench, next to a teetering pile of wood boxes.

Ruth girded herself. "Daniel," she called. "Matthew, Joseph." She waved them into the wagon. "I've lost an apple in the load, there in the middle." She pointed in their close-packed goods. "By the flour. It'll rot." That should keep them.

Ruth tied Esther's bonnet and snugged her close, face against her dress, the two of them together under her shawl. She counted on looking like one heavy person. Esther wormed in and didn't peep.

The cart came steadily closer.

As they pulled abreast, Ruth tipped her own bonnet down, just a sliver of the strangers visible. Four of them. They could easily overpower Aaron.

In the face of their stare, she shrank once more in her oh-so-fancy flesh, her wagon shamefully big and filled with necessities these people had surely never seen.

Aaron looked easy in the saddle.

Ruth crushed Esther under her arm. A muffled voice came out. "Mama." She dug her elbow into Ruth's side.

The men slowed their swaybacked team. Eyes in grizzled faces crawled over Ruth and the horses like fingers pulling at her clothes, unbuckling the horses' harness, rooting through the wagon. Cousin Ely's greed paled before these men, his greed more like inheritance without Ruth and Aaron actually being dead.

The malnourished boy chewed a mouthful of who knew what. If eyes could kill, they'd be dead already.

He tipped up his face, pursed his lips, and squirted an arc of black juice onto the trail, where it sat in a glistening pool. Ruth shrank farther into her shawl. The men laughed with the high cackle of guinea fowl.

"Right fine horses," the driver said. He slanted his mules across the trail. Aaron stopped. Jehu nose-to-nose with the mules, the team jigged in place.

"Sure could use one." The man nodded to the back of the cart. "Coffins is too much for mules. Wanna trade?" They snickered.

Joseph popped his head out from the canvas, his smile big and welcoming. "Ho, who are *you*?"

"Joseph!" Ruth hissed. That Joseph—he'd invite them to dinner. Aaron shifted in the saddle, the jerk line in his hand.

"Don't think yer mammy wants to know." The men cackled so hard the young one staggered against the three coffins stacked like soup bowls on the flatbed. The pile wobbled and the tops leaning behind the bench fell against him. He gave a yip as if he'd been bitten.

"You bust them things," the driver said, "I'll bust you."

"Sturdy work," Aaron said without a smile. "Business looks good."

"Can't complain." The oldest chewed on a stick. "Don't s'pose you're in need."

"Thank you, no."

"Not enough to go around, huh?" The hat-man lifted the side of what may have been a brim.

"Double up the young'uns." The kid clicked his tongue. "They're small, three in a box easy, line 'em up head to toe."

"Yer missus, she'd share," the old one said. "Got a small someone aside 'er now." He spat a piece of his stick.

Dear God, what was he suggesting? Throats slit as they tried to escape, all the coffins put to use? Or maybe the men would flog the horses onward, the wagon bucking, seven bodies left in the woods to rot.

To end in the woods, when their journey had hardly started, and no one would know. Ruth's head spun.

Jehu pawed the trail. Aaron's eyes flicked from the haulers to Ruth. He twitched the jerk line. Jehu, unrestrained, heaved into the mules. They cranked their necks, noses pointed at the sky, small front hooves lifting. Bridles clashed. The mules stumbled backward, lurching the cart. The skinny boy tilted. He raised one leg, the foot bandaged. He tried to regain his balance but tipped out of the cart, landing on the ground by the wagon's front wheel. The boy screamed.

From inside the Conestoga, Maus's screams joined his.

"Stop!" Ruth yelled at Aaron.

The boy lay clutching his knee above the bandage. Below his clenched fingers, the filthy ravelings showed dirt and pus, his foot a festering mass. He wailed.

Ruth lifted Esther behind the seat. "Talk to Maus." Ruth climbed down.

The old man climbed from the cart and stood at the boy's head, elbows akimbo. "Stop yer yap, boy—yer not dying."

Ruth kneeled by the boy's foot. "It's infected," she said. "He *could* die."

"Plenty more where he come from." The old man worked the stick from one side of his mouth to the other. "They go easy, can't get attached."

"But you do," the hat-man said. "Don't ya?" He looked into the woods.

"I reckon." The old man spat his stick on the trail.

"Daniel, get honey and vinegar," Ruth called. "Matthew, clean rags."

Aaron calmed the horses while Esther watched from the bench, Joseph on his knees beside Ruth, who stripped away the dirty bandaging.

"Don't!" the boy screamed. "Don't touch it."

"You'll lose your foot," Ruth said. "Maybe your leg."

"Not much use to nobody, then." The old man squatted and, with his knees, he held the boy's shoulders to the ground. "Do yer derndest," he said to Ruth.

"Daniel, hold his leg." She motioned to Aaron. "Over here—hold the other one."

With the boy screaming, she rinsed the dirt and pus, picked blackened flesh, and slathered the wound with honey, then wound the foot in clean rags. "That's the best I can do. He's got to keep it clean. And you—" Ruth pointed at the old man. "Change the bandages."

"Yes'm," he said. He and the man in the hat lifted the crying boy and laid him on his back in the top coffin. "Makes a fine bed," he said to the boy. "Enjoy it—the next fella won't."

Ruth stood, and for the first time noticed the tang of unwashed men and new wood overlaid with the stench of infection. She coughed.

All the pale men climbed in their cart, and the driver pulled his team onto the road.

"Obliged," the old man said.

The hat-man tipped his hat. "You here ag'in, we got pos-sum stew."

"You come west," said Joseph. "We'll have pickled pig feet and headcheese."

"Joseph," said Aaron. "Don't boast."

Ruth retrieved Maus from the hammock and nursed him as Aaron got under way. The blood in her veins ran quieter, but questions persisted. What could she have done had the men been what she feared? Scream?

Who would hear?

Fight? It wasn't their way.

They would have suffered whatever God had in store. They had to trust.

She did trust, but it wasn't any less frightful.

❧

Two weeks later, the Appalachians behind them, they de-scended to gentle hills. Peepers unleashed their calls, a wel-come harbinger of summer. The hours filled with sunshine and neck-slap. By a small river, birdsong lifted. Their spirits re-newed.

The land, all waving grass, foretold a world of plenty at the end of the trek. Blessed Idaho. They breathed pollen and sneezed, their noses full of yellow life-giving dust.

Ruth savored the sweetness, for Pittsburgh neared. They'd managed past Shippensburg, Bedford, and Somerset avoiding the towns, but now the trailhead loomed, south over the river, a place clogged with more English than she'd seen in all her born days. *Lord give me strength.* And before the staging field, the city of Pittsburgh.

Back in New Eden, she hadn't wanted to hear a word of Pittsburgh, and now she didn't want to see it—not the city, not the confluence of trails where the godless dribbled in, not the staging field or the horde of people who expected—no, *demanded*—something for nothing.

She couldn't rely on such people. But wasn't Aaron one of them now?

She'd thought so just before leaving. The final packing done, Ruth and Aaron had fallen into bed. From heavy sleep the banging of shutters woke them. Then thunder. Lightning flashed so bright the bedstead, bureau, and chair turned white and disappeared, leaving Ruth dazzled.

Wind tore at the house. Slates slid off the roof, *whoosh*, and smashed on the flagstones. And again—*smash*.

Aaron had covered his head with his arms. "I don't have time for this."

Water dripped on the pillow between them. "Blast."

Ruth threw off the covers. A candle held high, they peered at the ceiling and quickly pushed the bed aside. A puddle formed on the floor.

From the kitchen, Ruth fetched bread pans, cake pans, bowls. Aaron brought buckets from the barn, and they caught what water they could. Through the house, room by room, they checked for leaks.

No stains evident, they returned to their out-of-place bed.

Poor Aaron. He couldn't ignore the leaks. One slate maybe, not a whole section, and she couldn't help. The baby drew a knee across her belly as a reminder: no roof work for her.

No matter; their neighbors would come. No one would

dream of not coming—not just an obligation, but a feeding of souls. All would be fixed, departure put off for just a few hours.

Then came a clanging, muffled in the wind. She shook Aaron. "It's Delia—I know the bell." At the window, Ruth looked west toward her farm. No flare to the sky, but it could still be fire. They threw on clothes.

Aaron rode out as Ruth knew he would. She gathered food before harnessing Noah to the cart.

She toiled up the stairs to Daniel's room, ran a hand over his back until he sat up and rubbed his eyes.

"See to the chores come morning," Ruth said. "Papa's gone to Horst's. I'm going now."

"When will—?"

"We don't know."

Wind whipped through the buggy as Ruth urged Noah to a canter. In her hurry, she'd forgotten her bonnet. The wind tore at her cap and shawl.

Dawn came as she neared Delia's lane. Ruth looked for fire, for smoke, and found none, but the weathervane, usually straight up, now pointed down at the dooryard trees. The whole barn canted east into sheets of rain.

The place swarmed with men and women shunting pigs, sheep, and cows from the barn while chickens skittered underfoot. Horses bolted in wild attempts to return to their stalls.

Ruth guided Noah through the bleating and squealing. His ears rotated, yet he remained calm in his blinders as they reined in at the kitchen door.

Inside the empty kitchen, she wrestled tables together. She unloaded her baskets of food slated for their departure: corn bread, pickled eggs, biscuits, cheese, apples. She set out plates and forks and napkins, and sliced a ham from Delia's larder. She found loaves of bread in the breadbox and started slicing as the door banged open.

Along with a torrent of rain, Delia blew in, an infant lamb under each arm, her cap gone, hair like river grass in her face. The wet lambs cried and wriggled in fright.

Ruth slammed the door. "What happened?"

"Barn's collapsing." Delia, out of breath, set the struggling lambs on the floor. Their little black feet ticked and slipped on the wood as they careened in panic under the tables. Ruth caught one as it fell on its side at her feet. She sat cross-legged, the lamb secure in her arms above the baby. Delia tossed her a towel, caught the other lamb, and sat beside her. They cooed until the lambs breathed easy.

"The mother's lost," Delia said. "We heard rending in the night." Her hands full, Delia pressed her knee to Ruth's. "I'm glad you're still here. And no shun." She lifted her eyes to Ruth's. "Horst wanted one, an example to the rest of us." Her lamb squirmed.

Ruth had given her a wan smile.

"Don't worry—he hasn't persuaded the others."

The door blew open again, less force and no rain. Aaron, three neighbors, and Horst clomped in. Horst closed the door on lowing and neighing from the yard. "It's the whole sill," he said. "Rotten."

"Fixable?" Delia looked up from her lamb.

"We'll tear it down and rebuild," Horst said. "Two, maybe three days if everyone comes." Ruth snuck a look at Aaron as he helped himself to bread and ham. He layered them together, took a bite, and went out the door, hammer in his other hand. The rest followed.

"Looks like you're staying," Delia said.

Ruth's lamb broke free and skidded into a corner where it trembled on crooked legs. "For today." He would help. He'd continue; it was who he was despite his dreams. Yet doubt had clouded the room.

Well after noon, the sun had broken through. Ruth drove Noah past the barn. Broken beams poked the sky, and men crawled all over them.

Ruth returned to her littles, the boys at chores in the barn. In the house, Esther sat at the table counting eggs.

"Have you eaten?" Ruth said.

"Matthew ate pie," said Esther. "I ate eggs."

"You cooked?"

"Raw." Esther licked her lips. "With honey and apple. *I* went to the cellar."

By dark, Aaron, thick with dirt and sweat, returned. He counted slates Daniel had stacked by the kitchen door. "Should be enough," he said. If there weren't, friends would share, though precious time would be lost in the gathering.

At the table, Ruth loaded a plate with stew, passing it to Aaron. "And Horst's barn?" she said, almost afraid to ask.

Aaron cut corn bread. "He'll salvage." On top of a mouthful, he gulped milk. "We'll replace the eastern sill and uprights."

"How long?" Ruth asked.

"Another two days to get under cover."

"I'll help," Daniel said. An echo of small voices followed.

"We can't afford the time." Aaron stretched his neck and pulled at his shoulder.

"You'd leave?" Ruth had held his eye.

The last meat off his plate, he spooned the gravy into his mouth and leaned his head back against the chair. He scratched his beard and covered his face with his hands. He rubbed hard, then pushed his fingers up through his hair. "Another day might be a blessing. For you too."

Aaron had worked all the next day, his eyes on the valley ridge whenever Ruth spotted him. He worked at a fevered pitch, highest on broken beams, faster than the others, setting the claw of his hammer, wrenching the boards free and throwing them down on a growing pile. With the Fold and others from down valley, he salvaged the beams, cut broken ends, then reassembled them with pegs and raised them, sheathing with boards the littles had pulled free of nails. Sweat poured off him, staining his shirt down the whole of his back.

That night in bed, Ruth had rubbed salve into his blistered palms. "The others will manage," he said. "I told them, we go tomorrow. Ely can fix his own roof."

She stared at him. It was one thing to leave, another to leave in the face of a neighbor's need.

"It's not right," she said.

"I did two days' work in one—you saw me."

"Persuade yourself, not me." She'd looked away. If he could do this, how much worse would English be?

After she blew out the candle, Ruth had turned her back, Aaron stiff and silent beside her. *Our barn won't rot*, she told herself. But in Idaho, God only knew—

She hadn't the heart to dwell on it then, but now, as they approached the English, she did, and rot wasn't the worry. In Idaho, they'd have no bell and no one to hear it if they did.

❧

Approaching the city, Ruth needed a tighter rein on her fears. That's all they were, runaway horses on her runaway tongue. She and hers would be separate even as they followed the same trail as the English rabble. They would care for themselves.

As they closed in on Pittsburgh, more English filled the road, on foot, in carts and wagons, on horseback singly and in groups. The first one came abreast in a small one-horse cart, passing them, the cart full of peas in baskets, and beans and lettuce. From under her bonnet, Ruth peeked secretly at the faces of a man and his wife. The woman wore a dark blue dress, her head uncovered, the man in darker brown shirt and pants. Granted, not black, but nothing outlandish, the only bright color on their cheeks full of health and in the smiles for Aaron and the littles, who smiled in return. Thank God, the couple hadn't the look of Appalachian hollows. And neither did the ones who followed.

Once assured of this, Ruth wondered at their clothes. Some looked ready for church in the middle of the week, some work-worn, some ragged. With each one they passed, her heart raced less, and her vigilance eased enough to let her watch the birds with Matthew.

The woods beside the trail dwindled, allowing a wider view of unfamiliar birds as they fled the wagon's approach. One bright bird with a black mask perched haughty on black feet, a crested red singer.

He teased the eye, flitting twig to twig in the evening as Ruth collected deadfall, Maus in a sling. Now she saw the bird, then not, like cardinals at home, happy as they called, *What-*

*cheer, What-cheer.* Anything seemed possible in the late sunshine.

"What bird is that?"

"Matthew, don't be wandering."

Day by day the maze of roads gathered. Houses jammed together, tiny fields between. No barns now. Who lived without a barn? What did they eat?

As they crested a ridge, twenty-eight days from home, the city lay below them, splayed between cliffs, a gray quilt of houses in road-cut squares. Buildings lined the three rivers crossed at intervals by bridges. Long buildings at the water's edge made wide rectangles, and inland more houses grew taller with windows stacked row on row, and taller still, high-spired churches, all the buildings wound with smoke, the smell sharp as a burning barn.

Veering from a growing number of wagons, Aaron headed to the southern bridge, its massive stone arches supporting fewer travelers than those upriver. They left behind the loaded wagons destined for markets, or no loads at all, destined for only they knew what, their uncountable wheels rattling the decking of other bridges.

Into the narrowing city streets, herds of them jostled, a rabble bleating with the cry of sheep to slaughter, swarms of them, herded by what? Perhaps the hooded people of Opa's Old Country found their way to this country. Why wouldn't they? Opa had.

❧

As a child, snuggled in Opa's lap, Ruth felt no harm could come to her. Opa had bested evil, had come to New Eden, a land without fear, and raised his family.

"Tell more, tell the dungeon," she'd said. "Tell the talking rats."

It hadn't been hard to coax him, and yet, sitting by the hearth, he'd sigh deep from the toes of his thick socks. "My four-legged friends looked for crumbs I couldn't afford to drop." Ruth saw his rats big as lions, her grandfather, like Daniel in the den, surviving on faith in a cell where night delivered day with no sun to mark the difference. The walls seeped, and he sipped at the cracks, barely able to moisten his lips.

They dragged him from his cell to the high stone room filled with instruments of conversion, where grinning Baptists did their worst. On the rack, arms above his head, they tied his wrists, turned the notched wheel until his feet came off the floor, then tied his ankles. A hooded figure hauled on the lever, her grandfather stretched near parting until, like the apostle Peter, he denied, denied, denied what he held most dear.

*Don't be scaring her,* her papa had said as he sewed harness by the fire.

Many years later her brother told her the rest.

Until then Ruth hadn't known the scope of annihilation in the Old Country, the murder of Anabaptists an accepted practice. The year before he left for the sea, Opa stayed clear of his parents' home, wanting them safe, but he couldn't leave without saying he lived and he loved them.

He went to their house close-packed with others in Augsburg. He'd slipped into the yard and peered in the little panes of the living room window. His parents had to be alone, no visitors.

At first the wavy glass confused him, making a shambles of everything seen through it. He pressed his face to the glass.

He tried another window, and another. The house empty, every room a wreckage of furniture, wood chairs splintered, stuffed ones leaking their innards from slits in the cloth skin, tables with missing legs.

At the back of the house, the outside door ajar, he pushed into the kitchen, and confirmed the worst. A dark trail, thickened and checked like old paint, told him clear as the written word that he'd never see his family again.

Reeling, he fled, all the while waiting for a hand on his shoulder, praying for a quick death and an end to fear.

Ruth prayed it wouldn't come to that, not in this new country.

# PART II

## Keeping Plain

## CHAPTER 7

# Early June—Hurry, Hurry

S o strange rushing toward what she feared. Ruth tried to resurrect the smell of scythed hay, their house, their barn. It wouldn't come. Here the scent of every kind of manure hung in the smoke. Could this be the smell of the west?

Across the river, the city thinned to fields, and in the distance a brown wound cut the green: the staging field, and in one corner a smattering of covered wagons.

These depleted masses, could they ward off highwaymen and Indians? Ruth dreaded any English, yet she wanted the many they'd been promised. She wanted safety—their numbers, not the English themselves. One evil warding off a greater evil.

At dusk they approached the grouped wagons and their

dray animals on picket. Aaron slowed the horses. He scanned the perimeter. Up close, the milling crowd seemed bigger. Ruth's belly fluttered as if she'd swallowed the red-crested singer.

"Stragglers," Aaron said. "We'll have little to choose from."

For *this* Aaron had deserted Horst and Delia? But how was he to know?

☙

Before marriage, Aaron's father had taken Ruth aside. "Sometimes the boy doesn't think." When she asked Aaron why his father would have said such a thing, Aaron changed the subject.

The truth had come out one night courting in her father's house. They lay together fully dressed, the bundling board between them, their voices barely audible. Moonlight came through the window. Aaron reached his hand over the board and took hers. She stroked his curled little finger, the stunted one he'd always kept in his fist. "Will you tell me what happened?" she asked.

"Must I?" His fingers closed.

"You must." She flattened his hand and kissed each finger in turn, including the stunted one. For long moments he said nothing. She heard his legs chafe. His knee hit the board between them.

Finally he said, "When we were little littles, my sister and I chased a rabbit into the hedgerow. She wanted it, and not for supper." Aaron hid his face behind the board. "We couldn't find it. We searched the underbrush until Mama rang the bell for supper. That's when Anna saw the hole. I knelt and looked in. Don't, she said. But she wanted a rabbit more than anything, and being the big brother, I reached in. Then—*ach*." Aaron gave a humorless laugh from behind the board. "I yanked my hand, and there hung a baby badger, my finger in its teeth." He lifted his head. She touched her forehead to his. "The finger healed badly," he said. "And Papa said, '*Gedankenlos*, that's you.' He'd never called me that, but he was right—what a brainless thing to do. If Mama Badger had been home I'd have lost the whole hand."

"Are you sorry you told me?" Ruth said.

"No." He sounded relieved. "I should have told you sooner." He kissed her nose.

She stroked his hair behind one ear and he pressed his lips to hers. He looked like he might crawl right over the bundling board, but she knew he wouldn't. A piece of her had wished he would.

Had it been a sin, this call of the flesh? Under its spell, she imagined his touch a hundred different ways on a hundred different nights, and she herself touched upstanding nipples, the sizzle guiding her hand down the smooth skin of her belly, through tightly curled hair, her fingers searching between her legs, and slipping into the shuddering warmth.

She could never tell Delia. She hardly dared tell herself.

And it wasn't only then that the call came. As she healed from Maus's birth she heard it whisper in the crowded wagon. She could see it loud in Aaron's glance as she settled her nightdress tight on swollen breasts. A kiss stolen when others' eyes were closed heated them both. Dwelling on it made the call louder. One more thing she need hold at bay.

Aaron had stayed on his side of the bundling board and they'd gone on whispering and planning. "... fruitful, ten children at least," he'd said. They would eat peaches and pears, the taste of sun in every mouthful. She knew her future, and it was good.

❧

*Pittsburgh Trailhead*

*Dan'l Dearest Brother,*

*If you gather our entire congregation AND their stock it wouldn't amount to anything next to Pittsburgh's staging field. Such a jabber of neighing horses oxen lowing chickens squawking and bright painted wagons. Oh the red topboards the blue sides women in bright dresses even dust stained you can see the color. Many teams have bells topping the harness rows that jingle with every movement. Dare I admit it is a joyful song.*

*Your sinful Ruth*

❧

Closer still, these travelers weren't the specters of Appalachian hollows either. The people of the wagons were like the ones going into the city, only their clothes were dustier, their faces more tired.

As Ruth watched them, she did feel sinful, her heart swelling with the tinkle of bells. Their ring not the *clack, clack* of Bathsheba's bell, these more birdlike, full of unexpected joy.

Ruth built a small fire, using deadfall she'd saved along the trail. "It's a meager flame," she said. She set the cauldron low over it and cut onions into a chunk of melting fatback, the fragrance of pork an infusion for beans, giving a meaty taste where no fresh meat remained.

Aaron clapped Joseph's back. "Come, little men, more wood." They all headed for the western trees.

"Esther, you stir." Ruth listened for Maus asleep in the wagon, a wary eye on the throng. *Whoa, now, rein in your suspicions . . .* The mountain cat showed more threat than any here. That cat *did* want to eat them; even so, she'd found *him* a delight to the eye.

Ruth attended to dinner while women in long dresses shook dust from blues and reds and yellows in startling patterns. The women chattered between wagons. Coming together and breaking apart, they joined new clusters, a friendly peck on the cheek, a clasp of hands, their bodices brought close.

When they looked her way, Ruth dropped her eyes. They didn't look dangerous, except for their colors drawing her eye. Their smiles and the warmth, one to the other, made her miss Delia and their confidings.

One woman stood out from the rest, all in gray and a black armband. She had the look of Delia at a distance, the same full body, round cheeks. The woman could be kin perhaps—not blood, no, but kin of the mind. Mennonite without a cap on her lightly salted hair. Older than Ruth's twenty-nine years.

Age showed more in the furrow of the woman's forehead than the hair. As she passed closer, laugh lines crinkled by her eyes and around her little bow mouth with its ready smile.

Ruth busied herself, and when she raised her head, the woman was gone.

Here, against nature, most women pranced gaudy as male birds, and the men sauntered in drab shades of brown. Standing, stiff legs spread, they extended a hand to one another, watchful and curious as yearling bulls. Over them all, a man named Hugo.

"Ask Hugo," they said again and again. Hugo rode easily among them, wiry, a man too weathered to tell his age. The full-face beard didn't help. He dressed in fringed leggings, a worn coat lapping over his saddle's cantle, and a wind-beaten hat. In his wake, a tall boy greeted all who passed. The boy also in fringed pants and a loose shirt. He had a head of dark yellow hair wisping around his smooth face.

"Evening, Sadie," the women called.

Sadie? The boy gave them an openmouthed smile, rushing to one and the next. He gabbled at men and women alike. But no. Ruth saw long braids down his back, a slight thickening of hips.

A woman. Could this be? She put Ruth in mind of her father's yearling Morgan, leaping sprightly about the paddock, so unpredictable you couldn't get out of its way.

Then in the midst of a greeting, Sadie glanced over a friend's shoulder and caught Ruth's eye. One look would invite a snake to play. Ruth returned her attention to dinner, but from the corner of her eye Ruth spotted Sadie's advance, bee-straight over the packed ground, fringe on her pants flying. At her approach, Ruth backed against the wagon's front wheel. She gripped the spokes behind her, her cheeks lumpy and hot.

"Esther," Ruth whispered. "In the wagon."

"Why—?"

"Now," she ordered. Thank heaven Maus slept.

Sadie trotted up close. Ruth jammed a heel in the wheel

spokes and hiked herself backward onto the seat. Her skirts caught beneath her heel. She wrenched them free and slid to the middle of the bench.

"Skirts are a problem, aren't they?" Sadie hopped right up after Ruth. "Well, then," she said. "I haven't seen *you* before."

Sadie's sharp nose and blue eyes were so close, Ruth had to lean back, tucking her chin to keep her in focus. Ruth gulped for breath, her eyes wide. "*Ach, mein Gott, mein Gott in Himmel!*" The words flooded out, her grade-school English lost. She braced herself on the seat. Sadie latched on to Ruth's hand. Their calluses grated.

"You poor dear," Sadie said. "A death in the family and here you are, going . . . Where are you going? You do speak English, don't you?"

"*Ja*— Ah, yes." Ruth extracted her hand and clasped it to her throat.

"You'll be hot in all that black, what with summer coming. How much longer?"

Ruth took a deep breath. At home it was already summer. "A week, I guess." Her voice squeaked.

"You don't know?" Sadie tipped her head. "When did they die?"

"Who . . . ?" Ruth's eyebrows twitched, then rose. "Oh—no one died."

It was Sadie's turn to frown. "But black—surely you're not—" Sadie gave a little gasp. "Not Mormon, are you?"

"Mormon?" Ruth took a deep breath. "I'm Plain."

"You're plain . . ." Sadie paused. "Indeed you are, but who admits it, no matter how true?" The edges of Sadie's face softened. "You're funny," she said, "so you can't be Mormon."

Ruth slid as far from Sadie as possible, and nowhere else to go unless she jumped off the bench and ran around the wagon. She couldn't do that. As Ruth leaned away, she saw the woman in gray watching. The woman narrowed her eyes and caught Ruth's.

Ruth gave a silent plea for help. The other adjusted her black armband; then, all smiles, her ample body shook in a good-natured advance.

As the woman closed in, Sadie peered in the wagon. "A lot of stuff you got there." She put her hands to her mouth. "And a *baaaby*—ooh, a baby!"

"No." Ruth stiffened. She raised her elbows under her shawl. She swung them like horns and leaned toward Sadie, blocking any possible reach for Maus.

"Sadie." The woman in gray, now beside the wagon, put a hand on Sadie's knee.

Ruth wilted with relief. Without a word, a friend already.

"Now, Sadie, let the poor thing take a breath." The woman waggled her puff of hair, loose in front and netted in a hard ball at the back of her head. "Sadie comes with our Hugo."

"*Wife*, Hortence—that's what you meant," said Sadie. "So." She looked at Ruth. "You know Hortence, do you?"

"N-no."

"Preacher Johnston's wife. You two should get along—you have the same stylish dress." Sadie laughed, clear as harness bells. "A godly sort of dress, but which one is more godly?" She put a finger to her chin. "Hortence with a white collar, or all black. Hmm?"

"Come down from there, Sadie." Hortence's eyes pinched, deepening spidery lines, no doubt from facing the elements without a proper bonnet. "Sadie hasn't the sense God gave a goat. You pay her no mind. She's—"

"Mama, Mama." Joseph charged up to the women. Matthew followed, puffing hard. Sadie and Ruth climbed to the ground.

"You should see . . ." Joseph said. "A child . . ."

"English, please," said Ruth.

"A child with a real tail." Matthew jigged with excitement. "All furry and skinny. His father keeps him on a tether."

"He chitters, not German, not English," Joseph said.

"He cranks noise in a box."

"In the wagon," Ruth said. "Time for lessons—you make no sense." She pushed them inside.

Sadie said to her back, "That's Leonardo the organ grinder."

Organ grinder? Ruth shivered. Whose organs?

❧

That night, cook fires pricked the staging field. Ruth hovered by the wagon, dinner to tend to, and after dinner she bathed Maus. Pushing up her sleeves, she cradled him on one arm, faceup, and dipped him naked in the washtub. She rinsed the folds of his neck. He waved his arms as if testing the air, and kicked with the glee of discovery.

She swabbed him with a wad of sheep's wool, under his fat little arms, over his full belly, pale and wide like a frog. She ran the wool around the promise of his manhood, and into the creases of his legs. He gurgled happily, folded his knees to his belly, then lashed out with ecstatic feet. Water splashed.

Droplets hit his face, and he gasped, his brow drawn in

concern, legs and arms gone rigid. Frozen a moment, he seemed to rethink, then grasped the joy of water and thrashed again, showering himself and Ruth.

After Ruth swaddled Maus and tucked him in his hammock, she brought out her mending. She didn't notice the other women. Not till she'd finished stitching the last rent in Joseph's pants did she feel their attentions. They passed wagon to wagon, singly and in groups, and slid their eyes over her before moving on in the light of a large fire.

Other large fires dotted the field, but Aaron and the boys had helped stack logs for this one close at hand. Hauled from the woods, the logs now blazed like a barn. The builders gathered to it.

"Decision time," Aaron told Ruth before joining them. "We'll find out who will go where, the best routes, and choose who should lead."

With the littles in bed, Ruth climbed the seat for a better vantage. She could see the men's faces lively in the firelight. At first, their voices stayed low. They passed a bottle. The liquid flashed when each man tipped the long neck to their lips, bright as if they drank fire. They passed the bottle hand to hand to Aaron, who sniffed and passed it on.

Laughter erupted. Voices grew loud. One above the others, a bearish man, shouted, "Shows what you know—you couldn't *choose* a longer route."

"Longer, yes," Hugo said. "Easier through the mountains, safer." He settled his gun belt low at the hip. "But a few dead wouldn't trouble you, would they, Carver?"

A softer voice pleaded, "Gentlemen, gentlemen, keep

peaceable." The man, thin and bent, wore black clothes like Aaron, but, unlike Aaron, he wore a high white collar. Hortence stood behind him, the only woman in the group. Her white collar matched her husband's and caught the firelight as did the preacher's. Her chins and ample breast shook as though laughing, though nothing seemed laughable. She nudged her husband toward the arguers.

"Save it for Sunday." Carver's lip curled.

"Please, Preacher," Hugo said. "Step aside. We'll settle this."

The crowd tightened its circle around Hugo and Carver. Carver slapped a stick in his palm. He drew a jagged line in the dirt. "Straight through the mountains," he said, and kicked a hole in the range with the toe of his boot.

Hugo shook his head. "Only a fool—"

Carver lashed the back of his hand across Hugo's face. Ruth gasped. She clamped her hands over her mouth as Hugo's hat flew. He staggered sideways. Blood trickled from his lip, and he wiped it on his sleeve.

The preacher reached toward Carver. "Now, brother, that's no way to—"

"This ain't your concern." Carver raised a fist.

Ruth covered her eyes.

"We're brothers," Preacher said. "Let's talk this out."

Ruth separated her fingers the smallest crack.

"He's right." Hugo rubbed his jaw.

A man of peace, Ruth thought, except for the gun.

"You ain't no brother to me." With both his palms, Carver thumped Hugo in the chest. Hugo staggered back into the crowd.

Round-eyed behind her fingers, Ruth whispered into her hands, "*Worse than roosters.*"

How easily she cast aspersions, and Ruth no better than a chicken herself standing there on the bench, her eyes glued to the sight of blood. She shut them.

"That settles it." She heard the growly voice. "I lead."

Surely Aaron couldn't follow the likes of Carver. Still behind her fingers, she opened her eyes.

Hugo picked up his hat and stepped into the cleared circle. "Those who want"—he dusted himself off—"go Carver's way. I'll cross the Mississippi at Davenport, then to Omaha and follow the Platte. No fights and no shortcuts through the Rockies."

Ruth separated her fingers more.

"Sapsucker." Carver pointed at Hugo. "You can't defend *yourself,* much less them." Carver waved his arm at the crowd, and his hand smacked Hugo lightly on the cheek.

Hugo sighed. He turned his back. "If that's how you want it," he said, soft and resigned. Then, with a slow step, he swung around as if he had one more thought and slammed his fist at the bridge of Carver's nose. The man crumpled like a sledge-hammered ox.

Ruth dug her fingers in her eyes. *English contagion, so soon, dear Lord.* She sank to the bench, face in her hands, and prayed.

She stayed hunched there until fingertips touched her back. She shrank.

"What's the matter?" Aaron asked.

She didn't answer.

"You saw, didn't you?"

She'd not only seen; she'd *looked*. How could she tell him? Her limbs felt stiff as salt blocks under her skirts.

"It's a shame, this fighting," he said and wrapped his arms around her. She folded into him.

Next time—and there was bound to be one—she wouldn't look. And the littles, she had to shield them, stand guard against temptation.

"Hugo's rough." Aaron kept his arms around her. "I just hope he knows the best way. We're already so late."

"You want shortcuts?" Ruth pushed Aaron so she could see his eyes.

"Not Carver's." Aaron took her hands. "I'll check the maps with Hugo."

"Is that best?"

"English won't infect us," Aaron said. "I promise. In Idaho, we'll be at the center of hundreds of acres." He kissed her forehead. "Dawn to dark, you'll never see an English."

He always made it sound fine.

"Blessings will follow," he said. "We'll be a congregation, just us, until the others follow. You'll see." He glanced about and kissed her nose, her chin, and down her neck.

"*Fssst*," she hissed. "The littles."

He laughed and shrugged his shoulders. "Your brother will join us, and my sister—they'll see the light."

In the soft glow of the candle, Ruth wanted to believe, but Dan'l had been adamant against their leaving. Aaron's sister worse.

Ruth said nothing. She wanted Aaron to part the Red Sea and show them all a better land.

He rubbed her cheek. In the past she would have kissed his

work-split nails, then his lips. Instead she unfolded his hand and kissed the nub of his little finger. He closed his fist.

How could she protect him?

❧

*June*

*Dearest Dan'l,*

*English are made of strange cloth. I shuttle between their warp and weft. I had worried Aaron would succumb and it is I who show the first taint. Hard as I try not to my eyes stray to things they shouldn't.*

*We start tomorrow fifteen strong with a different language one wagon to the next a tower of Babel fallen on its side. We planned to be last in line separate from the rest but we are hemmed in assigned 7th. In camp every passing eye takes in the black of our clothes the cut of the wagon and the strength of our horses. I see their eyes full of admiration and suspicion.*

*God watches over us. We are free of head colds when many are not. Praise be.*

*Your loving sister,*

*Ruth*

❧

A day for Hugo to organize his followers gave Aaron time to ride into Pittsburgh and restock before leaving. Ruth stayed with the littles.

The next morning *"Up and at 'em!"* rang through the dark, and after a cold breakfast the field came alive in the clatter of decamping. Ruth hurried at milking Bathsheba. Joseph and Matthew collected the tripod and cauldron, now cool from last night's supper. They rubbed their sleeves in the dawn chill, the day clear, the sky growing blue.

Daniel and Aaron threw harness over the horses, threaded buckles, attached chains. The six horses stamped their feet and blew through widened nostrils as others passed, headed for the line at the field's edge. "Aaron, get out there."

Hugo leaned from his horse and hit their wagon twice with the heel of his hand. "Line up—blacksmith behind, Preacher in front. Go!"

Wagons seethed toward the westward road, like cattle herded into a chute, Hugo's group and Carver's and other leaders' leaving the same hour.

"In here now," Ruth called to the boys. "You'll get run over."

The boys ran clutching their hats. "Do we have to?"

"Until we clear the field," Aaron said. He swung onto Noah's saddle. "Ready?" He checked behind.

The boys scrambled aboard. Daniel and Joseph stood back of the bench, behind Ruth.

"Let's go." Esther, her bonnet askew, and Matthew, kneeling at the frontboard, pumped up and down as if to speed things along. Ruth held Maus. His cry added to the bleating crowd.

A horde of boys in every size ran between the moving teams.

Matthew pointed. "Why . . . ?"

"Hush, now," Aaron said. He started and stopped in the stream of animals and wagons, giving a turn, taking a turn, watching the wheels, angling close, too close, barely slipping through a space, veering Jehu away from a team with laid-back ears, the lead stretching his neck, long teeth bared.

Women's voices rose above the crunch of wheels and lost themselves in the braying of mules. A boy jumped in front of a team crowding beside Aaron. The team spooked sideways. The wagon jolted. The driver swore. He cut his whip at the boy.

"That's why you don't run loose," Ruth said.

Once out of the crush, Hugo's line of wagons wormed its way west, big wagons with six horses, smaller ones with four horses or mules, the smallest with two, and the blacksmith pulled by a pair of oxen. A few wagons were as new as Aaron's, many hard used and weathered gray, the canvas slapped with patches. Small wagons in every stage of decay moved along except for one cart with a shed top like an Appalachian house on wheels. It teetered slowly. Hugo assigned the driver to the second slot after he begged to come along.

"He's a hazard," Aaron said. "He'll slow us."

To Ruth, another member of their small group meant another person against marauders.

Her wagon, like the one in front, bucked and heaved in the ruts, Maus in his hammock, enjoying the pitch. Aaron was right. Many had gone before, and no one attended the roads.

Ruth's boys at the tailgate stood poised to jump to the ground. "Now can we?"

"Off the side, and stay close." Ruth feared they'd go over the tailgate, stumble into the path of the blacksmith's oxen, or, worse yet, run with the pack of boys.

Esther looked over the edge, and up at Ruth.

"When we stop, you can get down."

"But—"

Aaron swung off Noah, the team continuing to pull, and lifted Esther to the ground.

The pace walkable, Matthew and Esther ran to the edges of the road. They picked grass and with flat hands fed the horses as they trudged. Daniel walked beside Jehu and tested the straps for chafing, while Joseph watched other boys ranging ahead.

"At this rate, we'll never get there," Aaron fumed.

The morning stretched before them. The sun crawled up their backs, beat overhead, and angled into their eyes. Esther's gamboling slowed to a hard-breathing walk.

"Ready to ride?" Aaron said. He swooped her onto the seat beside Ruth. Matthew flagged too, and Aaron twirled him high on his shoulders, a firm grip on the boy's ankles, and fed them both on stories of gooseberries, raspberries, and peaches to come. Matthew hung on to Aaron's head.

"I like riding," Matthew said. He shaded his eyes, taking in the fields and growing woods. God only knew what else he saw from his high vantage.

He gave Aaron a nudge with his heels. "I'll have a faster horse in Idaho."

"You're right—we're slow. I'll have a word with Hugo." He dropped Matthew in the wagon and went forward, leaving the jerk line with Ruth.

~

That evening they camped by a stream. While others crowded close to the water, Aaron made camp as separate as the encroaching woods allowed. Ruth set the tripod and chopped vegetables. Aaron lit the fire before he and the boys watered Bathsheba and the horses.

The cow fed and tied to the wagon, Ruth sat to her milking while meat simmered. She served lamb and green beans on tin plates, the family cross-legged by their fire. They sopped the last gravy, reveling in the fresh provisions, when Joseph's eyes wandered beyond his plate to the gaggles of young roaming the camp.

They passed in waves, feet pounding. The girls squealed like shoats, and watched the boys, rangy as yearling calves, pushing and shoving and butting one another.

Aaron paid them no mind and leaned against the wagon's front wheel, a candle on the bench above his head. He held his Bible high, catching the light, his head tilted, beard at an angle. His lips moved as he read.

With a towel, Joseph swiped at the plates Ruth had washed. His eyes followed the young. Though he didn't move, Ruth could feel him slipping as if caught in the rip of a swift river.

She put a hand on his shoulder. "Your shirt's torn."

"No, it's not."

Ruth poked a finger in the hole and wiggled it on his skin. "It's time you mend for yourself." She retrieved her sewing basket as another gaggle of boys spun past.

"Eyes on your work," Aaron said. "Not *English*."

Close to the fire, Ruth patted the ground. "Come, sit."

"In a minute." The towel slack at his side, he watched the boys vanish beyond the firelight. Ruth reached for his hand and tugged.

"You all need practice sewing," Ruth said. "Not only Joseph."

"I have to make water," he said. He hung up his towel.

"Don't dawdle." Ruth resisted the urge to go with him as he cut behind the wagon. Aaron let the Bible fall against his chest. He frowned and scratched his beard as Joseph disappeared in the same direction as the boys.

"Daniel," Ruth said, "get the scrap cloth from my mattress." Ruth passed threaded needles to Matthew and Esther. "And don't wake Maus."

"I'll make another doll," Esther said.

Ruth glanced at Aaron. He looked at her, then in the direction Joseph had taken, and made no comment on Esther's words.

Daniel passed cloth to Matthew and helped him cut squares the size of his palm, one for each of them.

As time passed, Aaron's face darkened. He set the Bible aside and strode after Joseph.

Heads bent, Daniel, Matthew, and Esther attended their basting. Daniel added more sticks to the fire. Orange sparks wafted into the star-speckled dark.

"Daniel," Matthew said, "help me scissor a horse." How could Ruth tell him no, if on her square Esther could make a doll? But if Matthew had a horse, what would come next? Where would pictures on a quilt lead? Pictures on walls, paint on their skin like Indians?

Ruth had finished stitching the edge of a square when Aaron rounded the wagon with Joseph dragged by his ear. Aaron, mouth down in a grim line, pushed Joseph to the ground.

"You'll not be running with *English*," Aaron said.

Joseph sat looking at his lap. Ruth passed him a threaded needle. "Take off your shirt and get busy," she said.

He stitched, his eyes on his work as if nothing could be more important. Aaron went back to his Bible.

Daniel, having knotted the final stitch on his black square, leaned close to Ruth. "Could I make a tree on mine?" he asked. "A white oak?" He smoothed the cloth. "I don't have to." But he looked so hopeful. "I brought acorns from Gropa's tree. We'll have real oaks in Idaho."

Ruth squeezed Daniel's hand. How thoughtful he was. She could see them, five or six white oaks towering over their new house, Gropa with them again, a place to survey the spread of their land, generation to generation.

The trail stretched less steep than the Appalachians. Aaron wended their way up, and, cresting, they descended into valleys, an undulation the horses took in stride, their mettle shown to those who labored under lighter loads.

By late the fourth evening from Pittsburgh, the woods opened to a large lay-by, the flat ground a welcome change from tilted camps in the trees. Here the wide sky deepened to blue-black as Hugo pulled the line in.

Ten or so wagons already occupied one end, forcing Aaron to settle closer to his group than usual, no room for the separation he preferred. The day had been long and dusty, dust caking in the horses' sweat. Daniel washed them down and picked clods from their hooves while Ruth soaked meat in milk. She dipped the strips in cornmeal ready to fry while Aaron got the fire going.

After dinner, Aaron and Ruth bent their heads. They built a wall of intention and tried not to look when a hubbub started.

Men and women of the other group gathered at their big fire, a wagon set close with its tailgate made flat.

A young man climbed on and stood holding a shiny stick sideways to his mouth. He blew on it and, moving his fingers, filled the air with the call of a thrush gone wild. On and on, birdsong. Another fellow climbed up with an upside-down washtub. He stretched strings from the bottom and beat them with his fingers, the sound of a grouse thrumming in the rough.

The two men swayed; the people sitting around them swayed.

"Mama, is it birds?" Matthew asked, craning from the seat for a better view.

"No, people."

Daniel stepped on the seat. High on tiptoes, he held to the first bow as another fellow joined the two. "He has a box with strings," Daniel said, and a wail came from the box when the fellow sawed with a stick. Matthew and Joseph hopped up beside Daniel.

"Let's go see." Esther set her plate aside.

"No," Aaron said from the ground where he sat, his supper plate beside him. "It's not something we do."

"Why not?" Esther asked. "I like it."

Aaron scowled at Ruth, as if she could block their ears with her crumbling wall of intention. The melody invaded her body, making her want to sway like those gathered near the players.

"Time for sleep," Ruth said. "We've a long day tomorrow."

The noise from across camp grew louder as voices rose to the music. The seated people stood and leapt about in intricate patterns, coming together and breaking apart. They ducked under one another's arms, all the time turning in circles.

While the littles changed clothes, Aaron read the Bible aloud, his words unable to drown the music. Ruth sewed.

Hortence stalked close. Not waiting for the psalm to end, she said, "Of all the—"

Aaron paused.

Hortence pointed toward the music. "That Sadie." Her eyes went to slits. "Singing and clapping, and dancing, for Lord's sake." She brushed at her long gray sleeves as if the music had settled and soiled her frock.

Esther peeked from the canvas. "I see her—there she is." In her white nightdress Esther stood, tiptoes on the seat. She twirled one leg, then the other, and waved her hands above her head. "Ho, Sadie!" she called in high excitement.

"Bed. Now." Aaron's voice a growl.

Esther shrank behind the canvas.

"Dancing?" Ruth said to Hortence. She wanted to look, but didn't.

Hortence patted Ruth's hand. "Thank heaven, we can count on each other."

Hortence must not have caught Ruth's little unintended sway. "How kind you are, watching over us," Ruth said.

"Yes, a responsibility I'm glad to bear," Hortence said. "But that Sadie, she needs a whipping."

"Hortence, you don't mean that."

"Oh yes, she does," said Sadie as she huffed and puffed into the fire's light. "She means it and she'd like to do it herself."

"I'm too much of a lady." Hortence drew in her chins. "Which is more than I can say for you."

"Say what you will." Sadie gave Hortence a saucy grin. "I'll let Hugo be the judge. He knows what's under the fringed pants."

"Sadie!" Hortence flexed her fingers, as if searching for a whip. "You've no decency."

"I'm sure you could teach me." Sadie bowed to Hortence. "Maybe Ruth could help."

Ruth looked wildly from one to the other.

"You," Hortence bristled. "You are the Devil's own child."

"And as we all know . . ." With a half curtsy, her hands spreading an imaginary skirt, Sadie bowed low. "*You* are God's mother."

The edge of the canvas lifted at the topboard and one of Esther's eyes appeared. "Is Frau Preacher really God's mother?"

Aaron glowered at Sadie. Hortence adjusted her bodice, and huffed off.

"Esther, go to sleep," Ruth said. "Sadie was—"

"Hortence likes you," said Sadie as Hortence disappeared in the dark. "Count your lucky stars."

Aaron read on until the littles' breathing slowed.

In bed herself, Ruth put a pillow over her head. The lilting tones passed through the down, filling her with a honeyed warmth as she drifted into sleep, where dreams of devils and angels with whips held sway.

## CHAPTER 8

## *Doors*

*Saturday*

*Dear Dear Brother,*

*Without a flinch our horses took to the trail and the Ohio River waters. We followed the south side north to Rochester and forded there. Then followed the north side to Liverpool. There we left the river heading west toward Canton. Hugo will leave this letter at the way station and I wish it God speed.*

*We look forward to Sabbath. The preacher's wife Hortence says even on the trail Sunday is a day we observe. Not according to our ways I'm sure. Sadie our leader's wife is everywhere at once and not to be avoided try as I might. She says Hortence is pious as*

*the day is long come winter solstice. Hortence is my*
*right hand in most matters. She gives me courage.*

*I am ready to hear news of New Eden. How is*
*Rebecca? What mischief with your littles? Matthew*
*Daniel and Joseph miss them. Matthew fell from the*
*wagon while teasing an ox with a carrot. He brought*
*the whole line to a halt and now we are known for*
*more than our black clothes. Joseph tried to stretch his*
*tongue to touch his nose as oxen do. His doesn't reach*
*and he would use his finger if I let him. I don't. Esther*
*keeps trying with her tongue.*

*We are blessed to have Bathsheba, she is such a pet*
*and fresh milk keeps the littles strong. My milk is*
*plentiful and Maus thrives. It seems like forever since*
*we left you. I must remember not to say forever out*
*loud as Esther will think it time to turn back no matter*
*how many times I tell her no.*

*My love to you and yours.*
*Your Ruth*

The Sabbath, and so much to do, no hour of rest could be
found, much less a day. Aaron took the littles hunting firewood. Ruth filled the washtub on the far side of the wagon,
away from wandering eyes, and elbow-deep she scrubbed the
first batch of shirts in tepid water. Hair tickled her nose. She
blew at the lock escaping from under her cap. The horses
grazed on picket.

"Move 'em out," Hugo called.

Surely not. This was the Sabbath. She heard the clatter of start-up.

"Aaron," she shouted, then wiped her hands on her apron. She climbed the wagon for a wider view. Hands cupped to her mouth, she called into the woods: "Aaron, they're leaving."

Aaron broke from the trees, the littles behind him. He dropped his armload of wood, and they all ran. The bigger boys faster, Aaron dragged Matthew and Esther by the hand. Their legs too short to manage even that, he scooped one under each arm and joggled across the lay-by.

Ruth wrung out the clothes and tipped the washtub. Daniel and Aaron threw harness on the horses, fumbling the buckles in their haste.

"I thought this was the Sabbath," Aaron said to a passing driver.

"Come dark, you'll see."

Aaron high-highed the horses out of the lay-by, catching up an easy matter for Jehu, Noah, and the mares who hated being left behind. The trail too narrow to pass safely, Aaron held them to the end of the line.

"Easy, now." And they settled to a fast walk.

As the way steepened and the wagons slowed, Ruth at the rein, Aaron and the boys ranged ahead, passing Sadie as she dropped back on foot.

"Ruth!" Sadie's cheery call made Ruth's stomach clench. She knew Sadie wasn't a devil as Hortence had suggested. But what *was* she, in her pants, with her dancing? A living, breathing piece of temptation Ruth best hold at a distance.

Sadie bounded closer, hair fraying under a floppy hat, the

ends of her braids tangled in a yellow cloth around her neck. She closed the distance. "I wondered where you went," she said.

Ruth, last in line the way she wished they always were, now regretted their placement. No Hortence near enough to help. Ruth slapped the rein on Jehu's rump, and he picked up the pace.

Undaunted, Sadie sprang to the running gear. Her hands on the frontboard, she hiked herself up, both feet flying over the top. Fringe of her leather pants flicked like the tongues of a hundred snakes. She landed beside Ruth.

Jehu slowed, his nose at the tailgate of the wagon ahead; he knew what to do. Ruth dropped the rein over the seat and pulled a cutting board on her lap. She took bread and meat, a knife from her midday basket. At every jolt she steadied the board with the heel of her knife hand and clutched the bench with the other.

Sadie slid toward Ruth, her eye on the cutting board. "What's that?" She pushed up the slouch of her hat. "Dinner? Oh, say it's not so."

"Pickled pigs' feet," Ruth said. "Would you like some?" She couldn't not offer. "We've more than enough."

"You eat pigs' feet?" Sadie tucked her chin and twitched her nose.

"Don't you?"

"Not ever."

"We in New Eden do. Try it."

Sadie took the board in her lap. She poked the brown gelatinous block with its flecks of meat, and scrunched her whole face. "I don't know," she said, and cut a small piece.

Her doubtful face held no offense; how could that be?

Something clear in her eyes, a curiosity without one malicious mote. She wiggled on the seat the way Esther did when contemplating a new sweet, half suspicion, half excitement. But she'd sung; she'd danced. What could Ruth think?

"Well, I'll be." Sadie mouthed the little piece of pig foot, her tongue flapping the roof of her mouth. "It's good!" Sadie grinned, open and seemingly ecstatic with this new treat.

Ruth bent her head, a shy smile escaping. "Next to cake, it's Aaron's favorite."

Sadie shifted the board behind her and slid closer to Ruth. Sadie cocked her head and peered, her look saying, *What's beneath all that black? There's bright plumage there somewhere.* As if Ruth were exotic as a pickled pig with feathers.

Ruth flinched as Sadie reached a finger toward her head. "What a pretty little cap," Sadie said. "Can I try?" She took off her own hat. It had to be Hugo's.

To keep her at bay Ruth lifted the stiff white cap off her hair. The long ties trailed.

"Your part's so straight, and look at that hair." Sadie craned around Ruth, her eyes picking at tightly bound hair. "Must be long."

Ruth looked in her lap, her cheeks hot. She felt naked without her cap. Only Aaron had seen her hair down since they were married; even talking about it seemed indecent.

"How long? To your waist? To your rump?"

What would she ask next? Ruth had to answer. "Long as a lifetime," she said.

Sadie reached out an inquisitive finger. "You never cut it?"

"It's not done, not ever." Ruth deflected Sadie's hand with the prayer cap.

Sadie took the cap and turned it front to back. "So fine."
She fingered the material and set it gingerly on feral curls.
"Doesn't quite fit, does it?" The cap sat atop the bush of her
hair, one long tie hanging in front of her cheek. Ruth covered
a smile with her fingers.

"Silly, huh?" said Sadie. "My hair needs taming. Another
job for Hortence and her whip." She laughed and handed Ruth
the cap. "On you, it looks good—sets off your eyes, cornflower
blue, same darker starburst."

Ruth didn't know what to say.

From her neck, Sadie unwound the yellow cloth nearly as
thin as Ruth's cap. "Here, try my scarf—it'll make you as
pretty as your eyes."

"Oh, I couldn't." Ruth held up a hand.

Esther poked her head from the wagon. "Oooh, it *is*
pretty." She crawled between them and settled Dolly in her lap.

"It's yours," Sadie said, and tied it around Esther's neck.

Esther tipped her head like a magpie, better able to see the
scarf trailing on the chest of her black dress.

Ruth shook her head. "Esther, you mustn't—"

"No, no," Sadie said. "Look how happy she is. I can't take
it back."

"You don't understand. It's a matter of . . . She's not allowed."

"It's just a piece of cloth."

"Esther needs no adornment," Ruth said. "She is as God
made her. That's enough."

Sadie wilted in her seat, her eyes sad. "I'm sorry. I didn't
mean—"

"Dolly could wear it." Esther untied the scarf. "Couldn't
she? Please, Mama?"

"Dolly needs all the help she can get," Sadie said. Brightening, she knotted the scarf on the doll.

"Well . . ." Ruth twisted her fingers. "The yellow's almost white. And it's for Dolly, not Esther. We'll see what Papa says."

Come night, men, women, and children milled near the central fire. All, it seemed, except Ruth, Aaron, and their littles, who stayed apart as they should be, a gap of ground between them and the others.

Hortence moved from family to family, touching each person, one minute chortling with a little wink, the next frowning. She gave Ruth a smile and a *Come over* wave. Ruth shook her head and continued washing dishes, while Aaron pushed the littles to scrape their teeth and dress for bed.

Hortence's face puckered, and then, quick as a sheepdog, she herded the others' children to the big fire, where they pushed at one another, sniffled, and wiped their noses on their sleeves. They sat, then jumped up to sit next to someone else, their parents paying no mind.

Barking coughs rang through the circle. Great handkerchiefs came out and went back into pockets.

Preacher Johnston came from his wagon, bent as usual, his steps slow. "Gather 'round," he said. The adults sank to the ground and sat facing him, the fire at his back. Their babble of voices softened.

He looked over the crowd. With a deep breath, he straightened. His chest expanded, and like a different man he intoned, "We are all God's children." He opened his arms, encompassing the group before him, then opened his one arm wider. "All of

us." His eyes swept over Ruth, a dooryard away from his congregation. "We are His people and the sheep of His pasture."

So many godless looking to Preacher Johnston, and Ruth
had to wonder: Could they be His people too? Her God, their
God?

"The glory can be yours too, you who are baptized. And
woe unto those who are not; hellfire will be theirs down to the
smallest baby." His voice reverberated into the woods surrounding the lay-by, and again he looked over at Ruth with her
unbaptized children. His congregation looked too, but were
they merely curious or threatening? Here it was again, those
who baptized their young condemning the Anabaptists, the
way Opa had been in the Old Country.

No, her children would not be baptized. They would
choose at eighteen, the way everyone in their Fold did, and
until then no one could deny them the glory of God's love. It
wasn't theirs to withhold.

Ruth stopped listening. She barely heard Hortence read
from the Bible, or the preacher's view of what she could expect
in the world to come. She did catch his last words, ". . . and the
land will be ours." She didn't know if he spoke of the west the
way Aaron did, or the greater Promised Land.

The others repaired to their wagons with little chat and
much coughing. None passed their way, not even Hortence.

"Was that the whole of their service?" Ruth asked Aaron.
At home that would have been the introduction.

"Did you want more?" Aaron stretched.

"No, it made me queasy."

With the passing days, the land leveled to minor hillocks. The grass-lined trail curved to the right around one and left around the next, grasses tall enough to cut the view of those ahead. At times, Ruth saw only slivers of white canvas bobbing above the grass, and then even those disappeared, leaving the wide, wide land empty of all but the brown seed heads swaying in the wind. Ruth found the openness pressed on her chest.

The others disappeared for minutes at a time. She strained to see them, to hear them. The wheels of her wagon turned and turned, the sound like the grinding of millstones, Ruth the grain. All that space—it weighted flesh and bone; even shifting position was a chore.

She dreaded the call to nature, squatting in the grass, her legs shaking. The thought of it tightened her bowels. She'd cross her legs until she had no choice but to run.

In one of those solitary moments, Aaron and the boys conferring with Hugo, the wagons ahead disappeared, and Sadie bobbed into view. She walked the trail in the wrong direction. By the time they reached the west, Ruth figured Sadie would have traveled twice as far as anyone else.

"From up ahead, you look like you're floating in grass." Sadie laughed and hopped aboard. "Do you s'pose that's why they call wagons 'prairie schooners'?" Legs extended, she crossed her boots on the topboard, at home as she could be. "Not your Conestoga—the small ones like ours," Sadie said. "Hugo calls ours his ship."

Ruth said nothing. Undaunted, Sadie went on. "Your Aaron's a help, scouting ahead with your boys. I hope they find a shorter route." She peered behind Ruth. "Aw, look—Esther, so sweet, napping with the baby."

Ruth fidgeted under her chatter and a growing call to nature. She stood, craning her neck, hoping for Aaron's return.

No Aaron. No Hortence. Ruth sat, her legs tight together, and waited for the need to pass. But the need turned spasm. Ruth clenched against it, and as it faded another built.

"Ruth, what's the matter?"

Ruth set her teeth, head bent, the spasm full of urgency followed by pain. She couldn't ask.

"Ruth?" Sadie leaned forward and looked up into Ruth's face.

"I . . ." Ruth didn't have a choice. "Could . . . could you watch . . . ?" Ruth nodded at the littles.

"Why ever not?" Sadie said.

"Whoa, boy," Ruth called. She yanked the brake handle. As the wagon stopped she jumped, catching her skirt on the metal handle. The cloth tore. She hit the ground and looked back.

"Go." Sadie waved both hands, shooing Ruth into the grass. "Don't hurry—we'll have a fine time, won't we?" She turned to Esther, who, fresh from her nap, blinked in the sun.

Ruth plunged into the grasses. Their feathery tops ebbed and flowed around her. The nodding heads whispered to the sky as Ruth squatted among them. *Why, why would I ask a wolf to watch lambs?*

What made Aaron think they could be separate? The grasses gave answers too soft to hear. How she missed Delia. Ruth gasped for air. In so much open space, where was the air? Her chest heaved.

Despite Sadie's admonition not to hurry, Ruth did. She followed her inbound trail of broken stalks back to the road. Birds twanged as she ran. Her black skirts caught at her knees, impeding her, making her heart race. "Esther, Esther, I'm coming."

Finally, panting by the wagon, she found Esther laughing in Sadie's lap as she jiggled Maus's hammock.

"Mama, look." Esther pointed at blackbirds landing on the grass stems, bending them, pecking one seed head to the next. The birds shook red-tipped shoulders, their song a reminder of Lancaster and the fields of summer.

"Did they follow us?" Esther asked.

Sadie hugged Esther. "I'll bet they missed you and came to find you."

Esther climbed to the ground. "Here, birdie, birdie."

Matthew returned and circled in, landing with a blackbird flap of his arms.

"You're so lucky," Sadie said. "Having children." She beamed as if having Ruth's littles close lent joy to the day.

Ruth took Maus from his hammock. Sadie didn't reach for him, or ask to hold him, but looked on him with such radiance, seeming to celebrate Ruth's own devotion, that Ruth laid him on Sadie's lap. Sadie folded him to her. With a grateful nod, she inclined her head over his and closed her eyes. She rocked him, her smile soft as thistledown lining a bird nest. She'd make a good mother; why hadn't God granted her children?

❧

At midday, Aaron, Joseph, and Daniel returned to the wagon. Hugo called a halt and the wagons crowded together at the edge of the road. Sadie walked up the line, a lightness to her step, almost skipping. Hortence passed with a squint and pursed her lips.

When she reached Ruth and the family, Hortence rested a hand on Ruth's arm, the one holding Maus. With a glance at Sadie's back, Hortence said, "You're too trusting. Not wise, not wise at all. She's . . ." Hortence lifted her chin and averted her gaze. "I won't say more. I think you know." Then, looking deep in Ruth's eyes, Hortence broke into a chortle. "You and I, we know these things. We feel the Presence." Her face turned serious again. "That one, I can't vouch for her intentions."

"Oh dear." Ruth looked at Aaron and back at Hortence. "She seemed . . ."

Esther pulled at Ruth's other arm. "What are intentions, Mama?"

"Nothing you need worry about." Aaron picked her up and hugged her.

"Good." Esther wrapped her arms around Aaron's neck and whispered for all to hear, "I like Frau Sadie."

Hortence rolled her eyes heavenward. Then back to earth, they settled on Maus. She put hands on him as if to lift him, then smoothed his hairless head.

"Sadie was good with Esther," Ruth said. "And I needed—"

"Of course." Hortence retreated. With half-closed eyes, she averted her face. "I just thought you should know." She waved a plump hand as if shooing flies. "I should mind my own business."

"But Sadie offered—"

Hortence popped her eyes open and gave a jolly smile. "Just know that you can depend on me. Anytime."

"Hortence, you're a true friend." So much like Delia with her ready hands. Hortence not so alarmingly English as Sadie, yet unaccountable clouds lay beneath her sunny smile.

"I wish Hortence were Plain," Ruth said to Aaron as he stowed the leftover food. "I feel separate."

"As you should be," he said.

"No, coming from her—something I can't touch." Ruth frowned. "Her heart is open yet I feel a closed door."

"You make no sense," Aaron said. "She can't be open and closed at the same time."

"She doesn't finish what's on her mind."

"Perhaps she's careful not to tread too close, thoughtful of who we are."

"That might account for it."

Ruth missed the company of women, not just their help in time of need, but the gentle words of a knowing confidante. So nice to find Hortence concerned about saying something unkind.

# CHAPTER 9

Mid-June—Odor on the Wind

The feeling of separation disappeared. As good as her word, Hortence stood close, there when Aaron was forward with Hugo. She had the preacher camp their wagon next to Aaron's. Hortence always ready when Sadie approached, stepping between Sadie and Ruth with a cheery "Let me."

Every time Hortence saw Maus she pushed up her sleeves, cloth bunching at the elbows, fingers working the air as if scratching an itch. She patted Matthew on the head. He ducked from her reach, and, her arms empty, she encircled Esther, who shied from the soft bosom and gasped for air.

The boys had a way of disappearing, until the day she brought cake after the midday meal.

"A bite for each," Hortence said. "Now run along—your

mother's tired." She plucked Maus out of Ruth's arms. "With so many children, and sickness in camp, it's no wonder you look drawn. Poor Ruth, let the baby ride with me."

It was true; Ruth was tired. She hadn't slept well last night, mosquitoes singing in her ear, and the littles restless. Besides, Maus seemed all right. Ruth ignored the twinge she felt in the face of her new friend's generosity. Ungrateful. Churlish even.

For the afternoon, Aaron drove. He promised an eye out for the littles while Ruth rested in the wagon.

She slept.

After they stopped for the evening Ruth woke with a start. Feeling logy, she hauled herself from the bed. Her breasts swollen hard, Ruth left to find Maus. The preacher's wagon wasn't in its usual place. She heard Maus's hunger in full cry. It stopped for an instant, then rebounded more furious with each breath.

Ruth followed the sound across camp to Preacher Johnston's wagon, Hortence there in a chair, with Maus in her lap. She pushed a piece of corn bread in his mouth. Corn bread, good God. Ruth ran.

Maus shook his head, spewed crumbs, gagged, and screamed.

"No spitting," Hortence said. She shook her finger at him as Ruth scooped him from Hortence's lap.

"I best nurse him. He's not on food yet." Ruth thumped his back. "Thank you, Hortence. You've been most kind." Maus screamed.

With each outburst, Ruth felt milk leak from her breasts. "I had a good sleep." She turned to go.

Hortence gripped her arm. "They're never too young to learn solid food."

Hortence's children must be grown now, none being on this trip.

"How many do you have?" Ruth said.

Hortence's eyes narrowed. She chortled and gave a knowing nod toward Maus. "It's your funeral," she said. "He'll be a screamer."

"I'll keep it in mind," Ruth said. Well-intentioned advice, Ruth was sure, but she couldn't accept this kind of help no matter the intention. But she didn't want to hurt Hortence's feelings either.

❧

*Week two out of Pittsburgh*

*Dearest Dan'l,*

*We are well, while others succumb to fits of cough. I worry for our littles. Young ones seemingly fine one minute cough til blue the next. Their mothers give them physic pills. The collywobbles follow. Parents' faces are pale as their sick children.*

*Hortence attends the sick. Though they cough she holds them close. She is an angel of mercy. She says most times the littlest will die.*

*God be praised, none have died so far.*

*Your loving,*

*R*

❧

The day was uneventful through porridge. Esther, still in her nightdress, sat on the bench beside Matthew and dressed her doll. He helped tie the black apron and tied on the yellow scarf Sadie had given her. At least it wasn't red, too fancy to be ignored. Aaron had yet to notice, and it was Esther's treasure.

Ruth cleaned the cauldron while Daniel harnessed the team. Joseph watched, learning the order of chains where they hitched to the tongue. Behind the wagon, Aaron, preparing to shave, gathered a bowl of water on top of the oat bin, hooked the leather strop, and sharpened his razor. He wet his cheeks and upper lip, daubed soap, and after one last strop, set the blade to the two-day stubble above his beard.

Hortence, in the closest wagon, called, "Let me take the baby—we're ready to go and you're in the midst." She came to Ruth.

"Thank you, I couldn't impose," Ruth said.

"It's no imposition." Hortence scooped him out of Ruth's hands and, short of a tug-of-war, Ruth had to let go.

Hortence headed toward her ready wagon. "What's that smell?" she said. She sniffed Maus. "Not here."

Preacher Johnston came from behind his wagon and shouted, "It's a—"

Sharp whinnies pierced the air. Two of his four horses reared. Chains shook as all the horses, held together by harness, lunged in opposite directions. In the midst of flying hooves a small skunk, tail high, white stripe down its back, skittered in circles.

Hortence screamed. She clutched Maus and ran. Ruth raced after.

The preacher fumbled his jerk line. Out of control, the

horses careened at Aaron's team. Daniel, the closest, grabbed for the flying line. The line went taut. Holding tight, he lost balance and fell. The panicked horses dragged him bumping over the ground, first on his side, then flipped, belly to back to belly, dirt spewing till the line snapped and Daniel lay in a heap.

The preacher's wagon bucked after the horses, a shower of belongings flying from the tailgate into the billowing dust. Stench filled the air. Everyone coughed.

Aaron, bare chested, his face above his beard covered with soap, headed after the runaways and managed to swing onto the preacher's lead horse. "Easy, boy, easy now." He worked the stub of the jerk line, slowing the horses in a circle, and stopped.

Ruth's horses, using sense of the ages, had crouched their haunches and retreated. Their wagon moved smoothly backward out of the way.

Daniel lurched to his feet. Head in his hands, he stumbled toward Ruth. Hortence dropped Maus in her arms and snared Daniel's jacket.

"What were you doing?" She shook him, her cheeks bright pink. "You frightened our horses."

"Hortence!" Ruth swung the baby to the shoulder away from Hortence. "He tried to help."

Daniel raised his head, blood welling between his fingers.

"Joseph," Ruth called, "take Maus." She guided Daniel to the grass. They sat, turmoil at a distance. Ruth pulled his hands from his face, blood and dirt down his front.

She wadded her apron against a gash running from his eyebrow up into his hairline. "Can you speak?" she said, as if asking him to pass the salt.

"Only when spoken to," he answered.

She smiled. "That's when you *may* speak." Her icy calm melted to real relief.

Matthew, his eyes streaming, joined them. "Where's the skunk?"

"It's gone."

"Not the smell," said Esther. Red eyed, she crawled to Ruth and tugged at her arm.

Aaron knelt beside Daniel, squeezing fingers down each of his limbs in turn. "Feel all right?"

"Yes, Papa."

"You'll be worse tomorrow." Aaron looked around. "Matthew, rags. Joseph, water."

"Esther," Ruth called. "My sewing kit."

"Do you have to?" Daniel edged away.

"Yes, there's a flap," Ruth said.

"Big as your pants' back door." Matthew handed Ruth the clean rag.

"Hush, it's not that big." Ruth lifted the blood-soaked apron. "Lie back," she said, and flushed his face with water. The wound gaped wide, a spot of white at the bottom before it filled again with blood. She pressed a clean cloth over his brow.

"Was that bone?" Joseph asked. He leaned in close, holding Maus.

"Yes. Now be quiet."

The curious from other wagons gathered, though Ruth hardly noticed in her concentration. She threaded the finest needle from her cushion. Lighting a match, she burnt the needle's tip. Aaron, kneeling, held Daniel's head.

With the pressure off, blood oozed again. Ruth pressed the

needle against the edge of the wound. "Here we go." She dabbed it and slid the needle into the skin. Daniel bared his teeth, short breaths sounding so like Ruth in labor.

She pushed the needle through the first side, then the other, and knotted the thread on top, one fine stitch after another, blotting away blood as she went until a neat row of fourteen black bristles held the flap smooth.

"Too late for anesthetic, I see." Hugo, newly arrived with Sadie, offered a bottle of whiskey. Uncorking it, he splashed the stitches. Daniel yelped.

"And a gulp for the pain," Hugo said. He held the bottle to Daniel's lips.

Daniel coughed. "No more."

"Liquor!" Hortence's voice carried across the onlookers. "For shame."

"It's medicinal," Hugo said.

"It's corruption." Hortence stamped her foot. "God says so, and no black dress can hide the sin."

Ruth flushed. Heat rippled at the roots of her hair.

"So good of you to explain, Hortence," said Sadie.

"It's true, then." Esther looked with wonder at Hortence. "She *is* God's mother."

"No." Sadie made a snorting sound. "But she'd like to think so."

Aaron helped Daniel to his feet. "Let's get you in the wagon."

"Hurry on," Hugo said. "Get these horses sorted. We're late."

Aaron settled Daniel while Ruth stowed the sewing kit and dirty washrags.

"Isn't Hortence your friend?" Aaron asked.

Ruth's eyes welled. "I thought so."

※

Ruth read the trail. She swayed with the wagon's rhythm, the bone-jarring lurches going unnoticed. She wished she could read Hortence as well. This, her one possible friend, now full of hard looks.

The other women surveyed Ruth the way Joseph inspected a spider, poking it with his eyes, with his finger if he dared, then running away to count its legs from a distance.

Joseph usually ended with the insect crawling up his arm, but here the women and men kept away. Could this kind of separate be what God had in mind? It didn't feel good.

※

Three nights later, many in camp had fallen ill. Ruth woke to the sound of barking coughs throughout the lay-by. From under the wagon, she bent an ear toward the loudest, someone near, hacking on and on, harder and harder until they gagged. Vomit rumbled, and another cough began.

Several wagons away, a man lifting a bundled child stepped to the ground. He marched in circles and patted the child's back, hours of it before the bark turned to a whoop, bringing more heads out to look.

Hortence and the preacher appeared bleary in night-dresses. Hortence gathered the child from its flagging parent, while Preacher went with him to the wagon.

Murmured prayer threaded the camp, Hortence the loudest calling on her Lord. She'd been up the night before and would most likely be up the night after with other children. She had a knack for calming them, if not the cough.

Ruth kept honey and vinegar for cough, but God only knew if it worked on the whooping.

At home, Ruth would have helped. She had to try.

She walked across camp, the beaten ground hard under bare feet. She too wore a white nightdress. "Hortence," she whispered as she approached, "I could take a turn." Ruth held out her hands.

"You're not needed," Hortence said, her lips so tight they hardly moved. Her eyes sagged with exhaustion. "The Lord will help me."

"I'd like—"

Hortence turned her back.

Ruth let her hands drop to her sides. "If you change your mind, come find me."

Among English, staying separate was right, but not helping couldn't be more wrong. And not being allowed to help felt worse.

As Ruth crawled under her wagon, she heard Hortence pray, "Lord, protect Maus and his family. Please guide them to Your Path."

Ruth ran this kindness through her mind, weighed against the cold of Hortence's back.

Her words like Ruth's own prayers, God's path the one, but this English path could not be Ruth's, and the kindness smacked of a twisted arm.

In the morning Ruth's fellow travelers cast red-eyed glances her way. All dragged at their chores, and by the end of the long day their attention hit like stones.

As Ruth stirred soup for dinner, Sadie joined her at the fire. "Beware," a woman called from across camp. Ruth flinched, knowing they talked to Sadie.

"They listen to Hortence," Sadie said. "You and yours don't cough."

"You don't cough," Ruth said.

"Your health is the talk of the camp, not mine. They listen to Hortence and worry."

"And you?"

"I listen to my heart, not Hortence."

From where she stood, Ruth could hear Sadie's heart and the warmth of her words. Could she be a skinny English Delia?

❧

Rain and wind made quagmires in the trail, the days long with little progress. Outside Findlay, a week short of Fort Wayne, the halfway mark to the Mississippi, their wagons stayed in the lay-by and suffered under splattering hail.

Ruth sat on the milking stool. She covered her head and shoulders and back with canvas like a tent. She leaned into Bathsheba, poor brute, dripping from horn and jowl, belly and teat, diluting the milk with cow-scented rain.

"You're a good old girl," Ruth said. "You take it all and no complaint, you and Esther's Dolly. But you, I can talk to." Her hands closed in rhythm on the cow's warm teats and shot milk into the pail. "Your ears bend to my secrets, and you never confuse me with words, your back never cold under my hand." Ruth rolled her forehead on the cow's wet hide, down from the spine and below the ribs where her belly was soft. "You, mine own Bathsheba."

The pail full and foaming white, Ruth covered it and put it in the wagon, before dipping water from the barrel into the washtub. Why not stand in the rain, let God do the work? She hated to think how long clothes would take to dry.

Ruth, hidden behind her wagon, started in scrubbing on the washboard. She wrung the clothes and dumped the tub, refilled and rinsed and wrung once more. Her hair, without her cap, lay in a night braid down her back, lank and heavy, her dress as wet as the pants she washed.

The other travelers held to their wagons, their tempers heated and spilling from under canvas. Ruth made her way into her wagon, a wet mound under one arm. "Give me a hand," she said to her littles, each immersed in their own project. Matthew jumped his wood horse over Esther's doll. Daniel set aside the Bible he'd been reading to the back of Joseph's head, and took the clothes from his mother. He passed a shirt to Matthew, pants to Ruth, hung a pair himself, and extracted more for each, until the pile hung on pegs set in the bows. She knew they wouldn't dry for days.

A flute, sweet as a thrush, played from a distant wagon as families hunkered under cover. Would Sadie dance in the rain?

Ruth stopped work to listen. She missed the thrush at home, hidden in its woodland haunts, but here, this bird could live in a pocket, if one dared, and if one dared have a pocket, which Ruth didn't. Nevertheless, the flute came to her ears, should she care to let it in, and even if she didn't.

But she did, its sweet taken along with a salting of hail, made for a wet and blessed day while the Sandusky waters retreated. With rain and the river, hardwoods grew lush around Findlay, the area famous for boar, Hugo told them.

"Tonight, we hunt," he said.

The men set out in the dark, the crowd a bristle of guns. Aaron, without one, stayed at camp. He seemed oblivious to resentful faces after Hugo outlined the division of meat. Share and share alike.

The men stayed out all night, dragging into camp as the women began to stir. Each man went to his own wagon and none carried a boar or even a piece of one.

"Why should the forest share with hunters unwilling to share?" Hugo said loud enough to be heard at every breakfast fire. "We did find signs of Indians," he announced. "So, from now on, we circle the wagons." He turned to Aaron. "That means you too.

That night, they circled in a lay-by and hobbled the stock. They tied the horses and oxen on picket outside the ring.

Aaron tied Bathsheba to the far side of their wagon.

"Aaron?" Ruth took his arm. "Will Indians . . . ?"

"Don't worry," Aaron said. "If the threat were great, we'd picket in the circle. Bathsheba too."

Ruth sat to the cow's side and filled the pail. Daniel rode herd on Matthew lighting the fire, and Joseph wiped down the harness, rubbed on tallow.

The cauldron on its tripod close over her fire, Ruth melted the fatback and browned earthy turnips and sweet carrot along with the onion. A mash of potato in water thickened the soup. One strip of dry meat deepened the flavors even more.

"Salt?" Esther said. "I want to salt."

"*Shhh.*" Ruth touched her lips with a finger. "Maus's napping." She closed the salt jar. "Dry meat has its own salt." Dry, a disappointment after the promise of fresh pork. The thought of her home-smoked bacon had to be washed from her mind.

The family sat, bowls balanced in their laps, and joined hands. "Bless this meal to our use, O most merciful God." On the trail, meat in any form was a blessing.

Ruth felt eyes on her and turned to see Hortence bearing down, hands folded in front of her wide breast. Her round body swayed, mouth prissed into a smile, her eyes pinched.

"We pray for you in your good health," she said and rolled past. She stopped, her back toward Ruth and the family. Hortence sighed. "For the children's sake, won't you pray with us?"

"Thank you," Aaron said. "We'll manage without your prayers."

Hortence spun around as if he'd kicked her. "Everyone needs prayers."

"Yes," Aaron said. "We have our own."

"Mine are . . ." Hortence waved a dismissive hand and stalked into the night.

Ruth leaned close to Aaron, and said, "She couldn't think hers be better than—"

"*Surely* not." He kissed her cheek, his smile on the sly side. Her own smile flickered.

Ruth's lack of charity sat heavy through the next day. By evening, she thought a word with Hortence could soften the air, but the idea made her heart trip. Stay separate, yes; however, this didn't mean hostile.

Even in New Eden, the Plain remained pleasant to *English*. She should do the same here, say thank you for their prayers *and mean it*. After all, they believed in the same God; only the stepping-stones differed.

Perhaps Ruth had misheard Hortence's intent. She tried to rehear the tone. As she repeated the words too many times, they became nonsense.

"An untended sore festers," Aaron said as they stood together after dinner. He slipped his hand around her waist, leaned down, his head to hers, a long moment breathing softly, then gently nibbled the ridge of her ear.

How he eased her heart, infused her. Her thirst great, she rested against his chest and drank him in.

"I know the festering sore," he said. "Ours lasted too long, and I'm sorry. And I'm grateful."

"Grateful?" Ruth tilted her head, and he kissed her.

"Yes." He kissed her twice more. "You believed in me, trusted me."

Ruth returned her head to his chest. She didn't want him reading her face.

She loved him. To her core, she loved him and accepted who he was. But trust? Could she call that trust?

❧

The last line of light on the horizon long gone, movement in camp slowed. Now was the time to tend the festering. Ruth and Esther walked the camp's edge. Preacher's wagon had been shifted to the far side from Ruth and Aaron. The canvas tops reflected orange of the fire, each wagon separate, black voids at either end where who knew what might lurk.

Esther skipped beside Ruth, clearly tickled by this unexpected treat, out in the night on a grown-up mission. She should be in bed, but having Esther along would blunt an untoward tongue.

Ruth forced a nod at every eye that caught hers in the flickering light. She tried a hesitant smile. Not a one returned. Esther waved, undaunted by hard stares.

The walk felt like miles, but a shortcut by the central fire came too fraught with hazard as people rose to make ready for bed. Talking to Hortence would be more than enough uneasiness for one night. Ruth wished she had Esther's comfort. Nothing daunted her, not Hortence, not Sadie.

The thought of Sadie filled Ruth with confusion. Strange, she found herself looking forward to seeing her on the trail, or maybe just having it be tomorrow, the confrontation with Hortence done, her trepidations silly come daylight.

In a few months, she and Aaron would be on their own land, in their own house, in their own bed behind a closed door. *English* of no importance.

"Frau Preacher." Esther hopped and raised a finger. "There she is."

"Don't point."

The preacher held Hortence's arm as she lifted her skirts and mounted a set of steps to gain their wagon.

"Hortence," Ruth called as she hurried, wanting to stop her before she retired. This would be good, no time to sit and make conversation. A pleasant interchange and she could repair to her own comfort, Esther a good excuse to be off.

As Ruth came closer, the void behind the preacher's wagon gathered movement, a will-o'-the-wisp glimmering, and though she strained to see a shape, one didn't come together.

"Well?" Hortence said. She teetered on the top step.

Ruth's eyes stayed on the void. "I hoped we—" Yes, a definite movement. And no more said, a near-naked man screaming like Satan's own self leapt out of the dark, arms flailing, skin painted white with black hexings jagged as teeth, gourds in his hands buzzing like a fistful of rattlesnakes.

This creature stank of skunk, his loincloth red from the skinning, an apparition beyond Ruth's worst childhood nightmares. In those terrors, she couldn't move.

With a chilling smile, the man bared his teeth and sprang at Esther. Ruth lunged. Her arms up, fists high and shaking above her head, she closed the gap with giant strides, and, face in his face, she screamed, animal enough to frighten the Devil himself.

The Indian, for that's what he was, balked. His mouth sagged. White paint cracked around his lips. His white-ringed eyes bulged as Ruth, swollen with a mother's wrath, loomed over him.

His arms fell. The gourds went silent, his spell broken, and jackrabbit-fast, he sprang into the void from whence he came.

Ruth, like a tree, limbs in the air, didn't move. No one moved. Ruth's ears rang with silence. She blinked.

Esther, from behind, flung herself at Ruth's skirts. "Mama, Mama."

From all sides a cheer went up. Ruth looked around, dazed and confused in the ruckus as people rushed around her, crushing Esther against her, hugging her, and one another.

"What a she-bear," Hugo said. He clapped her on the shoulder. Other men did the same, jolting her, close to knocking her off her feet. Aaron swept along with the others, pulled her to him, taking the weight her jelly-legs refused.

"Indian fighter," said one man. A chant rose: "Indian fighter, Indian fighter."

"Pay no attention," Aaron said. "They don't know what they're saying."

Ruth shrank under their words. "Aaron, I'm not a fighter," she said. "I didn't strike him." Ruth leaned on his arm. "I didn't intend to strike him."

Hortence bustled into the crowd. She pushed them back, showing her teeth in the semblance of a smile, sweat on her upper lip. "Now, now," she said. "Praise God. Praise where it's due."

"Thank you, Hortence," Ruth whispered, and meant it. If Ruth could, she would crawl to her wagon and hide. Esther, on the other hand, soaked up the smiles as if they were sweets.

"Come now, Esther," Aaron said. "In the wagon with the boys. It's late."

Ruth climbed in beside them. In a welter of quilts, the boys, all up on their knees, clamored to know what had happened. "Papa wouldn't let us come."

Maus watched big-eyed from his hammock while Ruth tucked them in. "It's all over. Sleep now." Sitting in their midst, she nursed Maus and returned him to his hammock. All the littles settled, she joined Aaron by the fire with Hugo and Sadie, their faces long.

Aaron rose and lit a candle at the fire. "Come with me, Ruth." He threaded his arm through hers. "Prepare yourself."

Sadie and Hugo said good night and headed across the circle as Aaron took Ruth's hand and led her, her legs still shaking, over the tongue of their wagon.

Outside the circle, he held the candle high. "Hugo says it's what Indians do," he said. "They never meant us harm."

"Do what?" Ruth said, and then in the grass she saw Bathsheba's bell, the strap cut. Above it, her knotted rope hung on the side of the wagon, and no Bathsheba.

Ruth covered her mouth with one hand, the other on top. She could feel the skin of her face pucker against her palm, the shake of her chin. Above her hands, her eyes burned. Poor Bathsheba. Ruth fell against Aaron, her face in her hands.

"She'll be fine," he said. "She'll train a squaw the way she trained you."

Bathsheba could do that, Ruth had to believe; the pain of not believing would be too great. But, oh, how Ruth would miss her, the soft hair in her ears, the keeper of secrets, her constant friend. *Mine own Bathsheba.*

How would she tell Esther?

❧

*June, the third week*

My Dear Dan'l,

    *Toledo to the north we press on toward Fort Wayne. Our first Indian and no harm meant, but Bathsheba was taken. Beyond her milk, we are bereft. Esther cries, Matthew too. Daniel and Joseph hold their tears though they are there, as mine are. Aaron is subdued.*

    *Your loving sister,*
    *Ruth*

❧

The group pulled Ruth to them. A misunderstanding. Surely they would count themselves deceived once they accepted the truth. She would never have hit the Indian. They would shun her as quickly as they had taken to her.

Ruth went about her business as before. Two days later she smiled and ducked her head under a barrage of good wishes. Undeserved though they were, they did warm her, a welcome change from stony glares.

Four young girls stopped by the fire. They played with Maus and Esther, their eyes always on Daniel. He kept his head low, the scar on his forehead a deeper red with every attention.

Was he ashamed of Ruth, his mother the fighter? How could he not be? In his silence, the girls talked to Ruth. Daniel watched them watching him.

All too soon, she or Aaron would have to have words with him. Words about bees hovering over stamens, pistils with pollen tubes, the ovule, receptacles and sepals.

Maybe Aaron should do it. Yes, he could explain to the boys. Later, much later, she could explain to Esther. Or, knowing Esther, she'd be explaining to Joseph and Matthew well before either was ready. Ruth wasn't ready for any of it.

First she'd have to talk to Aaron and she wasn't ready for that either. Such talk had never come easy.

"I couldn't be that brave." A tall girl with yellow hair nattered on. "My dad says you saved us."

"No, listen," Ruth said. "The Indian didn't—"

"Don't be so modest," said an older woman just joining the group. "You're not what I thought."

Finally, someone who understood.

"You sat up on your wagon like a vulture," said the woman.

"You ate pigs' feet." All the girls giggled behind their hands.

"You're not so scary, except maybe to Indians." The woman laughed. "And you eat strange things, but Sadie says pig feet are tasty."

"Would you like some?" Ruth said.

This skittered them away, but a group of nine or ten gathered that night with presents for the littles, almost as if someone had died. One brought a bowl of blueberries and bread. Another brought pieces of chicken. Esther ate the meat from a leg and gave the bone to Maus. He gummed it for hours.

Ruth walked among them grateful for their offerings, and tried to explain she'd done nothing. No one would listen, and slowly Ruth gave herself up to their kindness.

Hortence, however, hung on Ruth's horizon like a puffy cloud. Fair or foul, hard to predict, and on this evening, with more than two or three gathered together, she bellied up to the group, all smiles.

"Lordy," she said to Ruth. "You really are a caution."

"Hortence is the caution," Sadie whispered behind Ruth.

"Do tell," Hortence said. Her shoulders under her dress gave a jolly shake. "Tell us how you managed, protecting us with your tiny fists." Her eyes went to slits above pinking cheeks. "We women want to know. I'm sure the men do too." She leaned her massive breast toward Matthew and patted his head. "Matthew must want to know why it wasn't his daddy." Her chins shook. "We'll ask your papa, and where is he now?"

"He's getting wood, but I can tell you," said Matthew. "He was with us in the wagon." He drew down his mouth and kicked at the dirt. "We missed the Indian."

"Leave her be," Sadie said. If she had hackles, they'd have been on end. "Aaron's not your concern."

Hortence, so accusing . . . Why? And Sadie, as if to the rescue? Had Aaron been with her, they'd have leapt between Esther and the Indian together.

These English. Ruth shook her head.

❦

Late that evening, she changed in the wagon and emerged in her nightdress. Aaron gave her a hand as she stretched a leg to the ground. The moon caught her, ankle to shin, lighting her leg white. She yanked the hem to her ankle, but yes, someone had seen. Hortence, by the big fire, watched without shame. She didn't bother pretending different. Her little bow mouth worked on a smile, disdain in the toss of her head.

"Heart full of spleen and sweet as a hornet," said Aaron. "I can't imagine what she thinks you've done." He wrapped Ruth in his arms as if they were in their own bedroom.

"Aaron," Ruth squeaked.

"Your leg's a fine sight," Aaron said. He bent, lifted the hem of her nightdress, and admired her ankle. "Let's give her something to gawk at." And he kissed her full on the mouth.

In horror, embarrassment, and a touch of glee, Ruth squeezed her eyes shut and nestled into his beard. "That woman's a burr in my chest."

He rested his cheek on the top of her head. "Seems like you do the same for her." He grunted low and amused. "Preacher stopped me today, said, 'I don't know what your missus did to my missus, but she's in a right fine swivet.'" Aaron held her at arm's length. "Whatever it is, Ruth, you best settle it." He kissed her again.

"How, when I've no idea what's buzzing in her bonnet?"

## CHAPTER 10

# The Last Week of June—Skirmishing

The wagon train passed into Indiana, Fort Wayne ahead, and Ruth pondered how she might settle Hortence's feathers. Ruth could sew up a wound, splint a broken leg, cook up a poultice, but this invisible infection stumped her. The fort would be a good distraction.

At first, she thought Fort Wayne was a place of respite, safe under the eyes of soldiers, a place to purchase fittings for broken wagons, to stock up on fresh peas and green beans, maybe an early tomato. She imagined a stockade fort with a big market, farmers trading goods and news.

"No Indian worries," she said to Sadie, sitting beside her on the bench.

"It's a city, not a fort, no soldiers." Sadie laughed. "Have you ever seen soldiers?"

"A few years back, out where Aaron said there shouldn't be soldiers. We had no part in the war."

She'd seen them gallop over a rise in Yoder's field, twenty-four of what had to be the Four Horsemen's closest cousins, blue uniformed, gold shoulder boards, brass buttons, faceless under brimmed hats, rigor to their bodies as if death lurked inside the blue cloth.

They carried long guns in scabbards, short guns in holsters at their sides, knee boots with cruel spurs they drove into their horses' sides, nothing meek about them, yet Ruth knew that *they* would inherit the earth.

A trumpet had sounded. She wanted them to be like Gideon frightening his enemy with noise, like Ruth with the Indian, dedicated to peace. But her brother had told her, in war, there's evil on every side. Like Gideon's rebellious men, some blue horsemen cut off heads of their enemies and put them on pikes as a warning.

Ruth skipped Gideon's men in the Bible when she read to her littles. Her loving God would not condone these acts.

He was a God of resurrection, of life.

❧

Two days to refit, they camped south of the city, across the river in acres of beaten earth. Aaron pulled his wagon from the others, not afraid of Indians so close to the city. Hugo said soldiers used to gather there, deploying for the civil war.

That first morning, before the family set out on foot for the city, Aaron counted paper money. He handed two bills to

Ruth. "Necessities only—we're short." She folded the paper and slipped it into her boot top.

As they walked together Aaron stayed gloomy. Ruth shifted Maus, squirming in her arms, and Esther cradled her doll. "Now, now," Esther crooned and patted Dolly's head. The tip of her treasured scarf peeked yellow from beneath the doll's black bonnet, telltale in the soft breeze.

"Dolly must be cold," Ruth said.

Esther wrapped the doll's shawl close at the neck, near dropping her in the process. "She's fussy." With only black showing, Esther squeezed Dolly against her cheek with both arms.

They walked across a covered bridge to the edge of the city. Halfway over, Hugo and Sadie caught up. Together they picked through hoof-turned dirt to the boardwalk and down a side street with its smattering of houses, low storage barns, and three stores. Each had a specialty, offering hard goods, soft goods, and foodstuffs, whatever travelers might need. The rest of the city spread daunting through a maze of streets Ruth wouldn't venture into.

"Sadie, look—there *are* soldiers." Two green-uniformed men without horses tipped their tasseled hats as they passed. "They look no older than Daniel," Ruth whispered to Aaron.

"Eleven? In the army?" Aaron laughed. "Not even the English."

Those fresh-faced boys didn't look so alike. "Is there a fort after all?" Ruth asked Hugo.

"Prison guards out of Sandusky," he said.

He and Sadie veered off to their own errands as three women crossed the street approaching Ruth and the littles. The women wore another kind of uniform, the shape of their dresses much the same, though the colors of wide-flowing skirts were different: one peach, one tomato, and one oak leaf brown. The peach neckline rose to a pale chin, while two other necklines dipped to the cleft of breasts, making Aaron red when one woman threw back her head and shook her shoulders.

"Jezebels." He locked Ruth's arm in his and scanned the boardwalk.

Esther let Dolly drop by one arm and reached a grimy hand to the tomato skirts.

"No." The woman whisked the billowing cloth away.

"When we get to Idaho," said Esther, "I want a red dress." Dolly swung at her side. The shawl loosened to a glimpse of yellow.

"There will be no red in Idaho." Aaron scowled. "And no yellow." He took Dolly by a leg while Esther clung to the doll's arm.

"This goes back to Sadie." He gave the scarf a yank and stuffed it inside his shirt. "I'll see to it." He strode off, the boys in tow. "Now, hardware."

"Does he have to?" Esther tugged Ruth's sleeve, eyes pleading.

"Yes, Esther." Ruth slid a finger over her cheek. "I was wrong, letting you keep it." Again, Ruth had made the situation worse, made everyone unhappy, most of all Esther, and that wasn't right. There were rules, whether she agreed or not.

Ruth went into the crowded food store, hoping they'd have crystallized sugar on a string, a *necessary* treat to soften Esther's disappointment, and one string saved for her birthday.

Before her other shopping, Ruth found the crystals on a

plate by the counter and bought six strings the length of her palm. The man behind the counter wrapped them in brown paper and handed them to Esther. "Don't eat it all at once," he said.

Her eyes lit at the suggestion. She looked at Ruth. A bit crestfallen, Esther said, "I share." Then, brightening: "And one for my birthday." She held up four fingers.

From the open window Ruth heard clatter from the street. Above it, Joseph's voice burst with excitement. She shopped her way toward the window, putting beans and lettuce in a split wood basket. From where she stood she could see Matthew, Joseph, Daniel, and a gang of boys armed with wood swords and guns, clustered around a mounted soldier.

Joseph slid his hand up the withers of the soldier's horse, fingers inching toward the stock of the long gun.

Suddenly the soldier wheeled his mount. Joseph tipped off his built-up boot and sat hard on the ground. Matthew and Daniel knelt beside him as the other boys crowded 'round. The soldier rode off.

"Hey, gimp, did you touch it?" a boy asked Joseph.

"One finger," Joseph said. "And don't call me gimp." Still sitting, he beat dust off his pants.

Ruth gripped the windowsill. "Where's your father?" she said to Esther, who stood at her elbow. "He should *be* there."

Another boy with a wood sword stood over Joseph. "Never touch a gun—don't you know nothing?"

"Anything," said Joseph. "Know *anything*."

"You a teacher, gimp?"

"Come away, Joseph." Daniel gave him a hand and steered him toward the boardwalk, but Joseph spun loose.

"You wanna fight?" the boy said. "Come on."

Where was Aaron? This had to stop.

"I'll run you through," the boy said. He poked Joseph's ribs with the sword.

Joseph grunted. "Ow, that hurts."

"Aw, does that hurt 'ums." The mocking boy hit him again.

Joseph dropped to the ground.

"Come on, gimp." The boy kicked him. "Fight."

Joseph rolled on his belly and swung his big boot behind the boy's knee. The leg buckled and the boy fell on his back in the dust. Joseph leapt on top, straddling his hips, and yanked the sword from the boy's hand.

Ruth dropped her basket. Dragging Esther by the sleeve, she rushed through the store and into the street.

"Joseph," she called. He paid no attention as he pinned the boy's shoulders to the ground, the sword across his chest. A hand on either end of the weapon, Joseph pressed down, his mouth by the boy's ear. "Don't. Call. Me. Gimp."

"I won't." The boy cringed. "I promise."

The rest of the gang milled about Joseph, aiming forefingers, their thumbs raised. They shouted, *"Pow pow pow."*

Up on his knees, Joseph swung the sword at them.

"Stop that." Ruth hustled down the boardwalk.

"Boom," another one shouted. "Mine's a cannon and you're dead." A boy clutched his chest and fell writhing in the dirt.

Joseph stood and pulled his opponent up by one arm. The boy grinned. "Die and I'll give you my turn with a gun."

"Hey," his friend said. "Dead means you're out of the game."

"Yeah, dead is dead," said another.

Ruth broke through the boys and grabbed Joseph by the neck. "Death is not a game." She shook him. At nine he should know better. "Esther, take Daniel's hand. Come, Matthew, we have provisions to find."

"I'm going to be a soldier," Matthew said. He walked between Joseph and Daniel as they passed through the boys and back toward the food store.

"You can't," said Joseph. "You're only five." He shifted his jacket straight on his shoulders. "Besides, you'd get blown to bits."

"No, I'll ride a horse of my own."

"You don't have to be a soldier to have a horse," Daniel said.

"I'll have a gun." Joseph aimed across the street with his finger.

"Stop that."

"For hunting, Mama."

Aaron hurried toward them. "What's all this?" He squeezed Ruth's arm in a tight grip.

"I'll marry a soldier," Esther said. "And wear a big dress." She threw back her head and sashayed down the walk, dragging Daniel by the elbow.

"You see?" Aaron said. His beard jutted at Ruth. "A three-year-old Jezebel."

"Yes, I see." Ruth pulled her arm from his grip. "I see we are not separate and cannot be. Perhaps we need blinders from here to Idaho?"

❧

*Week four, June*

*Dearest Brother,*

*We have yet to cross into Illinois. Idaho is far, and though I try, meekness escapes me. Aaron tells me I will not inherit the earth. I don't want the whole earth, just a few hundred acres and our family around me.*

*Today, flies inherit this camp. We had to move our wagon, the smell of night-jar overwhelming, even hazardous. Too many have stopped before us. Hugo wants to press on. The loudest say they are tired with the passing of whooping cough. Though it slows us, I do not begrudge them rest. We remain blessed with good health. May it keep.*

*Your most loving sister,*

*R.*

❧

Ruth knew money worries goaded Aaron, his sharp words little to do with her. He'd said as much, and the irritations of the previous day passed.

The littles tucked in, prayers said, Ruth sat on the ground, her back against the wagon's front wheel. She sewed another patch on Joseph's shirt. Aaron shared the lantern and oiled harness. "Have you seen Hortence?"

"I'd rather another Indian. I understand him better."

Aaron laughed. "Is she really so frightening?"

"*You* talk to her."

"It's your stew—don't let it burn."

Full of reluctance, Ruth closed her sewing basket and rose to her feet. Maus cried, this time a blessed reprieve.

She plucked him from his hammock and walked him around the edge of camp in the opposite direction from the preacher's fire. And as God would have it, Ruth spied Hortence, head down, a Bible pressed between her hands.

Ruth coughed so as not to startle her. "Hortence, I . . ."

Hortence stiffened. One hand went to her armband and tucked the shredded edge under.

Seeing a chance to unruffle her feathers, Ruth said, "Hortence, I'd be honored to make you a new armband. I've cloth in my basket."

Her eyes dove into Ruth's. "You," she said. "You think you have all the answers." Hortence puckered her mouth. "You in your black, and that white cap—God-given gifts, I suppose."

Ruth took a breath. "What does—?"

"I know your kind, parading around, looking down your nose, thinking you're better." Hortence advanced, head forward, the folded flesh of her neck stretching.

Ruth held her free hand up, palm out as if warding off a blow. She gripped Maus to her other side.

"Don't you come talking to me," Hortence said. "I'm ready for you." She thumped the Bible.

Her hiss and the stretch of her wattles put Ruth in mind of a snapper. She took a step back. Maus coughed, and Ruth brought him forward. She uncovered his head.

Hortence's face softened. "I didn't see him." Her voice filled with regret. She folded her hands in front of her breast. Maus coughed again.

"Oh, poor thing." Hortence advanced, stretching out a hand, a beseeching hand. "I'm sorry." She stroked his cheek.

Setting the Bible on the ground, she brought the other hand out, an offering, and like an offering of peace Ruth handed Maus over, letting Hortence cradle him to her, her face that of a different woman.

"You know, he looks so like . . ." Hortence leaned in and tickled his chin. She put her forehead to his. "Mine Ben." She whispered so Ruth could hardly make out the words. "My sweet boy."

"Well, well." The preacher's voice boomed as he came on them from the central fire. "A sight for sore eyes," he said. "I'm glad you've come to terms." He stood still when he saw the baby.

Hortence folded both arms around Maus as if she'd never let him go. She lifted her head, her eyes shining, and tipped the baby's face toward the preacher. "Doesn't he look like our Ben?"

Pain cut the preacher's face. Ruth could see it wash through his body from his gnarling brow to the curl of his fingers. She stood transfixed by the effort it took him to squash his grief, dig a more inaccessible hole where a sudden reminder wouldn't take him unawares.

Long seconds elapsed, filled with the click of Maus's tongue as in his hunger he rooted Hortence's chest.

Preacher Johnston's face rearranged itself to polite concern. "Thank you for speaking with my wife, Ruth. You must want to be off." He lifted Maus, gently prying him from Hortence's reluctant arms, and returned him to Ruth. The preacher put an arm around his wife's shoulders. They bowed their heads together and, retrieving the Bible, turned for their wagon.

Ruth cradled Maus as he chirped out cough after cough. "Another cold, my little man?" she said and walked back to Aaron.

"All settled?" he asked.

She sat out of the light and opened her dress. Maus latched on and suckled with eager slurps. "I wish I knew," she said.

❧

Past Joliet, soon at the Mississippi. Gaining the river, they'd be halfway. In the meantime, milkweed dotted the fields with orange and yellow flowers. Around them butterflies hovered, their wings veined with black.

This leg of the trip, many rivers crossed their way, the Eel, Tippecanoe, Yellow, Kankakee. The travelers, never short of water or mud.

To keep her family in clean clothes, Ruth spent the last of daylight most evenings downstream of camp. Tonight, well ahead of the dark, Aaron with the boys, she and Esther took turns with the washboard.

Sadie came down the bank, a pair of Hugo's pants under her arm and milkweed blossoms laced in her single braid. It swung in front of her shoulder as she knelt to the river.

Esther bounded to her and touched the flowers. "So pretty," she said. "I wish I could wear flowers in my hair." She patted her black prayer cap with both hands and sighed.

"I may have flowers," Sadie said, pounding the wet pants on a rock, "but you have a washboard. You're lucky." Again she dipped the pants. "Hugo thinks rocks work fine." She held up her dripping hands. "Look what they do." She waved raw fingers at Esther.

"Mama says her hands are rough as a cat's tongue," said Esther. She kept scrubbing Dolly's apron. "Last night Papa said a cat lick was fine with him." Esther looked from Sadie to Ruth.

Ruth's eyes went wide. Heat surged up her neck and into her face. How had the child heard? They'd been quiet, always quiet, whispering under the wagon, the hour way past bedtime. She'd thought the whole camp asleep when he'd crawled under her quilt, his hand like a mole, blind and searching beneath her nightdress.

It had been too long, since well before leaving, and then the baby. Their need great since healing, they made up for lost moments, awake when even bird and insects slept. Ruth gladly opening to his touch.

Sadie put a hand over her mouth.

"He was funning." Esther laughed and wrung out Dolly's apron. "We haven't got a cat."

"Time to go, Esther." Ruth gathered wet clothes, the doll's apron on top of the board, and tucked the bundle under one arm. "Now."

"You're all pink," Esther said as they fled the long trail threading the woods back to camp. "A fever?"

Her mouth dry, Ruth needed water—cool water, not the warm of the barrel. She spread the wet clothes on the grass outside the circle of wagons.

She would head upstream, around the bend where the water ran unsullied by the camp. With dusk coming, everyone finished drawing water, and Ruth would have a few minutes to herself. "Help Papa," Ruth said. "I'll be back soon."

Water swelled around rocks as she walked beside the

stream. A soft wind off fields to the west blew away bugs. The late June sun, a flat disk on the horizon, shimmered red.

The land might not be Pennsylvania, but it had its own magnificence. Wide swaths of grasses stretched in slow undulation, dark patches of woods to the south, lofty trees lining the river's path. And Idaho would be even better. Everything would be better in Idaho.

She thought of her fingers on Aaron and smiled, wishing the camp wasn't so crowded. It was a long way to their new home, to their wedding sheets spread on the new bed, to a time behind a closed door when they could run hands over each other's uncovered skin, his fingers exploring the hollow atop her breastbone and down the cleft, cupping her flesh, his lips following his fingers, her fingers in his hair pushing his head lower. She could feel the— *Foolishness!* She'd drive herself mad with this foolishness, squandering her moments alone, so rare they were. Squatting in the grass didn't count.

She need revel in the calm, absorb the quiet along the river, walk farther from where anyone might go, away from the crush of strangers and the clatter of her littles.

Ruth took the breeze off the water deep in her chest. The scent of flowers came with it from the edge of the path. The same kind Sadie had in her hair. Ruth couldn't resist picking one.

God's own flower; why not admire His handiwork? She held it to the edge of her prayer cap and looked in a still patch of water. Horrified at the sight of her face with the flower, she dropped the blossom. It bobbed downstream, an orange dot in the sun's red reflection. She prayed Aaron wouldn't see it floating by and know how she'd succumbed.

At home she hadn't time for such *English* temptations, always focused on work at hand. Her mind didn't wander. No wonder God wanted them separate. But the flowers were God's handiwork; could it be so wrong to admire them, want them close? He admired His own work. Was she putting herself in God's shoes? Supposing He wore shoes. Her thoughts went from worse to worse still.

She straightened her skirts and felt the untended rip where she'd caught the brake handle. It seemed easier to stop a fully loaded Conestoga than the swarm of unwanted desires.

Aaron would expect better of her. She expected better of herself.

Farther ahead she heard splashing, and rounding a bend she saw a figure standing hunched in the water, her back to Ruth. Drinking, Ruth supposed. But no.

As she drew closer, silent on the earthen trail, the figure splashed more water, first with one hand, then the other. Not drinking. When sipping water, a person scoops from in front with both hands, letting as little fall as possible.

Ruth shielded her eyes. Even in the fading light, she knew by the shape and the gray dress, the figure was Hortence. She'd piled her shoes, stockings, and shawl on the bank. She wouldn't be washing—that was done downstream, and farther below saved for more unsavory needs.

Hortence crooned a hymn Ruth had heard of a Sunday. She swayed slowly side to side with her self-made music, legs spread under her skirts.

Ruth stopped. She'd stumbled on a private moment, a religious moment she shouldn't interrupt.

She wouldn't want anyone interrupting her moments with God, especially someone who harbored contrarian beliefs.

Ruth turned to leave, but stopped when she heard a bur-
bling. Hortence laughed, indulgent and soft. Ruth looked back
as Hortence reached a hand in the water and splashed again.
Droplets pocked the surface around her. And again the burble.

Ruth knew the sound, the kind of sound Maus made when
she bathed him. But it couldn't be Maus; he was asleep in the
wagon. He was with Aaron and the littles.

Ruth turned full toward Hortence just as the woman bent
her knees, straightened her back, and raised her arms to
heaven, in her hands a baby. Water dripped from its naked
body. Maus's naked body.

"Welcome," Hortence said loudly to the child, to the water
and the trees, like a congregation. "Welcome to God's love."

## CHAPTER 11

## June into July—Unsettling

God's love indeed. Ruth choked. Breath stuck in her throat as if she'd taken a blow to the belly. Half a stone's throw from Hortence, she stood nailed to the riverbank, her arms out. She reached shaky fingers toward the ritual in the water, reaching until her arms could reach no farther. Belly to brain, her innards boiled.

She ripped one foot free. "Hort—" The name jammed in her craw.

Hortence wheeled, drawing Maus to her. She staggered. Her elbows flailed for balance, and the newly baptized boy bounced in her hands. With each rise in the air, Maus shrieked with delight.

In full throat, Ruth lunged. "Hortence!" Slogging through

the water her boots skimmed the bedrocks, and almost on Hortence, one boot slid between the smooth stones and caught.

Wild, she yanked free of the boot, lurched forward, and, near falling, snatched Maus by his slippery arm. He gasped, and Hortence, her footing lost, sat to her chest in the water. Her skirts rose around her, floating murky gray on the surface. She glared at Ruth, igniting the air like lightning. Ruth's skin prickled.

Betrayal. Her brother had predicted betrayal. Ruth's one friend, a Donner in their party of travelers?

Maus's delight ended and he wrinkled his brow, took an enormous breath, and bellowed. Hortence beat the folds of her skirts with her fists.

"He deserves better than you," she yelled. Drops streamed her cheeks, river water or tears, Ruth couldn't tell.

Maus naked over her shoulder, Ruth rubbed the smooth skin of his back. "He deserves better than both of us," she said. "But what he has is me." She waded carefully to shore, her arms locked over his back and legs. "And what I have, as far as Idaho, is you ahead in your wagon, so stay there, and leave me and mine be."

Hortence battled her skirts, while Ruth marched in lop-sided steps down the path, one boot on, one stocking foot leaving mud tracks.

Hortence shouted after her, "One day you'll thank me." She banged the water again.

Naked and red faced, Maus coughed and continued to cry. Stomping down the path to camp, Ruth examined him carefully and wrapped him in her shawl.

He wasn't hurt. Hortence had splashed him with water, a gift perhaps. The deeper meaning belonged to her, not Ruth, and for Maus the water was water.

It changed nothing for him and his relation to God.

Betrayal came with intent, the dismissal of Ruth as mother and protector, as if only Hortence and her beliefs held value.

There'd been no eating. Hortence wasn't a Donner. That had been Opa-talk. She hadn't harmed Maus.

Ruth couldn't wait to find Aaron. She would let herself overflow in his arms, let fly the outrage bubbling in her chest so fierce it hurt. The gall of that woman! He would be furious. He would be beyond furious.

What place might that be? And what then?

Would he forget the Ordnung? Take another's eye or a tooth without thinking, the way he'd smashed the cider jug last Easter?

The boil of Ruth's own anger frightened her, for who would be hurt if it bubbled over? Herself. At the core. She couldn't risk this for Aaron.

As dark settled, Ruth approached the wagon. She found Aaron and the littles squatting on the ground by the fire, working tallow into their leathers.

"Ruth?" Aaron said, surprise on his face. He got to his feet. "What's this?" He spread his hands as if to take the baby. "You have Maus?"

"I thought I'd spare you," Ruth said, her tone pleasant. Spare him the evening care, spare him guilt. Where had he been when Hortence stole their boy? She wouldn't tempt him to assuage her own anger.

"Mama, you're wet." Daniel kept working the tallow.

Esther scooched over to Ruth's feet. "Where's your boot?" Esther wiped mud from the toe of Ruth's torn stocking.

"We were having a drink," Ruth said. "Upriver and I slipped." A lie for a good cause was still a lie, this sin added to the wages she carried. "We'll find my boot tomorrow."

※

On his rounds two nights later, Hugo sat by the fire with Ruth and Aaron. "Two weeks to the Mississippi," he said. He clamped a pipe in his teeth and lit it. "I hope your food holds out; we're down to beans for breakfast, lunch, and dinner." He blew a stream of smoke. "I'm looking forward to Davenport. Mmm, fresh meat."

"Where will we ford?" Ruth asked.

A chirping cough came from the wagon. Ruth waved away the smoke.

Hugo tamped out his pipe and put it in his pocket. "We take the ferry."

Ruth frowned.

"*You* know," Hugo said. "It floats on the river like a raft."

"Wagons and horses and all of us?" Ruth could feel the raft, unsteady under their weight, tippy with the horses fidgeting worse than Ruth. She could see the slip of a wheel off the side, all of them sliding into the water, splashing madly until they sank.

"That's right," Hugo said.

A swarm of birds and bats took wing inside Ruth. *Two weeks.* She wanted to be in Davenport now, the wide waters behind her.

Ruth soothed Maus's cough with vinegar and honey and put the Mississippi out of her mind.

❧

After three days clear and bright, the trail smooth, they had made good time through the wide-open land. Now the trail too fast for walking, the littles crowded at the tailgate. Aaron rode Noah. He sat crooked on the saddle, his eyes north, then twisted and scanned south. "Look at it," Aaron said, a thrill in his voice. "Hay to the ends of the earth." He stretched his arms wide to the endless plenty.

His thrill and the thrill of the land lifted Ruth's heart. Sun drenched, her vision grew lush. Idaho shimmered above rivers, the nervous mountains and deserts. This land so rich, Idaho could only be more so. Aaron's dream surged through her, satisfying as dinner after a day at hard labor.

On the bench, she leaned back on her hands and tipped her face to the sky. She let the sun fill her bonnet with the scent of drying sheets so like afternoons in their New Eden dooryard. The same sun, there and here and in Idaho. Her Aaron, how could she have doubted him?

"Dan'l and Rebecca better hurry," she said. "The land could be gone."

Bird wings reigned for days as Ruth nurtured Aaron's vision, so easy in the midst of all this plenty. And yet bats returned, having nothing to do with Idaho or the Mississippi.

At the midday stop and through the afternoon Hortence passed Ruth's wagon five times when Maus was awake, coming close, but not so close Ruth could shoo her away.

Come evening, the wagons circled. Hortence haunted Ruth, though they hadn't spoken since splashing in the water.

Matthew started a dry cough, and Maus continued to work on his. Upwind of the fire, Ruth nursed Maus and spooned in honey when he finished. And a dose for Matthew. Beyond the heat of the day, they both seemed warm to the touch.

"They're not well," came a disembodied voice. Hortence from inside her wagon gave Ruth a jolt.

She felt Hortence hovering like the mountain cat, watchful, waiting. Not as frightening as the cat, Hortence was more of a tick with its head embedded in Ruth's ever-thinning skin.

Ruth caught her peeking over the tailgate, but before Ruth could accost her, she disappeared. Ruth wished she could be forgiving, let Hortence hold Maus for a minute, but a modicum of trust would be necessary, and even if Ruth could forgive, the trust would never regrow. With Aaron yes, but not Hortence.

Holding Maus, Ruth walked in circles around the family as they sat with their feet at the small fire. She rubbed his back and crooned, her steps flagging, while the others scraped their teeth before bed.

Daniel finished first, sipped water, swooshed, and threw his stick on the flames. "I'll do that," he said to Ruth. He stepped over Matthew and Joseph, handed his half-full cup to Ruth, and took Maus.

Aaron checked Esther's teeth. They both stood. He braided the almost four years of hair down her back. "Done," he said.

"My turn to hold Maus." Esther headed around the fire.

Instead of going behind Joseph and Matthew, she hopped over Matthew's legs, then Joseph's, but not high enough. She caught a foot on his knee.

"Watch—" Aaron shouted.

Joseph and Matthew pulled their legs to their chests as Esther's arms flew up, her hands white birds reaching for the sky. She pitched toward the fire, her nightdress flowing behind her, bare feet pointed.

Ruth's arms came up too, the cup gripped tight in her hand. She gasped. The boys gasped. Water sloshed.

As Esther arced toward the fire from one side, Aaron dove from the other. They met midair. His hands up like battering rams, he hit her chest. She bounced off his palms, her nightdress winding around her legs, and she hit the ground hard.

Aaron's movement halted, he dropped face-first on the burning sticks.

Esther and Aaron howled. Everyone else leapt as burning sticks scattered.

Hands at his face, Aaron rolled clear and lay on his back. Ruth, instantly beside him, kicked away the smoldering branches and knelt. She yanked his hands apart. The stench of burnt hair filled her nose as she doused him with the little water left in Daniel's cup. "Joseph, more water." Little red-ringed holes grew on Aaron's jacket and shirt. "Hurry, Joseph!" Ruth crushed the material in her skirts, the smell of scorch mixing with burnt hair.

"Here, Mama," Joseph huffed behind her. She sat on her heels to take the bucket and he threw the water over them both.

Rising on his elbows, Aaron sputtered.

"Good," Ruth said. "Bring more, and this time leave it in the bucket." She lifted her skirts. "It's out—now lie back."

Esther flung herself on Ruth's shoulder and snuffled as Ruth washed the ash from Aaron's skin, his gnarled beard crisp under her fingers. The others stood around them in a circle: Matthew and Joseph, feet apart, leaned their hands on their knees. Daniel stood upright holding Maus.

"Not so bad," Ruth said. "You'll blister, but no broken skin."

"Papa's beard," Joseph said. "It melted."

Aaron's fingers probed his beard. His face twisted as if pain lay in the hair's amputation.

"Not all of it melted." Ruth trickled water over his forehead.

"And his eyebrows." Matthew crouched in closer.

"Off with you." Aaron sat up, hands still at his beard. "It's bedtime."

They scuttled off, and after all were safely tucked in, Aaron paced by the wagon. "The shame of it," he whispered to Ruth. "It's mortifying."

"You're lucky to have a face. The beard will grow." She waited with a towel and scissors. "Now sit on the bucket."

"How can I show this face?"

"Who's going to see? English?" She pointed at the bucket. "They know nothing of faith and beards. They *will* think you strange with melted gaps. I have to cut it."

"It's not right." He sighed and sat on the bucket.

Ruth wrapped the towel over the shoulders of his nightshirt. She snipped the melted ends of his eyebrows and attacked the snarled beard. He winced with every snip.

"God will think I've broken faith."

"He knows better."

"You know me best, and once you thought so."

Ruth moved his head side to side. She held her hand cross-wise, measuring under his chin. "Two fingers long," she said. "You look newly married." She shook out the towel. "How do the burns feel?"

"Better than the beard."

❧

Flat, flat, flat, the ground stretched to the ends of the earth. One day like the next, Ruth blessed the interruption of a tree and prayed Idaho would have a touch of hillock and swale to hold them. This flat exposed the train to wind and sun and the glare of every eye that cared to look. The verge of the trail beaten hard and dried in the sun cracked the way Ruth imagined the desert would.

Days and more days, the wheels ground forward. Aaron kept his hat low, shielding his face as the blisters puffed, shrank flat, turned brown, and sloughed off to skin, looking constantly embarrassed. But soon enough the land recaptured his attention.

They moved farther back from the line of wagons. "This way you'll see the land unfold, not just someone else's tail-gate," he said. He didn't seem to crave the trees the way Ruth did, and though few grew here, she trusted many would grow in Idaho. The sky arched blue and huge above, without the weight she had once felt.

The trail led on through shortening grasses, the way stunningly straight till the wide track came to a point in the distance. Short of the horizon Ruth spotted a dot, coming or going, it was hard to tell, a mystery filled with anticipation.

As time passed the dot became a trickle of wagons. Drivers of Ruth's group craned their necks for a better look as the strangers crawled eastward under the glaring sun.

Murmured anticipation floated on the wind. Soon a chance to pass letters east, and learn of conditions ahead—springwater, Ruth hoped, with no taste of mud; perhaps talk of fresh food hawked by the trailside; perhaps music. She shouldn't wish it, but there it would be, impossible to keep from her ears.

These strangers could warn of fordings, and if someone set tolls too steep to pay. For Ruth and Aaron, any amount would be too steep, so much money from the sale of horses now destined for the Mississippi ferry.

Aaron had always found alternate crossings and forded where others feared to tread, Jehu and the team taking all, smooth as the open road, so the coming news held no worries.

The next day the strangers' wagons approached enough for Ruth to make them out. In the lead a three-horse team pulled cock-eyed horses with their noses dropped below their knees. The driver slumped on the bench, his thinning hair as ragged as his dirty clothes. He didn't look up.

A bony ox hauled the second wagon, no driver in sight. The last, its canvas shredded, lagged behind.

The front two passed at early afternoon. One man and two women in the first, and another two women in the second. They said not a word. Their hollow eyes in weather-dark faces snuffed Ruth's hope of good news and any surreptitious musical pleasure.

By evening, camp settled, the third wagon pulled in beside

Aaron's. Though Aaron offered a space in the circle, the driver refused. "Can't be bothered," he said. He left his horses in harness and lowered himself by Ruth's fire.

Two women followed, one young, one with gray hair, both in tattered exhaustion. They collapsed by the man, their eyes brown pools sunk in ravaged faces. Ruth handed the old woman a bowl of broth, her hands nearly too weak to hold it.

Sadie greeted the strangers and, without a fuss, picketed their horses. She fed them from Hugo's supply, checking their hooves as they chewed their oats. The animals settled, she returned to the strangers as Hortence, the preacher in tow, bustled across camp. Hortence carried a large bowl. "Come, everyone," she called and pushed past Sadie. "These folks are in need." At Ruth's fire, Hortence spooned portions of meat soup into bowls her husband set at the strangers' feet. "God blesses you," she said to each person served.

The old woman slanted her eyes at Hortence. "Does he, now?" She dropped the spoon in her bowl.

Sadie choked on a laugh. With a struggle, she removed the smile from her lips.

Others from Ruth's train offered bread. Their faces were at first filled with hopeful expectation, never mind the visitors' condition. Soon enough, all faces fell and questions stopped.

"You don't want to know what's out there," the man said. He bent over his hollow chest. "Salt grass, starvation, sickness."

"Charlie took an arrow," the young woman said. "I yanked it, burnt the hole with a hot knife." She wiped a sleeve across her mouth. "But sickness . . ." She rattled a cough deep in her chest. "The worst is sickness."

"You know colds," the old woman said. She nodded at Hortence, who nodded at her. "Neuralgias too. Hanna here broke her foot."

"But the fever," the old woman said. "Fever drops you 'fore you feel the blow."

"Took eleven of us." The old woman chafed her arms as if cold.

Hortence wrapped her shawl around the woman's shoulders and relieved her of the empty bowl.

The littles crowded next to Ruth, keeping her between them and the strangers, yet they leaned forward, their big eyes fastened on each speaker. The old woman crossed the shawl over sharp collarbones and wiped her eyes on the knitted corner. "No unguent, no salve, no poultice would touch it," she said. "We're finished."

The air hung wordless around the fire while sparks rose and fizzled.

When Aaron and Ruth changed for bed, he whispered, "Hundreds have gone before us, and only these three lost heart." They tucked in under the wagon, their faces close. "Three out of hundreds," he said, "a rate to make any farmer smile."

At home Aaron had worried and watched the sky over drying windrows of hay. He'd paced the night if wind knocked at the shutters. He'd ground his teeth at rat holes in the feed bin, but here, his brow stayed smooth. He seemed to trust God would carry the weight of bigger worries, leaving him free to spin dreams into reality. The Elders had trusted his faith. Late coming, Ruth trusted him, too.

During the next day, she sat close to Aaron, walked close within his shadow, warmed by his faith, and with a steady smile spread it to the littles, who seemed in no need of reassurance as they cavorted beside the trail. They examined bugs crawling in the grass, and followed the flight of large-winged birds as they hung in the sky, black and drifting in languid circles, their red heads pointing at the ground.

"I think they like us." Matthew waved both arms at the birds.

"You better hope not," Aaron said. He gave Matthew's rump a pat. "Vultures have a taste for the dead."

Ruth's lips froze, the smile brittle on her face. "Bite your tongue," she said.

They watched the birds circle and land in a dead tree. Seven of them rocked on the branches, eyeing something on the ground Ruth couldn't see. One dropped to it, and in a flurry the others pounced. Wings flapping, they swarmed over whatever it was, tearing the flesh, fighting over chunks, and, necks stretched, they gulped ropes of intestine. Ruth's midday meal threatened sour in her throat. She swallowed, and a nettle-like tickle brought on a cough.

That evening, as they pushed late into the setting sun, her eye stayed at the horizon. A flat line cut earth from sky as if there they'd come to the earth's end. The sun dropped to the edge and tumbled over, their track in shadow.

Beyond the lip of the world, what waited? An abyss with its dark rife with crawlers? Ruth couldn't pull her eyes from the last line of light as it faded.

That night, under the wagon, she lay awake beside Aaron. In the Appalachians she feared she wouldn't see tomorrow. Now, what the morrow might hold frightened her more. She saw herself clawing dark and endless corridors.

She shivered and curled her knees behind Aaron's, her nose against his back. One arm over the barrel of his chest, she took in his reassuring scent. Tomorrow, with more sun, her fears would burn away. She slept.

❧

Ruth worried over her words to Dan'l. She didn't want to scare him. Or herself.

*July, the first week*

*Dear Dear Dan'l,*

*Another five days. The land is slow rolling and cut with streams. Trees grow plentiful. Hot meals such as they are are an everyday event. We eat the same old soup. How quick we are to be ungrateful. Our stores should last us to Davenport. Then we restock.*

*Unlike himself little Maus fusses with cough. Aaron aches in every joint. They are both strong and will come right soon.*

*I hope to find a letter from you in Davenport once we cross the Mississippi.*

*Much Love,*

*R.*

❧

Aaron massaged his arms and shoulders as he walked beside Jehu. He slowed, falling back until he shuffled next to the wagon and held to the sideboard.

"Why don't you sit with us?" Ruth said. She passed Maus

to her other arm and scooched over. "Make room," she said to Esther, and nudged her to the far edge of the bench.

Aaron pulled himself onto the wagon and sank on the seat. Taking his thighs in his hands, he squeezed the muscle from groin to his knees. He shifted buttock to buttock and winced.

"You're worse," Ruth said. She felt a little queasy herself.

Aaron leaned to her ear. "I haven't been to the bushes, two days now."

"Matthew's always in the bushes. How can this be? You eat the same thing."

From his bed, Joseph came behind them. "When will we get there? My head hurts."

"You know when," Aaron snapped. "Not soon."

"Rest, Joseph." Ruth touched his forehead. "You feel warm too."

Ague nagged over the next few days. Matthew and Joseph flexed their limbs and complained. Maus, the most out of sorts, continued to cough, his brow more heated every day.

Ruth had a twinge of guilt as she pestered God with her prayers. They'd been so blessed when whooping cough rang from every wagon but theirs.

Night hung long, and pray though she might, Maus's sleep turned restless. He woke coughing as the others settled. Ruth put him to her breast, but he couldn't seem to find her nipple. She pressed it to his lips with her fingers. He mouthed it as if he'd forgotten how to latch on. He cried, his hot breath on her breast, and eventually fell asleep.

Over and over through the night he woke, and woke the others. Maus suckled so little, Ruth's breasts grew tight. God help him, he was miserable.

By start of the next day, short sleep made them all miserable. Ruth held Maus at breakfast, and Esther poked him when he fussed. Matthew's birds no longer swooped when he gathered firewood. Under way, Aaron on Noah, Matthew stayed in the wagon and contented himself with winged fingers.

Joseph rooched around on the next mattress. "It's good you fly," he said. "You'll never have a horse in Idaho."

"I will too." Matthew slapped his bedding.

Joseph's boot clunked the topboard.

"Stop." Matthew's voice broke. "That hurts." A flood of tears followed.

"No shenanigans." Ruth kept a stern tone.

"The strap comes next," Aaron shouted.

"Aaron." Ruth glared at his back.

He'd never shouted, and never, never would he use a strap.

He held to the saddle, little attention to the rein lying across Noah's withers, his body rocking with the horse's walk. Aaron rolled his head.

Jehu at lead, the team pressed on under Aaron's flagging guidance. "We'll make an early night," Aaron told Ruth. "Don't fuss. I'll be fine tomorrow."

In camp, they kept to themselves. He and Daniel drifted, heads down as they watered the horses. Aaron lifted his brow enough to watch the other men scout for wood along the stream.

"Save your strength," Ruth said. He made a tiny fire from sticks saved in their travels. Ruth warmed bean stew, while Maus, rocked in one arm, cried himself to an eerie calm. She dished a small portion on each plate, and they sat in a circle on the ground. Plates in their laps, none ate except Esther.

Matthew pushed the beans on his plate the way Sadie had poked at pickled pigs' feet, having yet to find them tasty. Esther scooped up Joseph's portion, and he dried his plate without washing it.

Ruth held out her hand. "I'll do it."

A group of boys ran past. Their shouts to one another might as well have been silent for all the notice Joseph took.

The spoon appeared heavy in Aaron's hand, and he gave up.

After supper, he didn't go to the big fire. "We'll be fine tomorrow," he said. "We're just tired."

"Don't count on it." Hortence appeared like a gopher out of its hole. "I heard poor Maus across camp." She craned for a view into the wagon. "What kind of mother are you?"

Ruth turned her head away.

Was there no moment safe from this woman's intrusion?

࿊

Another four morrows brought worse ague. By the fifth, Matthew and Daniel fought their pants and ran to every scattered copse. They came back pale and shaky. God, why must they suffer? And Aaron suffered the opposite.

At bedtime prayers, Ruth laid herself with the littles in the back of the wagon.

"Mama," Daniel said, breathless as if he'd climbed a hill. "Will my farm be far, like Uncle Dan'l at home?"

"If that's what you want," Ruth said.

"No," he quavered. His note of worry sounded more like Matthew, not Daniel's usual confident self. "I want it close. I'll need help."

"I'll help you, Daniel." Joseph rolled toward him.

"I will too." Matthew panted. "Together is better."

"I'll carry water," Esther said. Esther, the only one not moving as if tied to fieldstones.

"Now?" Matthew asked. "I'm so thirsty."

Esther climbed over the frontboard. "Aren't you scared out there?" Joseph wound his quilt tight to his body.

Esther dropped to the ground. "No—Papa's by the fire." She put a finger to her lips. "*Shhh*, he's sleeping." She tiptoed past him.

"Can't we always be together?" Daniel asked.

"Yes," Ruth said. "We'll have one big farm and live in a big farmhouse as long as you like." She wrapped an arm over Daniel and hugged him. "No one has to go anywhere, even when you're married."

"I'm having my own house," Esther said as she handed a cup to Matthew and climbed under her blanket. "I'm having dogs and cats in mine."

"I want pigs in our house," Matthew said.

"You'd have them in your bed, wouldn't you?" said Ruth.

"Yes." Matthew perked up. "Could I?"

"I don't think Papa would like that." Ruth tucked Matthew's blanket around him. "You may need a place of your own."

"That's all right. Pigs can stay in the barn."

Maus cried in his hammock.

"He wants pigs in the house too."

Ruth lifted Maus's nightshirt to change him. She felt raised spots, and in the light found seven red rings over his chest and belly.

"He's scalding." Ruth rested her hand on his chest. "He needs water."

"Give mine," Matthew said. "I don't want it. I don't want anything."

Ruth poured what was left in the cup on a cloth and bathed Maus's forehead. "He's still so hot." She climbed down from the wagon and filled a cup at the water barrel. Half-full, she noticed. A good thing the Mississippi would come soon.

They must drink more, wash away whatever this was.

❧

By morning, Maus pushed her swollen breast away with both hands. Esther ate her porridge while the others moped at getting dressed.

Daniel and Aaron dragged harness to the horses. They each heaved the leather over a horse's back. The first throw not high enough, the harness slid off, and they had to work on a single horse together.

Once ready, Aaron stepped to the stirrup, pushed with his grounded foot, and, holding to the saddle's pommel and cantle, hauled at his weight. He fell back. He took a deep breath and started again. Concerned, Ruth caught his eye as he brought both feet to the ground. "I'd rather ride with you today," Aaron said. He made a show of stepping lively to the running gear and onto the seat beside her. Ruth wasn't fooled, but fussing wouldn't help.

They decamped slowly, theirs the last place in line, a habit.

They slogged through the day, all in the wagon letting the horses do the work. The littles rested on their beds, moving quickly only to get to the bushes and squat. Maus cried, his simmering sweat gone dry. Again, he turned from Ruth's breast. She tickled his cheek with her nipple, but nothing would tempt him.

Ruth gave Esther dried meat strips and apple at midday. Lying in the wagon, the boys refused apple after a few bites. They wouldn't try the meat.

"When's Idaho?" asked Joseph.

"It's too long," Matthew said. "I want to go home."

"We're near halfway. Not long now," Ruth said.

Making camp that night, Ruth didn't bother with a fire. She heard the harness drop. "Leave it," Aaron said. "Feed and water, we'll see to the rest tomorrow."

When they'd finished, Ruth tried again to coax Aaron and the boys to eat. She wasn't much hungry herself. She too had fieldstones tied to her legs.

"Just a little cheese, Joseph," she insisted. "You have to eat something. All of you do."

Joseph ate the cheese and promptly heaved it up on his plate. "I'm sorry," he said. He set the plate on the ground, tears streaking his face.

"It's my fault." Ruth held him to her. "Don't be sorry."

"I don't want cheese," Matthew said.

"No one has to eat."

"I will," said Esther. She ate her portion and reached for Daniel's plate.

"Get changed." Ruth stowed the uneaten food. "Bedtime's right now." No one objected. "Tomorrow's a long day."

"We'll rest at the Mississippi," Aaron said. "I hear there's a wait to cross."

Night hours dragged, the wagon filled with the littles'
moaning. They rolled side to side, no real comfort in any position.

*Give them rest*, Ruth prayed. *They're so sick. God, what
should I do?*

Six weeks old and Maus lay quiet, breathing through his
mouth.

❧

After another dispiriting day, the wagons came through rough
land, a smattering of woods, of rocks and weeds and prickly
bushes. One section just off the road had been cleared. Rocks
stood in piles, many knocked over and scattered. Broken pieces
of board lay among them. Daniel, tired as he was, spied the wood.
"Good kindling," he said. "I'll go."

"No," Aaron said. "They're markers." Aaron followed the
others into the lay-by and made camp, collecting from the
woods for their fire.

The flames lit, Ruth forced her leaden arms to make a thin
turnip soup, something the boys and Aaron could keep down.

Sadie came by after their dinner. "You look a bit worse for
wear," she said, worry edging her smile. "You know, we miss
you up front." She folded her long legs and settled on her heels
beside Ruth. Ruth slouched against the wagon wheel.

"You're fevered." Sadie touched Ruth's forehead. "Hortence
says fever is God's punishment."

"For what?"

"She says she saw you bathing Maus upstream, naked as a
jaybird. Maus, that is."

"Did she?"

"I know it's not true."

"How so?"

"You couldn't, not you. Simple as that."

"But there's a nubbin of truth." Ruth raised her hands at the wrists in the smallest surrender. "She saw me, and she saw Maus, and we were upstream. There's where the truth ends."

Sadie shook her head. "But she persuades the others. She asked if any suffer fever. They said no, and she said, See, proof beyond doubt."

"How quick favors turn." Ruth gave a rueful smile.

Sadie rose on stork legs and stood over Ruth. "They're afraid," she said.

"Of me?" Ruth held her eye.

"Of Hortence and her God. They don't want what's happening to you."

❧

After no dinner, Aaron, all a-shiver, donned his white nightshirt and rolled himself in a quilt under the wagon. Ruth checked the littles inside under canvas, a candle held high. Esther slept while her brothers shifted in their fitful sleep beside her, except Maus, in his hammock, his dull eyes open. "So you're awake, my little sweet," Ruth whispered.

Her breasts, heavy with milk, strained the front of her black dress. She lifted him from his nest. "You must be hungry." She held a hand to his head, too hot, then checked him for wet. His continued dryness bode ill. He needed milk—he'd been without far too long. *Dear God, let his sickness be mine— please, please, return him to himself.*

She unfolded the front of her dress and gathered him in a

thin blanket. He rested limp in her arms, his breath shallow, no turn of his head to her breast. She pressed her nipple to his mouth. Milk sprinkled his yellowing face. "Please, little one."

She wanted to wrap herself around him, be his shield. With her touch to no avail, she protected him the only way she knew how.

*Dear God, I know You won't let him die. Please, he must eat.*

And yet he would not. Ruth held and held him, his eyelids drooping, not awake, not asleep.

*Don't let him die. I'll do anything. Anything You ask. I won't talk to another person on this train. I'll read the Bible morning and night, aloud to Aaron and all the littles. I'll . . .*

Matthew thrashed his legs, filling the wagon with stench. Ruth laid Maus in the hammock and rolled Matthew away from the others as he cried. His foot kicked Joseph, who curled on his side, coughing, coughing, and jostled into Daniel. Daniel clutched his belly. A soft grunt escaped his lips.

Ruth climbed from the wagon and lifted Matthew over the tailgate. Continuing to promise whatever God might want, she carried Matthew's shrinking body to the tall grass. At the edge of the clearing, she laid him on the ground.

"I couldn't help it, Mama."

"I know," she said. "You're sick." She stripped off his pants. The mess extended over the waistband and down both legs—everything had to come off. She covered his downy body with her shawl and ran for a bucket, rags, and lye soap.

With Matthew clean in a fresh nightshirt, she tossed his clothes in the bucket and carried him to the wagon, where Joseph curled, retching into his quilt. Even his long toes curled in his misery.

*My God, can You see us? We are here, separate as You insist, here in the lay-by.* Ruth thought of the hordes in Pittsburgh—not godless, she now knew. Everyone thinking God watched over them.

*Do You know my prayers? Do You hear my voice? Can't You find us bedded here in this wilderness?*

Matthew groaned beside her. "If God sees everything, why does He let us be sick?"

"I've been asking Him that," Ruth said.

"What does He say?"

"He whispers," Ruth answered. "And sometimes I can't hear."

## CHAPTER 12

# July, the Second Week—Dimming

R uth carried Matthew to the wagon and tucked him in, in time to take Joseph out with his quilt full of what his stomach wouldn't keep. Her gorge rose. She quelled it, as Daniel moaned for water.

"In a minute, Daniel." She washed Joseph and found another blanket, dropped the soiled quilt in the washtub, and helped Joseph with another shirt. She'd run out of nightshirts.

Sweat stood on her face. "You're too big to lift." She ran her arm over her forehead. "I'll boost you." Ruth rubbed her eyes, then laced her fingers. He stepped in the cup of her hands with one bare foot, and she hoisted him over the tailgate.

With Joseph settled, she offered a cup of water to Daniel,

who shook his head. He crossed his arms over his belly. His face twisted. "I can't," he said. Tears ran down his cheeks.

Esther breathed rhythmic and deep in her corner of the wagon, a grateful moment for Ruth. Before going to the wash-tub and attending the night's mishaps, she checked on Maus lying quiet in his hammock.

"Feeling better, my littlest little?" she whispered.

Maus's lids, near shut, showed a sliver of eye paler than his pale skin, his face a round moon, his mouth a tiny open O.

Feeling for fever, Ruth slipped her hand under his white nightdress. The flat of her palm moved belly to chest, and for one bright instant she praised God that Maus's fever had broken.

Her God had listened to her prayers, had answered her prayers. She lifted Maus, his head heavy in her hand. His arms and legs fell, limp beyond sleep.

"No," she told him, and shifted him to the crook of her arm. She leaned her ear to his mouth, her other hand frantic under his nightdress.

She knew, yet kept searching, her fingers over his ribs and around to his back. Her hands told her—they shouted—and she wouldn't listen.

She denied his quiet and lifted him to her swollen bosom, held his stillness against the quick of her heart, that it might infuse him. That it might wake what could never be woken again, and yet, with her arms wrapped around his cooling body, she prayed that it might be so.

Without a sound, Maus had put his hand in God's. He'd slipped away. How could she not have known? How could he have gone without her touch, without a kiss on his forehead?

She kissed the top of his head, rested her cheek on the soft center, and folded him into her warmth.

Through the hours before dawn, she barely heard the restive sounds of Daniel, Matthew, and Joseph. She sat among them in their waxing discomfort, and clung to Maus. No matter how she held him, folding and refolding his tiny body to hers, his heat seeped past her arms and into the air.

She stayed in the wagon until dark began to fade. Slowly she gathered her mind and, holding him to her side, crept off the mattress and over the seat to the ground. She knelt to rouse Aaron from under the wagon. On forearms and knees, he emerged into the clear morning, nightshirt twisted, his face flushed, eyes heavy, his lips dry. Ruth stood, unable to speak.

She wanted to comfort him, Aaron so exposed with his bare legs below a white hem, his naked feet, but she couldn't release her littlest boy.

"Maus?" he said. He seemed to pull the message from her unblinking eyes, eyes dry as chalk beneath her lids. Ruth pressed her lips together. She nodded.

"Oh, Maus." Aaron steadied himself against the wagon, then pushed upright. He folded them both in his arms, and they swayed, Maus in the silent middle, bathed in Aaron's uneven breathing.

Birds announced the sun, and with it the noise of early morning coughs, the splash of water, fires being built, cook pots clanging, as the camp came alive around them. A robin in the bushes sang cheery-up-cheerio and quickly hushed.

Person after person turned from their work, their eyes on Ruth and Aaron standing there, Maus between them. The camp went quiet.

"What are they doing?" A child's voice broke the silence. "What happened?"

"Bad luck," a man answered. "Get Hugo."

Ruth tucked her head into Aaron's chest, but she couldn't block her ears.

"Get the preacher," a woman said. "And Hortence."

Hours—no, minutes—later, Sadie stood beside Ruth and Aaron.

"My God, Ruth." Sadie's soft voice whispered in her ear. "This way." She put a hand on Ruth's shoulder, and they all moved as one. She led them outside the circled wagons, away from curious eyes. The other travelers returned to chores, their noises softened by the Conestoga.

A wail came from across the camp.

"No!" The preacher's voice carried conviction better than in sermons. "Not yet."

Hugo came with a bucket of water and soap, two shovels over his shoulder. Sadie tore a sheet of her own in half, one half set aside, the other laid on the grass with a washing cloth. "I'll start your kidlets' dressing," she said. "And when you're ready, I'll be across the road with Hugo." Hugo headed to the road with the shovels, Sadie to the wagon.

Ruth knelt by the sheet. Grasses plumped under the cloth, looking soft as goose down. She laid Maus on top and unwound his swaddle from stiffening limbs. She eased them straight, his thin body surprisingly long and gray as ash.

Aaron set the bucket and soap close. Ruth dipped the cloth. She wrung it, and swabbed Maus's broad forehead.

Still standing, Aaron held a hand to his own brow. He shook his head, stark eyes on Maus. He moved closer to Ruth.

She looked up, his grief a reflection of her own, a shared stone in their mouths holding them silent. He drew his hand down his face and over his lips to his beard. He yanked the graying hair.

Sadie returned. She squatted by Ruth.

"They're getting dressed," Sadie said, and one look at Aaron, she rose to her feet. "I'll help Hugo." She touched Ruth's arm and followed Hugo beyond the road to the burial ground.

"Mama." A small voice from behind Ruth. "Maus lost his tail."

Ruth sat back on her heels as Esther, carrying her dress, peered over Ruth's shoulder. The child wore black stockings and nothing more, her plump chest and belly pink in the sunlight.

"Yes," Ruth said, her mind falling back to newborn Maus, the cord attaching his body to hers, the cord she'd cut without a qualm, separating the two of them. She ran her finger around the healed circle on his sunken belly. "But he's still our Maus."

Aaron knelt beside Ruth. "You go," he said. "I'll do this."

She stood and lifted Esther. "Let's get you dressed."

Ruth took her to the wagon and set her on the bench, then stepped to the tongue. Inside, Matthew sat on his mattress, one leg in his pants, resting before sliding the other one in.

His jaw slack, Joseph stared at his built-up shoe as if he'd never seen it before. The laces hung loose.

Daniel wrestled a shirt over his head. He panted with effort, his face as milky as Matthew's and Joseph's.

When hiking herself to the bench, Ruth caught sight of Hortence. She advanced across the circle of wagons, the preacher tugging her gray sleeve. She pulled him along to Ruth's wagon, where Esther had laid her dress on the bench. She slid her arms up the skirt, into the sleeves, then over her head.

"You've lost him." Hortence latched a strangling grip on the topboard as if by sheer will she could lift her stubby body into the wagon and take Ruth by the throat.

"We didn't lose Maus," Esther said. "He's in the field with Papa." She wiggled her dress into position. "Sadie says it's a special day." Esther brushed hair from her eyes. "Maus gets to see God."

"Yes," Hortence said with a scowl. "No thanks to—"

"Now, Hortence." The preacher patted her shoulder. "You promised."

She shoved his hand away. "And you promised we'd see him properly buried."

"That won't be necessary," Ruth said. She ran a brush through Esther's hair. "You've done enough already."

❧

In a procession, the whole family, faces washed and dressed in wilted clothes, plodded out of the lay-by to the road. Lined in front of Ruth: Aaron, in black pants, jacket, and hat, led the way; Maus, wound in Sadie's half-sheet, lay across his arms; Hortence, one hand on Aaron's elbow, hurried beside him; Daniel, following, held Matthew's hand and from time to time looked back at Ruth; then came Joseph, shoulders bent, arms limp at his sides. Esther and Ruth, heads encased in black bonnets, ended the family. Ruth carried her Bible. The preacher came last.

They straggled across the road to the land with tumbled stones where Hugo and Sadie took turns, up to their hips, scooping earth from a hole. The group gathered around.

Esther leaned into Ruth. Ruth, with her hand on her daughter's shoulder, stood beside Aaron. Joseph and Daniel drooped on Aaron's other side with Matthew, their faces shaded beneath brimmed hats. The preacher stayed behind the family while Hortence inserted herself between Aaron and Ruth and stroked the shroud.

Hugo's shovel scritched down the inside of the hole. He scraped the bottom and threw the last of loose earth onto a pile. No one said a word.

Sadie gathered grass and lined the hole. "I wish we had a proper coffin." She brushed strands of grass and dirt from her pants and stood beside Ruth.

"Maus needs more grass." Hortence rubbed her palms together.

"This will do nicely," Aaron said. "We're grateful." He and Hugo knelt by the grave.

At the edge, on her knees, Hortence steepled her fingers as they lowered the small white bundle.

Ruth gripped her Bible in both hands, the hard cover gouging her palm. "Hortence," Ruth said. "Please."

Hortence raised her eyes, her look questioning. Ruth motioned her from the hole. Hortence hitched her body without shifting position and turned on Ruth. "Have you no heart?" Hortence fingered her black armband. "Look at you, stone-faced." Tears ran from her red-ringed eyes. "Where's your grief?"

Ruth dared not move lest ill-considered words spring from her mouth.

Sadie bent down. "Hortence, watch your step," she said under her breath. "You might fall in."

Esther put fingers to her mouth. The boys didn't seem to hear.

Aaron reached across Hortence and took the Bible from Ruth's shaking hands. He opened it and turned to the twenty-third psalm.

Hortence raised one knee, leaned on it, and stood. "Mr. Johnston will do that." She took the Bible from Aaron and passed it to the preacher.

"It's up to Aaron," Preacher Johnston whispered. He returned the open book. "It's his son in the grave, not ours."

Aaron smoothed the page and began. "The Lord is my shep—" His voice caught.

He waited.

Ruth pulled a handkerchief from her sleeve. She lowered the brim of her bonnet and held the linen over her mouth. Daniel sniffed, and she passed him the cloth.

"The Lord . . ." Aaron's lips trembled.

The preacher put a hand on Aaron's back, gently relieved him of the Bible, and read slowly and quietly to the end of the psalm.

Sadie spread more grass on top of Maus, and with a nod from Aaron, Hugo and Sadie took up shovels and gently filled the hole. As they tamped the earth with their boots, Hortence said, "Where's his cross?"

The preacher stood at the mound and signed a cross in the air while Hortence searched among boards scattered on the ground. "Here." She held up two slabs of wood nailed in an X.

Hugo took the wood, straightened it to a cross, and, using

the back of his shovel, banged it into the ground. With each beat of the metal blade, Ruth started.

"Now stones," Hugo said. He sent the boys collecting, and leaned close to Ruth. "Against wolves," he whispered behind his hand.

He and Sadie each picked up big rocks, rock after rock, and laid them on the mound. The boys added their smaller stones in a high pile.

"What are you doing?" Hortence raised her voice. "You'll crush him."

Sadie moved next to Hortence and spoke too low for others to hear. The longer she spoke, the paler Hortence's face went, her eyes widening.

"Time to go," Sadie said. She hooked Hortence's arm, and the preacher followed the mismatched pair to the road.

"Take your time," Hugo told Aaron. "Later, we're under way." And he went after the preacher.

Ruth stood by the grave, anger and grief in a welter she couldn't untangle. She took Esther in her arms, and the family clustered together, sharing the weight of body and mind, while the cairn held Maus in his turn.

So many others buried before him, so many bereft.

᠅

After the burial, Ruth and the family dragged back to camp. The little boys hauled themselves into the wagon and flopped on their beds while Aaron and Daniel hitched the horses. The day proceeded like any other, Esther beside Ruth on the seat.

"Move 'em out."

Aaron struggled to Noah's saddle, but made no move to

start. Grumbling arose behind them, and he waved the others on before urging his team forward. As he gained the road, he watched redwing blackbirds land on the makeshift cross. The birds chirped and cleaned their wings. They eyed the grasses for seed as if a piece of Ruth and Aaron's flesh didn't rest beneath the piled stones.

Ruth hoped the birds would keep their son company.

She sat straight on the bench, arms empty, hands in her lap. The wheels ground ever forward into the late morning, Ruth a milkweed, brittle stem, dry pod ready to burst.

She feared the scatter of black seed.

Her breasts leaked.

❧

In camp that night Ruth washed linens and blankets and clothes in the tub. Esther stirred another thin soup and chewed on a strip of dry meat she'd found. No one showed appetite for more.

After a small bowl, Matthew sat on a log, legs bent, elbows on his knees, forehead in his hands.

Joseph stopped his stiff prowl around the fire and kicked Matthew's log. "What are you doing?"

"Looking at bugs."

"I don't see bugs."

Without moving his head, Matthew waved him away.

Esther helped Ruth spread wet laundry on bushes to dry. "When do I get to see God?" she asked.

"Not for a long while." Ruth kissed her cheek and hugged her.

Matthew looked up. "I don't want to see God," he said. "I'm staying with you."

"That's our plan," said Aaron. He sat, his back against the

wagon's front wheel with Daniel. They faced the fire, and Daniel drew in Ruth's book, the one for unsayable thoughts she never dared write.

With a grunt, Aaron leaned his shoulder to Daniel's.

"What's that?" Aaron asked.

Daniel bent closer to his drawing. "A stool for Maus," he whispered.

Aaron put his arm around Daniel. "We'll keep it by the hearth."

Daniel drew his sleeve across his nose. "I think he'd like that."

"I know I would," Aaron said. "We can make it together if you like."

Daniel nodded.

"Me too?" said Joseph, and dropped next to Aaron.

"If you like." Daniel continued drawing.

"Come," Ruth said to Matthew. She opened her arm, inviting him in, and tightened the other around Esther.

Come morning, Ruth folded away the littlest clothes. She put the small patchwork quilt on top and closed the chest, in her ears the sound of earth as Hugo had filled the hole.

❧

The days unwound, one into the next, sickness latched to their bodies. Their fellow travelers, except Sadie and Hugo, left Ruth and her family to grief and their unsavory symptoms.

Slow off the mark, morning found them lagging farther and farther behind.

Matthew, on his mattress, whimpered. "I'm hot," he said. "Is this the desert?"

"It's just a fever," Aaron said from the bench beside Ruth. "You'll cool tomorrow."

"And your fever?" Ruth said. "Will it break tomorrow?"

"Yes," Aaron said without conviction. His eyes wandered everywhere but on Ruth. "God willing." He dragged his wrist across his nose, then pushed fingers through his hair as if that had been his intention all along.

"Have you been to the bushes?"

"Some."

"You're better?"

His breath hitched. He bent his shoulders and propped his hands on his knees, his fingers dug into the fabric of his pants. "How is it I'm better, and not Maus?" His head fell forward and he looked between his knees to the floor of the wagon, the muscles of his cheeks flexing above his short beard.

He slumped against the first bow, and, letting his head slip back, he breathed through his mouth. He stared at the sky, unblinking, then clamped his lids shut. His lips in a grimace, he covered his face with an arm. "I'm sorry," he whispered into the crook of his elbow.

Joseph moaned from his bed. Ruth crawled in beside him and rested the back of her hand on his damp forehead. "Hot enough to boil an egg," she teased, not wanting him to hear concern.

"My innards too. Make it stop, Mama."

But this was no eel she could slay, this thing she couldn't see. Beast from a hidden lair, it followed them, traveling without tracks, no way to hunt it, no way to kill it. Did it creep underground? Did it hover on the wind with vulture wings? Was it passed with the touch of a hand, a sneeze? Every exchange suspect, food or water, miles ago some taint they hadn't noticed.

By the tailgate, stoic Daniel stayed quiet, his belly puffed on a surfeit of nothing, the scar on his forehead livid against his pale skin. Ruth saw his pain in the tick of his jaw, heard it as his belly whinged. She touched the swelling. Within, she felt movement, as if some creature nested there and ate him from the inside.

"Don't worry, Mama." He didn't look at her. "It's better than it was." His lungs seemed to reach for air. He managed a weak smile before a line of blood crept from his nostril. He stanched it with a stained cloth he drew from under his pillow and tried to hide in his fist.

"What's that?" Ruth asked.

"Nothing." He shoved his fist under the quilt. "A bumped nose."

Another symptom to add to a growing list, his face going yellow as Maus's had.

Ruth left Daniel's barn door pants untied. His need ran quick, as Aaron's did now.

That evening Sadie brought a castor oil poultice. "This should help," she said.

Ruth laid it on Daniel's chest, replacing it through the night when his thrashing tossed it off. But change came only for the worse.

❧

The next day Aaron started fierce at his chores. His grip on the feed bucket left his knuckles bloodless as his face. He tended the horses, his eyes glazing listless as if the light of Idaho no longer showed in the distance.

"I'll finish here," Ruth said as they stood by the tailgate.

"No, you've enough work of your own."

"I'm fine," she coaxed.

"Sacks under those eyes say different." Lines deepened across his forehead. He kissed her cheek.

"Papa?" From inside the wagon, Joseph edged an elbow over the tailgate. He rested his chin on his arm. "When's Idaho?"

"At this rate," Aaron said, "I don't know."

"Come fall." Ruth smoothed Joseph's cheek. "We'll be there."

"The fall?" Aaron turned the bucket upside down and sat. "Yes, if we make the mountains in time, if we find water in the desert, if we get rid of this sickness. So many ifs, we may never get there."

"Aaron." Ruth stepped behind him, her hands on his shoulders, and rubbed her fingers into the space above his collarbones. "Hush."

❧

On the road, clouds blew in. By afternoon, a roll of distant thunder. Aaron sat the bench, the jerk line slack in his fingers. Jehu kept the team in line. Sensing the misery as horses will, he went slower and slower.

Ruth took the rein from Aaron's hand. "Hup, boy," she called, and a cough took her. She panted as if she were pulling the wagon. "We've got to keep pace."

Rain scattered on the canvas. Where drops hit the road they beat puffs of dust and disappeared. From deep in the wagon Matthew called, "Take me home."

"Home." Aaron slumped, his body a heap on the bench.

If Ruth could make the last months disappear, she would. She'd make the trek a thought they'd never brought to fruition.

Foolish wishes, a waste of their diminishing strength. There was no going back, not with Ely and his sticky-fingered bride lodged in their old house, solid as mortar.

That final day at home, dawn not yet seeping at the eastward sky, Ruth had lain weighted to her bed. She couldn't sleep. Her white nightdress snarled around her legs, her thoughts as dark as the hour.

Cramp tightened her distended belly. She'd thrown off her side of the patchwork quilt, swung her feet to the floor, and snuffed at her anger. Too much to do, she wouldn't dwell on Aaron's unchangeable mind.

He'd been so convinced, and she'd listened. She knew better, and yet he'd talked her around, Aaron with his gift for persuasion. But she'd let him.

In bed, he'd slept beside her, the quilt tucked under his angular beard. Smooth and soft his beard, the visible sign of marriage, the mark of his Plain faith. Resisting the urge to poke him, Ruth listened to the rumble of his breath, so like the sound of distant thunder.

Elbows out, she rested her hands on her knees, tipped her belly forward, and stood. She grabbed the bed's high footboard and steadied herself, the wood smooth under her fingers, then stepped around the dower chest to the window. She closed the sash as if to shut out a brewing storm.

No more foolishness, this last morning. Dear God, departure, on her like a fox.

Ruth's legs had felt weak.

Leaning against the window frame, she'd gathered her breath, took in the shadowed room, the pale walls, dark woodwork, a bureau, the chest at the foot of their marriage bed. Her father had made the bed where each of her four children had drawn their first breath. The bed where she had planned on birthing the fifth.

*Oh, Maus.* If only that bed had been his birthplace. She held a fist to her open mouth, pressed hard against her teeth.

She'd sat again on the edge of the bed and pulled off her nightdress. With the motion, straw in the ticking murmured. She ran her hands over the tight skin of her belly. "Late to your own birth," she'd whispered.

Dressed, Ruth took a deep breath and threaded her way around packed baskets, to the stairs and down, holding to the wall. In the kitchen, she lit a lamp, poked the fire to life under the cauldron, porridge set to simmer.

The littles clattered overhead. Aaron, down first, took the steps two at a time, his hair wild from bed. He opened the farmhouse door and surveyed his handiwork. He smiled. Aaron and his Conestoga skirted the edge of sin.

If only pride had been the worst of it.

Joseph had bounded down next, his built-up shoe slamming the treads. Fast as his father, he galloped out the door after Aaron.

Daniel stayed upstairs with Esther and Matthew. Matthew could dress himself, but early birds distracted him. Esther had trouble with laces and plaiting her hair; otherwise she shunned help.

Finally down, her black cap crooked, Esther said, "Now?" She put her head out the kitchen door. "We start?"

Ruth stirred the porridge. "Loading first."

Matthew dawdled on the stairs. "I'm a heron," he said. His thick legs stepping high couldn't have looked less like a heron.

Nudging Matthew every third stair, Daniel carried a basket—"Hurry along"—and he headed to the wagon.

By full light, Ruth's brother Dan'l pulled his buggy under the open shed and tethered his horse. His wife, Rebecca, holding her littlest, climbed out, followed by more of their brood. They rushed for the dooryard. Ruth embraced Dan'l before he lent Aaron a hand with the bigger chests and bureaus. She didn't look him in the eye—she couldn't bear to see the disapproval, the pain of their parting. She kissed Rebecca.

Cousin Ely arrived, tied his horse, and he and his new bride joined the group. All flitted like moths to the wagon's flame, the canvas top pinking as the sun rose. A few neighbors on their way to Horst's barn had promised a hand before saying good-bye.

Ruth walked room by room through the echoing house as the men carried out the last chest. Yes, she'd agreed to go, but seeing the house stripped to bare walls . . .

She held to the front doorframe, tears streaking her cheeks, the family's earthly possessions littering the dooryard. Dark wood tables, bureaus, chests and chairs, baskets and beds all askew on uneven ground.

The beds and bureaus, so big in the house, looked small without ceiling and walls as they waited for Aaron. He'd choose what would fit for the trek. More than two thousand miles, a distance Ruth couldn't grasp. Her fingers latched white on the doorframe.

Scrubbed to a shine the night before, the littles wove figure eights as they chased cousins around the furniture, then out the lane and back, their chests heaving.

Her littles so robust, happy, and full of health. Ruth pressed her fist harder against her teeth—that, or she might cry out.

Matthew had cocked his head in front of Ruth. "Let's go," he said.

Esther pulled at Ruth's skirt. "When do we get there?"

Ruth basked in their elation, bread she could eat.

Bathsheba had wandered the dooryard. She snuffled the bedding, nudged cook pots, the baskets of foodstuffs, dried fruit, pickled pigs' feet, hams, link sausage in loops. The cow rolled white-rimmed eyes and knocked over a basket of candles Ruth prayed would pierce the dark.

She'd wanted to scream against leaving, but struggle would make it worse. Her mouth dry, she'd had no word of comfort, not for the cow, and none for herself.

Should she have screamed, unleashed her tongue? Ruth's chest hurt with the holding of tears. *What if, what if?* She'd been through this before, during, and after the trek began. Too many times.

In the yard, she'd walked bowlegged, exhaustion increasing the longer she stood. Thank heaven for neighbors. Each man a brother, the women sisters, she hugged and kissed them all and waved them on their way to work on Horst's barn.

As they left, she checked past the white barn to Yoder's field, where the Elders might appear, should they come to pronounce the family shunned. Nothing so far, and no Delia either.

How could she leave without a good-bye? Delia, the one person beyond her brother she'd miss the most.

Ruth imagined the argument Delia and Horst could be having this very moment as the neighbors hammered on their barn. Futile for Delia, Horst being both brother and Elder.

Ruth tied Bathsheba to a hook on the wagon's topboard. Matthew tickled the piglets in the barnyard. Joseph hunted for the last goose eggs.

Esther sat on her grounded mattress, legs out straight, boot toes to the sky. Light curls escaped under her prayer cap. In her lap, she cradled old tattered Dolly. Rents in the faceless cloth looked like features. "Don't worry," Esther said to the doll. "You'll sleep in the wagon with me." She tucked Dolly under her apron, patted the bulge, and leaned back on her hands. "Gracious," she said. "What a ruckus."

Cousin Ely prowled the dooryard with his bride. Her eyes flitted about with possessive delight. *Their* dooryard now, Ruth reminded herself.

"It's a good thing," Aaron had said. "Keeps the farm in the family." This may have helped Aaron, but didn't soften Ruth's unpleasant turn of mind. Ely never her favorite.

The bride examined an iron fry pan. She looked in a chest, riffled through the linens, and closed it. Ruth would rather Bathsheba blow a wet breath in all they would eat than have this strange girl touch what wasn't hers. Ruth compressed her lips and walked through the bustling yard to the back of the empty house.

She'd put her palm to the fieldstones, soft browns in the uneven rock. She smelled the baked-in sun and traced smooth mortar lines between the stones, the walls made to last beyond the apocalypse.

Her mind bubbled with loneliness, with remorse and blame and a thickening of anger. Could this be her own private apocalypse? Slowly she'd walked her fingers along the wall.

Calmer, she returned to the dooryard. At the wagon, the young couple held their breath as Aaron's hand hovered over one treasure to the next.

Their possessions, once small in the dooryard, now ready for loading, seemed monstrous. They'd never fit.

"Our bed?" Ruth said.

"No, too big."

"Oh, Aaron, and the dower chest?"

"Too heavy."

Ruth's father had made both. Wedding presents. The men, now down to Daniel, Aaron, Ely, and Dan'l, moved rejected pieces out of the way. Dan'l gave her a down-mouth look. He knew how much it hurt, and she knew how much he disapproved, yet he'd come to help. Not like Aaron's absent sister, Anna.

Ely slid a look at his bride. Her eyes went a quick-stitch wider. A slight intake of breath, and her hands in little fists ticked together.

Ruth wanted to growl. Instead she salvaged linens from the chest, the fine wedding sheets her Oma had woven.

It wasn't pride that made her want the sheets and chest. It was love, the touch of family in the weave, in the smooth dovetails Ruth could feel only in her heart.

She made careful folds and pressed the sheets into a basket. Following her movements, the bride's eyes turned wistful. Ruth ground her teeth. These sheets were not meant for someone else's joy.

Aaron frowned.

"I know," Ruth had said. "We can't take it all."

"Christ gave up everything," he said. "This should be easy."

She didn't pretend to be Christ. Besides, what home did He give up, a man born in someone else's stable?

Ruth went hot from the inside. She cringed, a quick glance at the sky. What did she expect, thunderbolts? Not her God, a God of peace, a turn-the-other-cheek God.

While loading, she presented one small item after another, only to be told again, "Biggest first." Or "Too big—we need small, got to fill the cracks."

Too little, too big, she couldn't get it right. She left the footstool, Daniel's first attempt at furniture. She'd used it every day. At least she had Daniel. After all, that's what this was about—the littles—none too big, none too small, the treasures of her life.

Ruth looked again for Delia across the fields. Matthew brought his horse, the three-legged one Onkel Dan'l whittled when Matthew turned three. After two years of loving, the stain rubbed off in patches; it stood despite the broken leg.

"Cousin Ely might put him down," Matthew said.

When Dan'l and Ely hoisted the big table upside down over the lowered tailgate, Ely dropped his end. He grabbed a leg as the table slipped down the gate with a cross-grain screech. The leg snapped. "Ah," he said as if surprised. "I guess the table's mine."

Ruth turned her back. Poor Aaron. At this point even she wanted his Oma's table.

As the others finished loading, Rebecca offered a late meal

of bread and cheese from baskets she'd brought. Ruth couldn't stomach the smallest bite.

A fine drizzle began as Aaron and Daniel harnessed Jehu. They started with the hame. Aaron placed the wood collar over the horse's neck; then came the bridle. Jehu took the bit. Aaron pulled the leather over the horse's ears, adjusted blinders, and tightened the throatlatch. Daniel attended a myriad of other straps for hitching chains to doubletrees, the doubletrees linked to spreaders, then the wagon tongue. They did the same for four mares and Noah.

All harnessed, Aaron and Daniel attached them to the traces. Aaron ran the jerk line, the single rein from Jehu's bit, threaded through a ring on each harness, over the frontboard, and coiled it on the bench.

"Ready?" Aaron called. He patted the horse's rump. The stallion nickered.

Ely and his bride, busy as little weevils, toted their new possessions out of the rain. They said no good-byes.

Ruth kissed Rebecca and the baby in her arms, then the tops of other littles' heads. Anna and her brood still hadn't come.

When Ruth came to Dan'l, she clung to his neck. The baby inside her gave a kick as they pressed together.

"Feisty little critter," Dan'l said, and kissed Ruth on both cheeks. "I don't think it wants to go." He locked her in tender arms.

Her lower lip trembled, and she pulled it between her teeth.

"I want you to have this," Dan'l said. "For your thoughts." With a finger on her chin, he turned her face to his. "They're important to me." He handed her a leather-bound book. She opened the cover to cream-colored pages blank as a doll's face. Her eyes brimmed. Unable to say what filled her heart, she squeezed his hand and turned away. Her thoughts, important. Imagine.

At the wagon, she stepped on the tongue. Aaron gave her a boost from behind, propelling her over the low frontboard. Overbalanced, she crumpled on the bench beside Esther.

Regaining composure, Ruth straightened her dress and re-tied her bonnet.

"Look at us," Esther said, holding up the doll. "Little, bigger, biggest."

Ruth slipped her arm around Esther while she cradled her doll and nuzzled the stains of a long and loving life.

"Is Dolly having a hard time leaving?" Ruth asked.

"Nooo." Esther laid the doll in her lap, blank face down. "She's *tiiiired* of waiting."

"Any minute now," Ruth said.

The boys swarmed around the patient horses. Matthew cartwheeled into a somersault for his cousins. Joseph, with his heavy boot, climbed as if to the seat, but hopped on Noah's rump, arms spread, jumping horse to horse to Jehu, the way anyone else would hop stones in a stream.

The crowd of family gathered close, black hats and bonnets bent against the drizzle, their tentative hands lifted in farewell. If only Delia could have come.

Aaron swung onto Noah's saddle. "Hup, now," he called.

The horses had heaved, and for a blink Ruth thought the wagon wouldn't move, its wheels weighted to the spokes in New Eden earth. Not forward nor back, the day gray and cold and wet.

Necks arched, the horses strained against the harness and, with a jolt, the wheels broke free, just as the great oak had when Aaron hauled the trunk from the forest, the ground plowed with stubs of its severed limbs.

Momentum set in. They wheeled easily down the lane, the unseasoned boards and beams groaning.

"Wait, wait." The call had come from Yoder's field. A plump figure, black skirts flying, bonnet waving, rushed across the stubble.

"*Delia.*" Ruth sighed. Aaron reined in long enough for Delia to climb beside Ruth. "I had to come." They put their arms around each other, black on black.

"Horst can shun me." Delia's mouth to Ruth's ear, she'd whispered, "I could use the rest."

Beyond words, they looked in each other's eyes, chins trembling.

"Don't you start," Delia said, and gave Ruth's cheek a tap. They both gulped and widened their eyes, lower lids like vessels threatening to spill. They each laughed at the other's plight—what else could they do?

Now no Delia, no laughter, Ruth let her eyes well over. The wagon lumbered on.

As they'd neared Delia's lane, she'd touched the swell of Ruth's belly. "If it's a girl, name her after me."

"We will," Ruth had said. "I promise."

"You better."

Aaron stopped and Delia climbed down. The boys, who'd cavorted beside the wagon, climbed aboard and settled into their ark on wheels. Delia stood in the drizzle, tendrils of hair running in her face. She waved both arms. "Good-bye, Ruth."

She grew smaller as the wheels turned, her call carried on the wind. "God keep you."

❧

*God keep us indeed.*

If only Delia knew.

Aaron looked sidelong at Ruth. She closed her mouth and rested her fist in her lap.

"Maybe we should go home," he said.

"To the farm?" She turned on him.

"You'd like that, wouldn't you?"

"We're almost halfway." Ruth stared at him.

His dull eyes wandered. He picked at his shirt, loosened his pants, and held his belly. Harness creaked with every shift of the horses' rumps.

Ruth flicked the rein. "This is sickness talking."

His eyes lowered, his words lower still, he said, "But what if . . . ?"

Ruth swung her knees over, facing him. "Did you think this would be easy?" Her face grew hot beyond fever.

"No, but . . . Maus. I didn't know . . ."

"Maus, yes." Ruth's lips thinned to a line. "Would you have him die in vain?" Plunged into a deep, abiding cold, her whole body shook. She crossed her arms and they trembled at the bone. Her words jittered. "This bed is your bed. You made it." The words came through teeth she pressed together against their chatter. "Here all of us sleep and wake and eat and breathe. You can't unmake this bed."

Aaron covered his face with his hands. His body lolled with the motion of the wagon as Ruth watched the clouds roll together, dark gray folding into light, the light folding into dark.

Farther south, rain sheeted across open fields, flooding the long grasses. The horses lumbered on mile after mile, Ruth and Aaron side by side. The trail wound ahead toward a section of woods where the other wagons had long since passed from sight.

In his ark, Noah had watched the waters rise and he floated for one hundred and fifty days. Surely he had doubts before his dove returned with an olive leaf. And Noah wasn't tested with fever. Noah didn't lose a child.

Ruth rested her hand on Aaron's knee. "It's no small thing we do," she said. "And we do it together." His head still down, he slid his hand into hers, and she rubbed the nub of his little finger.

❧

Night threatened as Ruth pulled into the lay-by. A fire gleamed inside the circled wagons, the orange light flowing over the tongues where they slid under axles of the wagon ahead. Ruth scanned space after space and found none left open.

From the narrow slots, lines of people emerged forming a delegation. They surged out to meet Ruth and Aaron. Hortence, short and round, led the way, her husband behind her. She halted and raised her arm, a Bible in her hand.

"Whoa," said Ruth. The wheels stopped, but the horses' hooves kept moving in place. Jehu tossed his head. His bit rattled.

"You turn right 'round," Hortence said. "You're not welcome here."

A murmur went through the crowd.

"Isn't that right, Mr. Johnston?" she said. Hortence clamped the preacher's arm and steered him out front, shield and weapon at once. She gave sharp nods, one to Ruth, one to the group as if her husband's presence was proof against whatever Ruth or Aaron had to say.

Ruth made no move. She stared at Hortence. For a moment Ruth couldn't grasp what her demand could be. She shook her head, an attempt at clearing the spread of cobwebs clogging her reason.

Hortence drew herself to her tallest, her breast swelling, imposing in her fierce defense of God's truth. "Get ye hence," she intoned.

"Why is Frau God angry?" Esther peeked between Aaron and Ruth, a hand on each shoulder.

Aaron gagged on a laugh. His body rocked, his eyes hidden under the brim of his hat. "Hortence's sentences," he said, his throat full of phlegm, "recommend us hence." He coughed. "At God's insistence."

Hortence grew red faced. "Is sickness not enough?" She stood, stubby feet planted apart, body shaking beneath her gray dress. No pretense of a smile this time. "You're drunk."

"What's drunk?" Esther wormed a knee between them.

"Esther, get on your bed." Ruth pushed her toward the others in the wagon.

Aaron gripped the bench with one hand, tore off his hat, and jutted what was left of his beard. His eyes, focused for the first time in days, bored into Hortence. "Is this a shrew before me?" he said, the lilt gone from his voice. "A shrew, yes, full grown from a woman's rib."

Ruth touched Aaron's thigh. Once again, her fortress—sick as he was, always her fortress.

"Come, now, folks." Hugo in fringed leather leggings, and Sadie to match, parted the crowd. They strode through the opening to where Preacher Johnston and Hortence stood. "What's all this?" Hugo asked.

"It's the only way." Hortence pushed her face at him, her body still aimed squarely at Ruth. "They're a danger. Mr. Johnston, he'll tell you. Everyone agrees—we took a vote."

"That so, Preacher?" Hugo took off his battered hat and turned it upside down. "A vote?" He looked into its bowl. "I don't remember casting mine." He shook the hat and looked inside again, then at Hortence. "Or is it stones being cast?"

"Stones!" Hortence cried. "Me? I've been more than kind." She shook the Bible above her head. "If it weren't for me, their baby'd be in hell." Hortence faced Ruth. "You should be thanking me." Hortence clasped the book to her breast. "You're the stony one, snatching the poor thing, making him cry, making me cry." She pointed at Ruth. "Telling me I'd no right. Well, I—"

"Enough." Ruth's eyes burned. Rage, a tight bud, swelled in her throat and ripened. Like an Appalachian tree, she could see the bud ready to break into full bloom. She dreaded the bloom, and made winter of her mind.

Her hand twitched the jerk rein. "Gee," she said through her teeth. Jehu sidestepped right; the others veered too. The front wheels angled with the tongue.

"No," Hugo shouted. "You can't leave."

Hortence strode forward, the others close behind. They swamped Hugo.

"Back off," he said and drew his pistol. With a roar, the muzzle flashed. Ruth's mares shied and the wagon bucked, near spilling Aaron from the seat before Jehu brought them in line.

"Papa!" Esther from deep in the wagon. "What bangs?"

"Just Hugo," Ruth said. "Noising with his gun. Stay where you are."

The crowd retreated. They clustered, heads close, anger buzzing.

"They have to go," Hortence said. "God said so."

Sadie pushed through in front of Hortence. "What?" She put a hand to her ear. "I can't hear Him."

"While I'm leader, no one gets expelled." Hugo swung his pistol in a low arc across the group. The crowd shrank.

"Hugo, no fights." Ruth lifted her voice. "Not on our account." The group went quiet. Horses shifted in their traces, chains clanking.

"It's best," Ruth said. "We'll go."

Hortence raised her Bible. "God's will be done."

Ruth wound the jerk rein in her fingers, twisting until they whitened. She completed the turn and headed out the lay-by, her heart galloping. Aaron rested a hand on hers. "Pay her no mind," he said. "Hell hath no fury . . ." He let out a long breath.

He could easily be speaking of Ruth, her fury closer, more alarming.

# PART III

*A Wager of Bones*

## CHAPTER 13

*July, the Third Week—Goose Fat*

R uth urged Jehu into the growing dark, mile after mile west toward Moline and the Mississippi beyond. Aaron hunched beside her, bumping her shoulder with every rut in the trail.

She would keep the pace until he recovered. "It's for the best," she said. "Now we're truly separate."

"Yes, separate, and we'll be faster," he said.

Ruth's heart slowed to a trot, then a walk. Blood returned to her fingers, her shaking stilled.

In the last glimmer of evening, she saw a way off the trail. One twitch of the rein and she called, "Haw." Jehu and the team veered left into a narrow lane and entered the clearing by a sluggish creek. Grass surrounded the beaten circle with a lone tree she could use as a picket. Woods bordered the grass.

Ruth's knees and hips complained as she climbed down, her elbows too, and neck. For now the queasies had gone. Aaron put a leg over the frontboard, ready to climb down.

"Stay where you are," Ruth said. He didn't argue. She unhitched the team, dropping the tongue to the dirt.

Slow, buckle by buckle, she opened the straps, let the harness fall from each horse in turn, and led them to water. As they drank, she ran her hands over their thick shoulders and down their legs. She felt each hoof for stones wedged at the center of their soft frogs.

She knew their bodies as she knew her littles', having washed and fed them since birth, brought them through colic, through cuts and stretched tendons. It wouldn't do to have them fetch up lame. Well beyond the inconvenience, she couldn't bear to see them suffer, feeling their pain as she did with her children.

At the wagon, Esther helped scoop oats from the feed box. She gave each horse a taste by hand.

The horses settled on picket, the rope tied to the tree, no need of a hammer. Ruth dragged to the wagon, lit a candle, and laid out pickles and stale biscuits. Their stores near gone, Davenport couldn't come soon enough. Tomorrow she'd see about a fire.

Esther ate. Ruth dipped water from the barrel and took cups into the wagon while Daniel slept. She was loath to wake him. Matthew nibbled a bit of biscuit and dropped the rest. Ruth fished it out of his bed and offered it to Joseph; they couldn't afford to waste food. Without raising his head, Joseph turned away, no biscuit, no water.

Aaron held the ladle and drank scoop after scoop. He splashed his face, the water running from his beard.

Here they were, unto themselves as Aaron had promised, and nearly halfway along their journey. Ruth and Esther could manage an early start each day. Ruth need only say the word, buckle the traces, and the horses would do the rest.

In her blanket, Ruth lay awake next to Aaron. Her breasts ached, still swollen with milk awaiting Maus's insistent nudge. In time, the milk would dry, leaving her breasts withered until the next child. Born in Idaho, what child could make their family whole? No matter how many children, Maus would always be missing.

In the surrounding woods, leaves shivered in the wind, and on it Ruth heard Maus's cry.

※

A good sleep and a little time would cure Aaron, his strength renewed. But the following day, his eyes dull, he hardly raised his head from his pillow. Ruth walked the horses to the creek and sat on a stone while they drank. With flared nostrils, they blew at a skim of hatchling gnats, clearing a circle where they pulled in the clear water.

They finished, and when she stood, her head swam. She braced her hands on her knees and waited for the tilt to pass. She pressed on, not so much putting one foot before the next as dragging first one and then the other behind her. At the wagon, the spin took her again and she sat on the tongue.

This would be the Sabbath. She didn't know if it was, but this would be a day of rest.

※

The second evening in the clearing, the boys and Aaron lay in the wagon all day in white nightshirts. Fully dressed like Ruth, Esther stirred a puddle of mud with a stick. "See, I made soup, Mama."

"You're such a help, my littlest sweet." The last words caught Ruth. Esther, almost four, again the littlest little.

Ruth's legs gave, and she sat on the slanted tongue. Mud soup, rich and dark. But they needed something more. "We best make a fire."

"Mmm," Esther said. "Mud's better hot."

Ruth gathered her skirts and, hands on her knees, rose slowly to her feet. Esther looked up to the lay-by entrance. "Someone's coming."

The clop of hooves sounded before Sadie rounded the bend. Sadie hallooed as she came, tiny atop a heavy workhorse. She carried a covered pot. "Hugo saw your tracks," she said. "Oh, Ruth." Sadie rested the pot on the pommel of her saddle. "You didn't look good before, but now it's time for the knacker." She clapped a hand over her mouth. "Me and my tongue."

Ruth smiled. "*You* are a tonic, and I'm glad you're here, but you shouldn't be—you could catch fever." Ruth extended her hands, fingers up as if to push Sadie away.

"Pish-tosh." Sadie handed Ruth the pot and dismounted. "Chicken broth," she said. "And you with no fire. Where's Aaron?"

"Took to his bed. The boys too."

"You sit right there. Come on, Esther. We'll build one."

Ruth sat until they returned with wood. She took the lid off the broth.

"No, no," Sadie said. "I'm doing this. Let me feel useful." She busied herself with the fire.

Esther gave her mud a quick stir.

"What herbs did you use?" Sadie asked.

"Sage," Esther said. "But it's really a weed."

"A good cook uses what's handy." Sadie poured her broth into Ruth's cauldron. A chunk of meat splashed. "Esther, you stir while I sit with your mama." Sadie slid close to Ruth on the tongue, an arm around her shoulder.

"Where'd you get meat? Last I knew you had only beans."

"Funny how things turn up," Sadie said.

Ruth smiled.

"What?" said Sadie.

"I was thinking of the first day you sat beside me." Ruth put her head on Sadie's shoulder. "Now look at us."

"I thought your eyes would fall out." Sadie laughed until she teared. "It took an age to figure you. I couldn't imagine someone afraid of little ol' me." She wiped her eyes. "I shouldn't laugh; you felt bad."

"Worse came later."

"You know, Hugo feels terrible," she said. "We both do." Sadie looked at her hands. Esther's spoon clacked inside the cauldron.

"If Hortence was a man," Sadie said, "Hugo would have plowed the ground with her."

"Tell him this is best."

"Hugo's stone hit a few hearts." Sadie smiled. "We'll be days waiting for the ferry. Some might visit if only to drop bread at a distance." She stood and walked over to the fire. She rested a hand on Esther's back and looked over her shoulder into the soup. "You do good work." Sadie looked back at Ruth. "How's the barrel?"

"Good for now, but water goes fast on soiled sheets. The creek's too slow for washing."

"And Aaron?"

"The sun hurts his eyes," Ruth said. She sat silent, head down. Sadie took the spoon from Esther and stirred the soup. Ruth looked out to the woods and let out a long breath, slow, so Sadie wouldn't hear it.

Ruth couldn't talk of Aaron's nights, the cramping, his lips drawn on chattering teeth, how his legs flailed and his fingers picked at the sheet. The blanket pulled to his chin, sweat stood on his face, and in his sleep he cried for water in Matthew's voice.

Ruth had put a compress on his head and soothed him along with the others. Worrisome as they were, those nights she knew what to do, not like ones when he lay silent, eyes open yet seeming to see nothing, as if no vision kept him going. Ruth had to feed on her own vision.

Covering Ruth's secrecy, peepers by the water lent their steady conversation.

Sadie handed the spoon over to Esther and, returning, sat beside Ruth. She took Ruth's hand, held the roughened top to her cheek. Warmth flooded through Ruth.

"What a smile you have," Sadie said. "Just like Esther when she saw the scarf." Sadie gave Ruth a squeeze. "That very same smile."

Ruth's belly cramped. She didn't want to let go of Sadie's hand. The cramp grew tighter, low and insistent. She'd had worse. It would pass.

"Who'd have thought a scarf could make a child so happy," Sadie said. "I'm glad she didn't give it back."

"But Aaron, he—" The twinge turned spasm. Ruth jumped to her feet. "Sadie, I—" She rushed for the bushes.

"Take your time," Sadie called.

And this time she did.

❧

Midmorning, their third in the lay-by. The day grew balmy. All Ruth's men in the wagon, she knelt by the tub, her hands resting on the rim. She took a deep breath and plunged her arms into the water. Her head swam.

She wiped sweat on her sleeve, and from the corner of her eye she saw movement by the road. There came Hortence bustling into the lay-by, her collar shining, armband new and wide and black on her gray sleeve. The sight of her twisted Ruth's stomach worse than collywobbles. Ruth groaned.

"Mama, what's the matter?" Esther asked as she set down a half-full bucket of rinse water.

"Nothing." Ruth dried her hands on her apron, and waited.

Hortence advanced to a spot in the track where someone had apparently left a plate and crept away without a word. "Squash isn't good for fever," Hortence said loudly across the space between them, putting the plate in her basket. "These people have no mind. You need meat." She pulled out a small tub on the palm of her hand. "Stick to your ribs," she said. "Potted meat in goose fat, Mr. Johnston's favorite."

Ruth swallowed the rise of her gorge. Heat filled her and sweat grew on her upper lip. Her bowels tightened. She rose stiffly off her knees. "Hortence, you—"

"No need to thank me—Mr. Johnston did take a bite." She ran a finger over the top of the fat. "He does love his meat, and it's our last pot." She licked her finger.

"How kind." Ruth squeezed her knees and thighs together. She fought the wave weakening the hold on her bowels and her tongue. She couldn't lose control of either in front of Esther.

The bushes called from what seemed a growing distance. Moving her legs only from the knees down, she shuffled three little steps and stopped again, squeezing every muscle tight.

"Think nothing of it," Hortence said. Her chuckle had returned.

Ruth took two more little steps. Her voice pinched with effort, she said, "I'd hate to see your last meat wasted"—she took a breath—"on bellies too tender for gruel."

"Well!" Hortence sniffed and dropped the tub in her basket. "Some people don't know the Lord's charity when they see it." She straightened her shoulders. "But then you don't know the Lord as I do." She took out the squash, set it on the ground, and marched for the road. "Far be it from me to force you." She tossed her words to the air. "I wouldn't want to intrude."

Ruth bolted for the bushes.

Esther waved.

❧

That night, the fourth in the lay-by, an August stifle hung thick in the wagon though they hadn't reached the end of July. Outside, the dark hummed with emerging insects, bats in eager pursuit. Flitting, they arced over the white canvas and disappeared in the star-dotted sky.

Ruth leaned over the tailgate and breathed deeply. The air, like an elixir, helped thin the fog swathing her brain. Rest in the fresh air would do everyone good, lower the fever, clear their lungs of stench if not the plague of phlegm rattling the depths. "Come—out with you." She gave Matthew and Joseph a gentle tug on the arm.

Esther bounded from the wagon, her white nightdress flying. "Look—birds." She pointed into the night. "What are they doing?" No one mustered the strength to answer.

The boys burrowed deeper in their quilts and moaned.

"Up now," Ruth said. "You'll feel better."

Grumbling, Daniel led the way, and they slithered boneless over the frontboard. Once on the ground, they sank to their knees, arms limp at their sides, heads bowed, while Aaron and Ruth slowly smoothed mattresses where they fell. The boys fell on top.

"No hint of rain," Ruth said. "We'll stay the night."

❧

Dawn seeped gray through Ruth's dreams, and brought her full awake. She lay on her back, arms and legs heavy as logs on the ticking. Today they would refit, should any have the strength to ride into town. She had to get going; that's all there was to it. Once started, it wouldn't be so hard. She stayed where she was—another few minutes wouldn't hurt. The others, sprawled half off their mattresses, slept fitfully beside her.

By full light, her lazy eyelids barely ajar, Ruth smelled the coming rain. Her lids popped open. "Up now—quick, quick." She heaved herself upright. "Into the wagon."

Clouds crowded the sky and began to spit. Ruth and

Aaron threw the stuffed tickings into the wagon and urged the boys in after. How she hated steeping them in the wagon's odor. No matter how she washed their bodies and their bedding and the insides of the topboards, the smell clung the way the oak's brown leaves had clung before the felling, unwilling to give over their life.

Aaron seemed better, eyes clearer, his cough not such a rattle. Truly awake, he took off his nightshirt and wiped his face. He stretched.

Ruth had seen his sunken cheeks under the growing stubble above his beard, and still she wasn't prepared for ribs pressing his skin, the stringiness of his arms, the depth of the pit beneath. He tipped his head side to side and looked pleased. "Still works," he said. "Good thing I didn't die—I'd hate to meet God without a proper beard."

"Aaron!" came an excited call from the road, and Sadie rode in with more soup. "You're up."

"Don't tell my legs—they're still napping." Aaron hastily slipped a shirt over his head.

"He's better, thanks to your broth."

"I hear you're too good for charity." Sadie laughed. "Goose fat not to your liking?"

"She's rid of us," Aaron said. "Why plague us with goose fat?"

"Sometimes the loser wins."

Ruth frowned.

"She wanted a fight," Sadie said. "Without one, you stole her victory."

"Not my intention."

"Of course not. And when she tried again, you stole her

charity." Sadie rocked on her heels and laughed. "Made her so mad she threw the pot in the fire."

"I am sorry," Ruth said.

"There you go again."

"Not for Hortence, sad to say." Ruth twisted her mouth. "The waste of it, and I'm sorry for Preacher Johnston."

"You know, I'm going to miss you," Sadie said. "We cross day after tomorrow. But you'll catch us, now Aaron's better."

"With horses fresh, we'll make time." Aaron held out his palm. "And the rain stopped. This bodes well."

❧

Sadie's latest soup ran through them all except Aaron. Aaron not worse, not entirely better.

Ruth's lye soap used to a sliver, she settled for rinsing sick from the sheets and nightshirts. Now bloody, the stains remained.

That evening, Daniel sweated through his sheets. Ruth showed Esther how to wring out a cooling compress and hold it to his forehead.

"That's right. Now turn it over." Ruth wrung another cloth, and, crouching between Daniel and Joseph, she laid hers across Joseph's forehead.

"No." He writhed from under her hand. "I'm cold." He pulled at his blanket.

"If I had a scarf," Esther said, a resigned sigh escaping, "I could warm you." Her eyes wandered over the lumpy bedding, up the wagon bows, and settled on Ruth.

But Matthew's silence took her attention. Shades of Maus quailed her heart. She dipped her cloth in the bowl she shared with Esther and wrung it out. Ruth wiped down his face and chest. He didn't open his eyes.

Aaron brought her another half pail of water, set it close to where she sat, and laid himself next to Joseph.

"I'll warm you." Aaron wrapped his arms around Joseph and held his shivering body. "In Idaho our hearth will be wide enough to sleep on." Aaron readjusted his hold, his lips by Joseph's ear. "And the fire so deep we could roast a pig." He talked a good vision and she caught his eye. He reached over and gave her arm a gentle squeeze.

"No food, Papa. *Shhh*." Joseph waggled his head.

"What about candy?" said Esther. "You always want candy. Mama got a sugar string. For my birthday."

"That's right," Ruth said.

"Today?"

"No, five more." Aaron held up his hand, tapping the air with fingers and thumb. "Five more days. And you don't have to share."

"I don't want any," Joseph said. "I'm still cold."

Aaron wrapped him in a quilt Daniel had thrown off. "In Idaho, we'll make a tub so big, you'll sit to your neck in warm water."

"Big enough to swim?" Esther put her hand on Aaron's knee.

"Why not?" He covered her hand with his.

The wagon swam with dreams, Idaho in the heavy air like something fresh to breathe. The clop of horses' hooves sounded, in Ruth's mind like the herd they would have come Idaho.

"Hulloo," echoed into the lay-by. Ruth dragged herself to

the tailgate and saw Hugo as he rode across the clearing, his saddle horse dancing. He kissed his hand and blew in her direction. "I've brought bread and broth." He dismounted and untied a basket from behind his saddle. "Thought I'd lend a hand 'fore we make the crossing, though Sadie says you're better." He handed the bread to Aaron in the wagon and poured broth in the cauldron on the ground by the dead fire.

Ruth fell back on the mattress. "You're a godsend," she said, her whisper lost against the topboard, where she lay.

She heard him take the horses off picket and over to the creek where he filled buckets and replenished the water barrel. "I hobbled the horses," he shouted.

Why hadn't she thought of that? Why hadn't Aaron?

The leather cuffs at the fetlock with a chain between would leave them free to graze and go to the creek, but not so free as to run.

Ruth sank deeper into her bed, arms and legs heavy as water. The horses could fend for themselves. No worries about wandering. Jehu and Noah would keep the mares close in the clearing, oats an ever-present possibility they wouldn't forgo.

"See you on the other side," Hugo called.

"A day or two." Aaron, his words hearty, covering the distance.

Two days of rest, yes. She let her muscles unwind into the ticking. She could do this.

## CHAPTER 14

# Chickens Home to Roost

After another nightfall and another, the boys lay flat in the wagon, their blankets discarded. Ruth's fingers seared at the touch of Daniel's forehead. He coughed in spasms, the effort wringing him of further movement. As it was with Daniel, so with Matthew and Joseph, tongues brown. Brown and furry, their breathing shallow.

Matthew slipped into a deep sleep. Lying beside him, Ruth felt his chest. She didn't have to see the red circles—she could feel them. Aaron lay on Matthew's other side, checking as often as Ruth. Esther watched from the bench.

"Ma." Joseph could barely speak. He tried to lift an arm.

She reached a palm to his forehead. "He needs a compress."

"I'll do it." Aaron slid over.

Ruth sank in a wave of exhaustion. Night noises filled the wagon. She rested her head against a chest of drawers. She couldn't afford the comfort of pillows; she'd lose herself. And the boys . . .

She saw as if through the wrong end of a spyglass. In a sea of darkness, they lay in the belly of the wagon, ribs overhead, together at the center of a lantern-lit circle.

Concentrate. She fixed on the talk of peepers, the owl in the woods, a vole scuttling the grass, anything to tie herself to this world. But the sounds floated distant in her ear.

"Ma . . . Ma . . ."

Aaron was there. Aaron better, God be praised, back with the world on his shoulders. Her Aaron. He would lay the compress. She would rest, half an hour, she would rest.

She floated, head big as a pumpkin. Her ears rang. Jehu whinnied, then Noah. The mares answered.

Coyotes. Ruth should check.

She listened to her breath, the labor of its going out and its coming in. Her chest rose. Her chest fell. The effort a full day's labor.

She lay quiet under the weight of her own skin.

A dark beyond night settled. She let it wrap her, tender yet protective as a stone house, its inside soft with thistledown. No worry of coyotes. Noah alone would do more than Ruth against them. He could crush a skull with one blow of his hoof. For that matter, the mares could too. She heard them shuffling in the dark, and the mumble of voices.

Aaron seeing to them . . . again, as always, her fortress.

She sank into another world, hearing a buzz like distant bees talking honey, a crock-full she could scoop and drizzle on bread and scrapple. She heard her spoon hit the crock as if she couldn't find the opening.

She heard the clank of chains. Finally, after eight days in the lay-by, they must be under way, Aaron setting a fast pace, the clop of hooves, the ride unnaturally smooth. The clop softer, softer . . . They'd soon be there.

She let herself sink, the days passing in flashes, shattering bright to blessed dark. Cool water. Warm soup. The dark so full of peace, Aaron's loving murmurs in her ear.

⁓

Fear of the Rockies proved groundless. Their horses took the switchbacks easy as Pennsylvania foothills. The desert pushed their stamina, dear God seeing them through, ever there when things looked bleak. And Aaron, always Aaron, calming her fears.

They laughed through the snowcaps, tossing the white like spring petals, opening their mouths to the taste of the west. So delicious.

And on arrival, with summer finished, the grasses of fall were ready for scything. Asparagus fronds blew in a gentle breeze, no need to double dig the beds, the boys so happy, the promise of hundreds of stalks come spring. How could she have doubted Idaho, with apples the size of Maus's head? She surveyed their grasslands, the hundred sheep grazing; a stream, its banks strewn with rocks for their foundation. Oh, the fresh cool water, and fish for the catching. Woods, the lumber cut for the house, Aaron and Daniel and Joseph and Matthew setting the beams. They crawled the rafters, laying the roof, so like New Eden. Joseph snared rabbits. Ruth's heart overflowed, her eyes happy with tears, Maus clasped to her breast as she walked.

And there was Matthew—she heard him, his eagle cry; he must be soaring through the fields. But this was Esther's voice. "Mama?"

"Esther?"

So hard to rise from her nap. This marriage bed was not as she thought, still had the feel of baskets and bureaus beneath. A cup thrust at her mouth tipped, her fingers too thick to take hold. She frowned as water wicked into the quilt.

Oh, that desert thirst, recurrent and terrible. The remembered stench of sickness drowned the sweet smell of Idaho. Would it never leave her nose? She shouldn't nap; rest made her more tired.

"Mama," Esther said. "Mama, please."

Wet swamped Ruth's forehead. Open your eyes, she told herself. No, no, too bright. She heard a moan.

"Mama, you're awake!"

She felt small fingers pry one eyelid to a slit. There, inches before her, Esther's face loomed enormous in the candlelight. Beyond her, the wood ribs arched under the Conestoga's cover.

"This isn't Idaho," Ruth said.

She wanted to cry. She had weathered the mountains and the desert, smelled the land, built the house, and slept in their new bed. She'd known the joy of all she'd been promised, and now she had yet to cross the Mississippi. The mere idea of putting on her dress overwhelmed her. Tears seeped down her cheeks.

Dawn showed over the tailgate. Birds started their morning song. A warm morning, and in it, Ruth neither boiled nor shivered.

"Mama," Esther said. She sat beside Ruth, a string of rock candy in her little hand. "Can I eat it?"

"'May I?'" Ruth said, her words rote, her voice soft as if from some safe distance. She ran her hand over Esther's tangled hair, a wild child raised in the scrub, and possessed of skills that came from who knew where.

"Please." Esther folded her hands. "I saved it for today. My birthday. Papa said."

"Yes." Ruth rolled on her side and pushed up on one elbow. Her long braid flopped loose beside her. She shook her head, steadied herself, and took in the wagon end to end. She shook her head again and rubbed her eyes.

Dear God, another dream, this one of the worst order, clear as the dream of Idaho. She thought she'd been there, and this seemed equally real, though beyond the realm of what God could ordain. Three bundles. She slid her hand on the unclean sheet, rough on her rough skin. She touched her papery forehead, dragged her eyelids closed with her fingers and opened them again, the inside of the wagon unchanged with its three shroudings by the tailgate.

Esther pushed a square of material in front of Ruth's face. "I've been working, see." She held up a cloth square. "I finished Matthew's." Pleasure smiled across her face. "It's a surprise. I wish he'd wake up. He sleeps longest."

Ruth too wished he'd wake up. "He'll be so pleased," she said. Her eyes went to Matthew, the bundle closest to the wagon's sideboard. Shorter, rounder than the others, she knew him by his shape wound in a sheet, there lying next to Daniel in his quilt, Joseph beside him in his, the bodies laid with care, as if sacrificed to the Conestoga.

Her breath ratcheted in, and with it the scents of her babies, their once-boyish odors gone rank. She drew her knees to her chest, arms around her knees, and hung on, as if untethered she might abandon her body, leaving her in the wagon with no means to cope. A bad dream—what else would it be? She had to wake up.

Fresh air would help. She crawled toward the bench, blue sky harsh through the canvas opening. And there was Aaron stretched across the seat like a sleeping guard, the water dipper in his hand, his pants stained and stiff.

Ruth lost her breath. She couldn't swallow. Silence hummed in her ears.

Loud between her teeth, Esther crunched the crystalline sugar. "All gone," she said and held up the empty string. "Can we get more?"

Ruth held her head. "Not just now," she said.

She sat there.

She blinked, unable to move, unable to feel her fingers or legs, more hallmarks of nightmare.

Her jaw slack, she stared at nothing.

She clicked her teeth together, but her lips wouldn't meet, and she gaped.

"Mama?" Esther's voice dampened the tangle of cobwebs. "What are you doing?"

Ruth wobbled and brought her eyes to bear on Esther, gathered within herself, kissed the child, and moved her aside. Ruth crawled to the bench and sat next to Aaron. She touched his stiffening cheek.

"Oh, Aaron."

What last days did he suffer while she gamboled in the hills of Idaho?

"Papa said leave them be." Esther talked, and as best Ruth could, she assembled the time, a lifetime. Three days? The five Esther had said? Days of soup and water and sleep, and one by one their boys . . . first Matthew, and after a few days Daniel and Joseph. Esther left them be as Papa said, wrapped snug by the tailgate. Then Aaron's last night—it had to be but hours before she woke, Aaron's body not yet set in the way of death. He slept and wouldn't wake, though with the morning, his eyes looked sleepless upon the day. Oh, Esther.

True to fatherly duties, alone he'd washed each boy in turn. Ruth wept for Aaron's solitary vigil. She couldn't bear to linger on those hours as each child passed.

She touched Aaron's draped hand and the dipper dropped, hitting the ground with the clang of a small bell. Sun poured in the wagon as she straightened his limbs on the bench.

She snipped his pants up one leg and down the other, stripped the cloth, then the shirt, baring his gray skin. Flesh diminished, his delicious myrrh and aloes things of the past.

Now Ruth must wash him, alone as he washed their sons. Or did Esther help? Ruth couldn't ask and Esther didn't say. She sat on the sloped tongue and drew in the dirt with a stick. "Bad men," she said to Dolly, who sat on the ground, legs straight, leaning against the tongue.

Esther drew a circle and in it she made a turn-down mouth. "I hide," she said. "With Daniel." She pulled a pretend quilt over her head and peeked out at the doll. "Money." The word gruff and angry. Rocking forward, she poked Dolly with the stick, and in the same gruff voice, "Your horses."

Ruth climbed from the wagon. "Esther, did the bad men hurt you?"

Esther hoisted Dolly by the feet and stomped the drawing flat. "Dolly's dancing." At a three-legged crawl, she danced the doll's feet to another bare spot in the lay-by. They sat facing each other, both cross-legged. Esther held Dolly's stubby hands and swung them side to side with each word. "All gone, Papa said. They won't be back."

An eye on Esther, Ruth dipped water from the barrel into a bucket. Past Esther, the lay-by stretched empty to the tree and beyond. At the edge of the nibbled grass she could see mounds of chain and leather. The hobbles. Their importance ticked at her, but she couldn't take the meaning, her mind on Esther, on Aaron and the task at hand.

Kneeling beside Aaron, Ruth ran the cloth over each of his arms. Creases at his inner elbow held crystals of his last sweat. She smoothed his curled fingers, exposed his palm, the thick calluses, his broken lifeline. Was it always thus? How could she not remember? Hadn't she pored over his hands when they courted, tracing his nails, kissing each finger?

She started again with his feet. No time for remembrance; rigor would take him. His sulfurous feet, mile widened, the knife-pared nails, second toe longer than the first, the littlest snugged under the next, had been chafed raw.

She worked over his ankles to calves strung with starvation. His bent shins joined tendinous thighs, knees in sharp articulation. She washed with care the collapse of his manhood. Never again would she know the joy of him, or the children he had yet to father, the ones in need of more land.

Oh, God, how she'd loved him.

And trust? For so long, she couldn't.

But then she'd taken his vision as her own, and the two

seemed one, love and trust, two sides of the same knife, the knife now gutting her as she had gutted the eel.

Ruth worked from the valley of his belly to his laddered ribs. She pounded the anvil of his breastbone. "How could you?" She pounded with both fists. "How?" With all they had, how could he have wanted more?

Stop. She sat back on her heels. Stop now. Bend you to it, and don't flinch.

His face under her fingertips, she relearned his ridges and wrinkles, her forehead closer and closer to his. Her hands fell to her lap. She closed her eyes.

And beginning again, she plumbed his eye wells. Dried glue, left by his fever, crusted his lashes. The crust dissolved under her cloth, and she swept the lashes clean. Ruth rinsed and wrung the cloth. She took up his hand, brought it to her lips, and kissed his badger-bit finger before closing the others over it. With both hands she clasped his hand to her breast.

Once more without the cloth, she rinsed him, every bone and hollow caressed. Oh, those terrible hollows, how they caught and held the water.

Ruth blotted Aaron dry, his face and beard last. His beard so short, and Aaron about to meet God. Poor Aaron.

Ruth wedged the first of their wedding sheets beneath him. Her hair swung in the way. She knotted the braid behind her head, then wound the sheet over his legs, his body and chest. She stopped at his face and stroked his beard. He'd be so unhappy. She couldn't leave him mortified.

Ruth retrieved scissors from her sewing basket and returned to the bench. She spread her hand, measured from his chin to below his breastbone, and unknotted her braid. She measured the same length from the end of her braid. In a fist she held the mark, and with the other hand squeezed the scissors together over and over until she'd severed the hair.

"Mama." Esther crawled up the wagon tongue, her hands on the topboard. "What would God say?"

Ruth straightened the swath of hair and tucked one end under his beard. She smoothed the rest down to the white, white sheet and tucked it in. Esther watched.

As Ruth wrapped the shrouding over his chest, she paused for one last look. The burns on his face showed in patches slightly grayer than the rest of his skin. They'd healed well. She traced them and covered his face.

When Ruth wound the second sheet, Esther climbed over the topboard.

"Papa can have Dolly's quilt," she said. "But it's not finished."

"Papa would want you to have it," Ruth said.

"Dolly says he should, 'cause he gave . . ." Esther pressed a finger to her lips. Ruth thought she caught an instant of glee lighting the child's eyes as she climbed into the wagon.

Esther rummaged in the sewing basket and brought out the L of sewn-together squares. She passed the cloth to Ruth, squares with Dolly's outline, the fence posts, the house. "I think he needs it more," Esther said.

"I think you're right." Ruth folded the cloth. "This is Papa's Idaho."

The closest Aaron would ever come. Inside the final layer of sheet, Ruth placed the square over his heart, and with the last of the day's strength, she pulled him off the bench and into the wagon beside the boys. They would be company, and for them she was glad.

Their bodies at her back, she looked over the tongue to where it dug into the ground. The land west spread its promise before her in a burst of sun she couldn't feel. She saw only a vast emptiness, the ponderous wagon beneath her.

She'd let this happen. She'd overlooked his lapse in sense, her devotion like a stone bridge built rock by rock. She ignored the clatter of his tongue, for where would she have been without him, his smell of myrrh and aloes, his guiding hand at her back, the strength of his arms around her. And yet here she was without him.

In a fog of leftover fever, she wandered out to the field and picked up a strap from the mound of hobbles. The chain rattled up with it. She examined the leather, cut clean through, the horses freed of restraint. And where were they now? Facing what greater impediment? Oh, Lord.

Bad men, Esther had said. Haste in the stealing, they hadn't bothered to unbuckle the straps. She dropped the leather. She'd heard them in her dream, the voices, the diminishing clop of hooves, and all the while she thought herself on a smooth ride to Idaho.

Now with no horses and no money, even if she knew the route, how could she get herself and Esther and the wagon there? It was all she could do to drag herself back to the wagon and sit on the tongue, her forearms on her thighs, her hands hanging over her knees.

With Aaron gone, Ruth was a cow without a bell, a cow wandering in the night. She was cud worked through seven stomachs.

Dry eyed, she saw nothing, heard nothing, save Esther dimly as she emptied Aaron's rinse water.

❦

In the morning she bid her fingers rebraid her hair. They'd forgotten how. She dropped her hands at her sides. Without her prayer cap, her shortened braid had frayed thick as a foxtail.

She pulled boots over dirty stockings. Her black dress unchanged, she'd slept next to Esther. Esther had put on a white nightdress without being asked.

Ruth would as soon abandon her body completely, the way travelers before her abandoned their too heavy goods by the side of the trail, those things too treasured to leave behind, now too costly to keep. Her body too cumbersome for this world.

The one treasure she abandoned, so little and so light, and still she couldn't keep him. It tore at her, thinking of Maus alone and unfed.

But Esther, she must be starving. Ruth scrabbled the bottom of her basket of stores and found two half-consumed strips of dry meat, the sugar jar empty, dried peaches gone, the walnut meats too. Esther, now the capable one, the hungry one, where Ruth had no need of food.

While Esther drew in the dirt, Ruth mustered strength and cooked dried apples with the last of crushed oats. And there were graves to dig.

How, when scooping porridge sapped her?

"Mama, when will Papa and the boys wake?" Esther drew a picture of a house with a pitched roof and circles for stones.

"They've gone to live with God," Ruth said.

"No, Mama, they're in the wagon." Esther stood on the tongue and peered over the frontboard. "See?"

"They left their earthly bodies here, Esther. They have no need of them."

"And their heads, Mama?" She held her palms out, questioning. "Did He take their heads?"

"Oh, my sweet . . ." Ruth knelt before her and took Esther in her arms. How could she explain, life in death, death in life?

She couldn't grasp it herself. She couldn't grasp day advancing to night.

## CHAPTER 15

# *August—Waiting on Lazarus*

C ome morning, Ruth sat on the ground by the charred logs of a cold fire. She waited as if she might wake to an earlier life. *Christ, where are you?*

Esther crawled from under the wagon, where they had both spent the night. She pressed her face to Ruth's neck. "Tonight, let's sleep under the stars, Mama. My nose doesn't like the wagon." Ruth's gaze drifted to the sky.

Esther rooted in a basket Ruth had left by the wheel. "Here, Mama, a peach in with the apples." She held out the dried slice.

"I'll save it," Ruth said in a whisper. "For breakfast."

"Mama, this is breakfast."

Ruth smiled. She took a tiny bite. "Mmm," she said. Her

eyes wandered beyond Esther's shoulder. She chewed and chewed and held the morsel in her mouth.

"Swallow, Mama," Esther said, "or it's not breakfast."

Oh, hawk-eyed child. Now somehow older than Ruth, Esther knew the steps she should take come flood or come famine. That used to be Ruth, the one who insisted Aaron eat, those nights in the barn birthing colts. Aaron, his arm to the shoulder in a mare, turning a breech, so deep in the thrill of new life nothing else mattered. Or herself becoming the parent as her mother staved off death, and after, dressing her mother's body in white and sitting by the coffin.

Why had Appalachian men thought to squeeze three bodies in a coffin? And here, unprepared for death, Ruth had no coffin at all, unless you counted the Conestoga, Aaron there in his shroud with his boys. *Oh, please, Christ, won't you raise me a Lazarus?*

But she might wait millenniums on Christ. *Gird yourself.*

She lifted the shovel from among their tools. At the edge of the clearing she shoved the blade into the ground. She had dug such a pit before, taking roots of the oak. A week, it took then, at full strength.

For the third time she set her foot on the blade and could go no further. Fingers gripping the top of the shaft, she rested her head.

A shadow passed before the sun. She raised her eyes. Plain in black feathers, Matthew's languid birds waited to take on her task, should she fail.

Aaron, in his beloved Conestoga, had called them to the lay-by, to the wagon with its precious cargo, all fever tainted, their last fluids beyond the powers of lye soap.

In life nothing could stanch the spread. With death Ruth had to bury them. Seven days for such a hole, and she couldn't manage seven minutes.

Ruth let the shovel drop. Hands at her sides, she stood by the dent in the ground, her head heavy on her shoulders. The birds floated high above, patient under the afternoon sun, her slowness of mind no concern to them.

They knew their job, and she knew it too, how they'd fall from the sky and roost on the canvas, first one bird, then another and another. She couldn't let them.

She turned to the Conestoga, the wagon so small as they traveled west, now huge in the lay-by. What could she do? The sun blazed.

For a moment, she let her lids close. With a sigh, she picked up the shovel. Ruth dragged the blade on the ground as she walked back to the wagon. With cauterizing flame, she would send them on their way: Matthew flying among the birds, Joseph free to play and no heavy boot, Daniel ready to hold a hand should any be fearful, and Aaron ever westward with his boys, together in their Conestoga.

❧

"Little sticks, little sticks," Esther chanted as she gleaned the lay-by. Venturing only to the edge of the woods, she stacked her arms as best she could. She returned staggering under her load. "Where?" She puffed.

Ruth snipped the rank tickings and, on her knees, pushed straw under the wagon. "Here," she said. Esther dropped the kindling and jumped backward, her toes kept safe.

Ruth layered the small sticks in a crosshatch atop the straw the way Opa had taught her, then went to the woods for bigger branches.

"More?" Esther asked.

"Yes, more." Ruth moved to the other side of the wagon. "Here, beside me." Without thought of past or future, the job at hand all she could manage, Ruth filled the space from the ground past the axles to the bottom of the box. With the last sticks wedged under the oak boards, Ruth and Esther rested on their heels.

The wind rose, and Ruth's head swam with lingering fever. Night closed around them, and Ruth retrieved Dolly from the wagon, along with Esther's quilt, the only clean one, and a tin of matches. Esther tied Dolly's shawl tight at the neck and chewed the last strip of meat while she knotted her apron around slices of dried apple.

"It's time." Ruth rubbed her forehead.

Esther stood aside while Ruth kneeled to the straw and struck a red-tipped match. With a whiff of acrid smoke, the stick flared, and she watched the flame creep toward her fingers, the blackened wood twisting in the flame's wake.

It touched her finger and she shook the flame out. Peepers sang by the stream. A bat wheeled and disappeared.

Ruth struck a second match and, leaning to the task, lit the straw. The first few strands caught, and fire spread under the wagon. She lit three places on the wagon's far side and returned to Esther, where flames had engulfed the kindling and now crackled through the maze of branches.

Ruth moved Esther upwind with her quilt and Dolly to the far side of the lay-by. They sat close.

"Mama, will fire hurt them?" Esther said.

Ruth leaned against a tree. "Nothing can hurt them now."

Covered with her quilt, Esther curled against Ruth while the wind teased the fire till it roared. The green wood hissed, sap bubbling from the grain. The oak hadn't warped or checked, one worry that had come to naught after nearly a thousand miles. The wagon coming to naught, their faces shone in the heat.

Esther slid down with the hours. Her head on her mother's lap, she slept as flames cavorted around the oak planking. Wind-driven, the flames tagged the waxed canvas and leapt ecstatic through white skin.

In old Egypt, Aaron had told her, a wife laid herself on her husband's pyre, going with him to the next world. A better world, she could hear him say, not Idaho, a place you believe in. Yes, where she'd lie beside him, the two of them resting in peace. Temptation beckoned.

Ruth looked at Esther asleep in her lap, and the beckoning fingers wilted. No, she couldn't abandon Esther, and she wouldn't take her to the next world.

Ruth held vigil while flame gnawed the spokes and fellies. Charred brittle, the wheels collapsed with their axles and brakes, all crushed as first the tail end gave, then the front, the way a horse collapses before colic takes its life. The glittering mound of coals shifted and hummed through the night, sinking little by little, ending with the patter of falling ash.

❧

Dawn crept across the lay-by, banded pale pink and purple.

She must prepare.

Prepare for what? With what?

No answer. Even the birds stayed mute.

Ruth stared into the dawn. Like a burl on the tree, she would have stayed longer, but voices invaded the quiet. A group of English on foot, most likely farmers outside Moline, maybe thirteen strong, advanced like wary beasts, curiosity overcoming suspicion as they sidled toward the ashes.

What would they make of this capless woman in tattered black, hair wild across her face? And what of the mud-caked child beside her?

Esther sat up and stretched. Ruth stood, her legs stiff with damp. Dizzy, she braced herself, one hand on the tree, and averted her face from the strangers, though they lacked the vehemence of Hortence and her followers.

"Mama?" Esther whispered. Her hand slipped into Ruth's.

The colors of dawn faded to a clear blue ceiling. "We must go," Ruth said to Esther, and slung the quilt over her shoulder. Esther lifted Dolly from the ground and held her, one-handed to her chest, a piece of family she wouldn't relinquish. Ruth gripped the child's other hand, and one foot before the next she forged toward the crowd.

The English bent their heads one to another and shuffled their feet before a man stepped forward. "Can we . . . ?"

Ruth looked to the road beyond as if he didn't exist, and the crowd parted in some confusion. The women reached toward Ruth as she passed, concern on their faces. The men frowned and eyed the smoldering ash.

Like Moses parting the sea, Ruth marched on, moving forward always her instinct. Esther hurried beside her. She looked up. "Where, Mama, where will we go?"

Where indeed? Ruth didn't answer. Unlike Moses, she saw no destination, no direction.

Ruth had promised Aaron she'd make the trek. She'd chosen his way over her own, over the Fold, chosen him over the Ordnung's commandment. And now he'd abandoned her, cut her loose, as if to say: *Fine, you wanted to choose? The choice is yours.*

Now she could go home. But what home could New Eden be, with its heart in someone else's hands?

She could choose Idaho, follow Aaron's vision, the place she'd come to cherish. She'd lost much in the striving, so how could she not continue?

The man and his vision inseparable, in Idaho, she'd hold to Aaron. Though the way be long, he would light the dark land.

And dark land it would be with its endless grasses, no house, no barn, the fields devoid of her kind, devoid of Aaron. Could he light such a place, a place with no Daniel, no Joseph, no Matthew, no Maus, plowing and planting joy?

What choice? Her anger rose.

If Aaron were here, she'd pound his breastbone anew.

Even with sun above the trees, a dimness enveloped the road, the world as seen through a glass darkly. God forbid she saw it face-to-face. How could she look?

Ruth strode through the English, her mouth tight as if stitched with the strongest thread, for her thoughts, should they spill, would surely scald any who heard them.

She railed in the confines of her head. *Is that you, Satan, your hooves on my hair, your musk in my nose?*

Her stride lengthened.

*Is that your thigh with boils too close to count?* Spleen filled her like food, feeding her, as the sun passed overhead.

*Or is that You, God?* He who shunned His own children, their knowledge made sin.

Dry lips against her teeth, she hissed at the blue blue sky, her face hot.

*Tell me, am I Job?*

She pressed her palm to her forehead.

*Am I Job, that You hook me through the nose?*

*Job, and You boastful of my old devotions.*

Ruth pushed her sleeves above her elbows, her pace too fast for Esther's short legs.

*Are You so pride-filled before Satan that You toss the bones of my children in wager?*

She marched on, fever and fumes of rage blurring the distance.

*No more. No. I am not Your Job.*

❧

By dusk, clouds had snuck under her blue ceiling. The road passed through woods, further darkening the way. Ruth slowed in her own fog of resurgent fever, her head bent, the dirt track in front of her feet all she could see.

Subsisting on dried apples from her apron, Esther trudged beside her. She tugged at Ruth's sleeve. "Mama," she whispered. "English."

Ruth raised bleary eyes. A man and a woman carrying a basket approached. The woman came first, someone's oma, heavyset as the man, her hair soft and gray, dressed in flowered cloth. Where once Ruth might have cared, she hardly noticed now.

"Where are you bound?" the woman said.

Ruth made no answer.

"Moline's another two hours," the man said. His brown shirt had earth smeared on the front. He brushed it off. "Me and the wife been picking mushrooms."

Ruth moved out of their way.

"A blow's coming." The man looked up through the leaves. "Spitting already."

Ruth brushed past them.

"No. No, dear." The woman caught her sleeve. "You and the child, come with us." She nodded her head down the road. Ruth looked back. A lane she hadn't seen veered through the trees.

"If we hurry"—the woman gave a gentle tug—"we'll make it 'fore the rain wets us."

Esther tugged at Ruth's other hand, and Ruth let herself be guided down the long lane. Her legs increasingly weak, her mind had no will of its own.

"You'll stay the night, the both of you."

At dinner, Esther found her voice, small and chirpy. "We're going to Idaho. Papa said."

"Where is your papa?" the husband asked.

"He's in heaven with the boys." Esther looked up at Ruth. "Except Maus. He's by the road, isn't he, Mama?"

The woman put down her fork and exchanged glances with her husband. He stopped chewing.

Esther reached for a slice of bread from the board in the middle of the table.

"He has a cross to play with," Esther said. "Stuck in the ground just for him."

The couple went back to their meat in silence. Ruth slid hers around her plate while Esther sopped gravy till the plate shone as if she'd licked it.

After dinner, and a bath in a bucket on the porch, the woman handed Ruth and Esther each a folded garment. "Try these for now."

They drew the loaned nightshirts over their heads, the cloth worn soft. Ruth's shirt swam pleasantly. Esther's sleeves hung below her hands, the hem in a pool on the floor. She gathered the hem in her arms along with Dolly, rescued and wrung out from the wash bucket. "I do it myself," she'd said, her back to Ruth. The threat of help brought a stiff-armed resistance.

"This way." The woman herded them up creaky stairs to a spare bedroom. On a real bed, in a room with a door, snug under a roof, they lay between sheets smelling of sun. Esther sighed and closed her eyes.

Ruth lay rigid, afraid to sink into the ticking. She had to go on tomorrow. She couldn't yield to a weaker self; she might never regain her will.

The wind cried through the trees outside. Esther slept while Ruth listened.

No matter the wind before her, she must stand straight. Yes, that's what she always did, bulled ahead, relying on God to see her through, even when she railed at Him.

Outside limbs cracked and leaves whispered as a branch fell close to the house. Ruth had forgotten the lesson of trees: Give before the wind, lest in stiffness ye snap.

Though she be childbearer, cook, housekeeper, milker, horse trainer, sheep shearer, gardener, plowman, and field hand, she could not go on alone. She could not be a fold of one for Esther.

And if fever returned, as it had with Aaron? If Ruth succumbed, what of Esther then? Alone short of the Rockies. Alone in the desert, or among Indians of the Plains. Alone in Idaho. Chasing phantoms could destroy them.

That night, under the covers together, Esther stirred as another branch came down. She curled warm into Ruth and took her hand, holding it against Dolly, Dolly tight to her chest.

*My Esther, tether to this earth. You've suffered me gently, and I will take you home.*

She'd like to tell Esther, forever is over, but without Aaron and the boys, forever was just beginning.

## CHAPTER 16

## *Where Forever Began*

Gert gave her ink, pen, and paper. Ruth sat at the kitchen table and gripped the shaft with cold fingers.

*Dan'l,*
   *You are the only one I can*

How could a pen be this heavy?

*Aaron and his dream are*

She crushed the paper. No one told her a pen could be heavier than a shovel. Her eyes closed, she sat. She smoothed out the wrinkles and started again.

*Dearest Dan'l,*
  *All is lost. There are no words to*

She dipped the pen in the inkpot, held it over the paper, then back in the pot without writing. Her arms crossed on the table, she rested her head in the crook of an elbow.

A hand came to rest on Ruth's shoulder. Gert sat beside her and slid the paper away.

❧

Gert's letter took weeks to reach him, and weeks more for Dan'l to find Ruth. Those days unfolded as she and Esther remained in the tidy frame house with its covered front porch and red barn, Gert and Abe protective as parents.

Together, Plain and English melded. Gert and Ruth, at first nurse and patient, later baked together, their arms in flour to their wrists. Talk came slowly.

At dusk, the four of them often sat on the porch and watched Abe's neighbor scythe until dark. Some nights Abe went to bed early, his shoulders stooped.

The first time it happened, Gert said, "He thought the boys would stay." She blew her nose, the hankie stuffed back in her sleeve. "Chicago's a snare."

For a bit, they sat in silence.

"Them in their city duds, they come when the mood strikes, and acre by acre the farm slips away."

More silence.

"Thank heaven for Jordon." Gert nodded at the man scything. "He farms for a cut of the harvest."

❧

Ruth grew strength. She and Gert sat milking on stools, mornings and evenings, one cow to the next, Ruth's unease gone in the still of the old barn. She bathed in soft light flowing through small windows, the shafts filled with motes of dust she could see but couldn't feel.

Under Abe and Gert's gentle protection, Ruth spent her rage in silent work, mucking stalls, spreading manure. Unto herself, she slandered her unwanted Shepherd.

Gert, well versed in the ways of wounded animals, kept a respectful distance, touching Ruth lightly in passing, then moving on without the pressure of sorrowful looks.

At night, tucking Esther into bed, no matter how Ruth explained the absence of the boys and her Papa, Esther ended the conversation, saying, "It's long, Mama. When are they coming home?" She ground her fists into flooding eyes. "When?"

One night, after the tears had subsided, Ruth plumped Esther's pillow and straightened Dolly's bonnet. The candlelight caught a wisp of yellow at the doll's throat. Ruth gave a tug, and more yellow stretched from under the bonnet. "What's this?" Puzzled, Ruth's brows came together. "Why, it's—"

Esther stopped Ruth's hand. "Papa said, *Shhh*, it's a birthday secret. He said God would tell you. But you didn't see God."

"It's all right, Esther." Ruth tucked Sadie's scarf deep in Dolly's bonnet. "I won't say a word."

"A secret, just you and me and Papa?" said Esther.

Ruth kissed the worry from her forehead. "Yes, you and me and Papa." Another kind of unease held her. Lingering sickness, she thought, not herself yet. Her breasts still tender.

❧

Esther was herself and more. She dashed from the house wearing a dress bright as a garden. Bareheaded, she flitted barnyard to barn to the fields, her hand in Abe's when he had one free. Gert doted in the absence of her own grandchildren. Abe pretended not to, and Ruth could actually laugh at his feeble efforts.

Esther and Ruth's black clothes, tainted beyond repair, had been burnt. Gert altered one of her outgrown dresses for Esther, the cloth with tiny flowers. Esther beamed. A different set of faded flowers played across the dress refit for Ruth. Even washed pale, the pinks and blues pricked Ruth in places she couldn't scratch.

The fourth week, after evening milking, the chores done, Gert and Ruth walked the hedgerows in search of mislaid eggs. Ruth parted the long weeds. "Here's one," she said. A red hen scurried off her hidden nest and into the stubble of mown hay, leaving behind two eggs. Ruth put them in her basket.

A great squealing came from behind them. She and Gert stopped their search and watched Abe and Esther as they rushed hither-thither waving their arms at two young pigs escaping the barnyard. With a lot of noisy laughter and the help of Jordon, they scared the shoats through the open gate. Abe swung Esther onto the rail and, with her riding, pushed the gate closed. He leaned his arms where she sat. Their heads together, they laughed at the shoats scrambling for scraps from the noon dinner.

"Pigs," Ruth said to the air. "Matthew's favorite."

Without a word, Gert slipped her arm through Ruth's, and

for the first time Ruth's eyes welled. For long seconds she looked at the ground, then shook her head.

They turned for the house, walking arm in arm, their eyes straight ahead. A gentle breeze ruffled their hair, and the evening swelled with cicadas lamenting the coming end of summer.

Gert sighed. She tightened her grip on Ruth's arm as they climbed the porch. "The time will come." Gert opened the door. "And you *will* bear it."

Ruth squeezed Gert's hand and took the eggs to the larder. "What shall we make for supper?"

A few days later, her brother arrived.

Bread just out of the oven, she turned the loaves on their sides to cool, the English kitchen rich with yeasty sweetness and the bubble of stewed chicken. Wheels sounded outside. She wiped her hands on the apron covering her flowered dress. A horse nickered. Someone spoke, footfalls on the porch, and the front door blew open.

In came Dan'l, panting as if he'd run the whole way from Lancaster. He paused, door latch in hand, confusion on his face as his eyes seemed to search for the person he remembered.

"Oh, Ruth." He kissed her, hugged her long, then held her at arm's length.

She averted her eyes, not wanting to see the depth of his grief, or find her own reflected in his. His touch weakened her. His sorrow invited hers, a sea she dared not fall into. She would drown.

Again he put his arms around her. "My poor Ruth—you're so thin." He smoothed her cheek where it hollowed. "We'll get home and feed you. Come, get ready. Rebecca set a room aside."

Ruth's life planned for her, she should be grateful. Dan'l, her big brother to the rescue, nothing to worry her. Wasn't that why she'd written him, to take her home, put her in a buggy and take her where she belonged, the place she'd fought so hard to stay? Had she really thought he'd wipe away the last months, return her to her former life, make everything right again?

No, she'd let go of her senses, not wanting to see tomorrow as it would be, as it would have to be. Home wouldn't be home, not what it was. There would be no falling into the peace of her own bed, the last months banished, the world made whole by her brother's hand.

So tired when she tried to write, she'd wanted to drift back into the fog of sickness. She wanted to shirk the unshirkable, put it in someone else's hands, so much so Gert had to write the letter. But there were no other hands. She had to make decisions for Esther and herself. *Her* hand had to make the world whole, no one else, least of all her brother. It wasn't his life, but he'd feel responsible. He'd think he knew best. She'd made a mistake.

"Ruth?" he said.

She stiffened.

❧

As a boy, Dan'l had played the big brother, driving Ruth to stamp her foot. At five, she'd been at the creek with her tin of night crawlers, one worm wriggling in her fingers. After a moment's hesitation, her tongue peeking out of the corner of her mouth, she pierced the worm with her hook. Dan'l came running down the bank. "I'll do that." He took the worm, finished the skewering, then weighted the line and threw it in the water.

The first time, she thought him helpful. The second time, she said, "I can do it." The third, she said, with controlled tartness, "If you want to fish, get your own line." He'd looked so hurt, Ruth wanted to cry.

"I'll share my crawlers," she'd said.

She learned to appreciate his protection. One day at market when she was twelve, helping her mother arrange squash, corn, cucumbers, and tomatoes on their table, an English with ragged hair around his mouth latched eyes on her from across the square. He crooked a finger and called, "Here, puss puss." Dan'l yanked at her skirt and pulled her behind their buggy, his face redder than the stack of tomatoes.

"I didn't see a cat," she'd said. "Did you?"

"When you're older, I'll explain," Dan'l said and curled his lip. "English dog."

He made it his purpose, being close. After she'd married, Ruth missed him. And here he came again, his intentions nothing but good. Her rescuer.

❧

Now she couldn't lean into this comfort. Her breath hitched.

Esther flew in the door behind him, threw her arms around Dan'l's knees and Ruth's, near to knocking them down. "Onkel Dan'l, you came!"

"Of course," he said, and scooped her into a bear hug.

"You should see," she said. "English piggies."

Dan'l set her on the ground. She took his hand, stretching his arm toward the door. "Come."

"We've miles to the first way station," he said. "And pigs at home."

"May I have one?" Her face shining into his, Esther held to the hem of his black jacket.

"Yes, your very own," he said, and glanced at the door. "But we've got to leave."

"No," Ruth said, more abrupt than she'd intended. "Not yet." She turned to the fire and stirred the stew, the spoon shaking in her hand. "Dinner's about ready, and Gert and Abe would want to meet you."

The concern in his face increased. "I met them outside."

"No." Ruth rested a hand on his arm. "More than that. And surely the horses need rest."

Later, at table, Dan'l eyed his plate. "You cooked this, Ruth?"

When she said yes, he dug in with his fork, relief so obvious, Ruth flushed.

"How was your trip?" Gert asked.

"Fine." Dan'l focused on opening a biscuit. He buttered the steaming center in silence.

"Good-looking horses you got there," Abe tried.

"Mmm." And the conversation limped painfully on through dessert.

"You best gather your things," Dan'l said around the last bite of pecan pie. Pushing back his chair, he laid his napkin on the table. "I'll help."

"Won't you spend the night?" Gert, ever thoughtful. "Get an early start tomorrow."

"We couldn't," he said with a graceless smile.

They headed upstairs, Esther at their heels.

"Come, Esther," Gert called. "You can help with the dishes." Esther retreated to the kitchen.

Ruth stood in the middle of the bedroom she and Esther shared. Everything belonged to Gert, one big and one small flowered dress and two nightshirts on a hook by the door, a hairbrush on the dresser. Their only possession lay relaxed on the bed: Dolly, her head propped on the pillow, faceless and silent.

"They *seemed* nice enough," Dan'l said. His nostrils twitched.

Ruth came back at him. "You can't imagine."

"Sweet Ruth." His words low and cajoling. "You've been here too long." He stepped close beside her, latched his arm through hers, and with the other hand brushed a straying lock of her hair. "I'll take care of you." He patted her hand. Around him hung the scent of clothes too long in a trunk.

She could see it all, her life unfolding before her—

The trip home would pass in flashes of sun and windblown rain unable to breach the hard top of Dan'l's black buggy. Esther would chatter at Dan'l. He'd indulge her. He'd indulge them both.

A flutter of wings beat inside her. She couldn't tell which, birds or bats or butterflies. She only knew they rose from her belly and beat under her breastbone.

She knew she'd come to dread Dan'l's soft glance, his guiding touch on her sleeve. Yes, she loved him, but he would unravel her, pry at the walls she'd shored up so carefully.

In her silence, he would watch her from the corner of his eye, his concern brutal as fists. The generosity of strangers easier to endure. She'd want to ease his grief, but wouldn't be able to, not while staying composed herself.

The three of them would descend into Lancaster Valley. Craning at the windows, she and Esther would watch lines of white fence rolling with the land, the white barns and field-stone houses just like Dolly's quilt. And she'd see again Aaron's final layer of shrouding, the unfinished vision of Idaho folded in.

They'd be home, but not home as she'd known it. In Dan'l's house, there'd be the cold room where she'd sleep, Esther in with her cousins, Ruth's days spent helping Rebecca in the kitchen, evenings staying out of the way, hoping to keep her brother's life as it had been.

She didn't want to be an extra woman in his house, every day in every way a reminder of what Ruth no longer had.

She'd be a millstone, in the Fold or out, no standing, no money. Horst would say she was blessed to have a brother to burden, and she was. That blessing, its own kind of burden.

But she would have Delia, the best of all blessings, if Horst let her visit. Maybe others, all shifting their feet, their faces set in pity-filled welcome. She'd need a shield against the glare of that pity.

Where once English sparked a deep-seated fear, now it seemed the Plain made Ruth rub her hands in sweaty distress. She touched her uncovered braids wound at the nape of her neck, ran her hand down the flowered dress.

Dan'l smiled. "Don't worry." He patted her again. "At home all will be well. God understands."

"Does He?" Would Dan'l be like Hortence, faith burning in fierce devotion?

Hortence still burrowed under Ruth's skin, and yet Ruth envied her, envied how in the face of her son's death Hortence could believe without question.

Would Dan'l push faith under her nails, push it up her nose as Hortence had? Her tender membranes still rankled.

"Ruth." He shook her shoulder. "Come, now—why aren't you packing?"

He would run her life, expect her to obey as she'd obeyed Aaron. Questions squashed.

"I don't know." Her eyes met his. "I need time."

He shook her elbow. "You needn't worry. God has a plan."

"Plan?" she whispered. "Did He plan on taking my littles?"

"Now, Ruth." Dan'l grasped her forearms, his face stern. "This is grief talking."

She yanked free. "Was He punishing Aaron? Did the rest of us just fall in His way?" She couldn't believe in a God so careless.

"Please, Ruth. You don't know what you're saying." She turned from him, but he held her shoulders. "Come home now. I know it's hard, but Horst will help—everyone will."

Yes, everyone would help her into a black dress, cover her hair with a prayer cap, shroud her head in a bonnet, the brim like blinders narrowing her vision.

"Did you know Horst wanted us shunned?" She brushed at her twisted sleeves, her voice growing louder. "Aaron looked ahead. He thought for himself. Was that so wrong?"

"Hush, now. You can't think this way."

"You said my thoughts were important to you. You gave me a book to write them down, and now you won't listen."

"That's not true— this simply isn't the time."

"If not now, when?"

Dan'l took her in his arms, her body a bundle of sticks. Unyielding, her mouth set, she let him hold her.

"I shouldn't have written," she said and backed from his embrace. "I'm not your little sister, not the Ruth—"

"You are." He reached for her hands. "You're *my* Ruth."

"No, Dan'l." She crossed her arms, her voice soft. "I'm my Ruth."

"English have done this," he said, locking his fingers. "A few months at home and you'll feel better."

"Oh, Dan'l, if only it were that simple." She touched his fingers, but wouldn't take hold. "I wish it were, but it's not."

❧

"She's too tired to travel," Dan'l said to Esther the next morning at breakfast. "You and I can go home. Won't that be fun? Your mother will follow."

Ruth's bowed head jerked up. "No." She stared at Dan'l. "That's not what we agreed."

"It's best. You're in no condition—"

"I'll stay here with the piggies," Esther said. "They're in no condition."

Gert reached across the corner of the table and took Ruth's hand. "We all agreed Delia could come and stay if Horst would bring her."

Ruth knew Dan'l's mind. Delia would be protection against English. In the process, she'd persuade Ruth to the true path.

Ruth didn't care. The thought of seeing Delia gladdened her heart.

Spring 1869

Delia arrived at the end of harvest. Mouse quiet, she came in the barn and found Ruth with Esther feeding the pigs.

"Ruth!" Delia squeaked with excitement and swooped in, bonnet flying. "Ruth, Ruth!"

They swayed forth and forth hugging, stopped, looked at each other, and clasped together again. Delia soft and comforting.

Esther hopped up and down beside them. "Tante, Tante Delia."

When the two stopped hugging, Ruth asked, "Where's Horst?"

With both hands, Delia shooed away the question like so many chickens.

"But how?" Esther chirped.

"Sheer determination." Delia lifted Esther and hugged them both at once. Ruth flinched as Esther's knee dug into her tender breast.

"Nothing could keep me from you and your mama. Not now."

The same wonderful Delia, as if no time had gone by. As if their lives had not altered beyond recognition.

"You won't try dragging me off tomorrow?" Ruth laughed with only a trace of uneasiness.

"We won't be going anywhere. The stage coach hit snow in the mountains, so, no, I won't leave till well after planting."

"What will Horst say?"

Delia rolled her eyes toward heaven and turned to Esther. "So show me my room."

Esther flew her into the house, giving a quick hello to Gert and Abe as they prepared supper. Ruth followed, and they exchanged amused smiles.

Upstairs and into the room next to hers, Esther helped Delia unpack the satchel someone had placed next to the bed. They hung black clothes on pegs lined on the wall.

"We had to burn ours," Esther said.

"Why?" Delia asked.

"Fever." Ruth answered for Esther.

"And what do you think of your new ones?" Delia opened the folds of Esther's skirts.

With glee, Esther twirled, showing all the flowers. Her smile grew hesitant, her eyes earnest on Delia's. "Mama says God won't be mad. What do you think, Tante?"

"I think He has bigger fish to fry."

Ruth squeezed Delia's hand.

❧

After supper Ruth and Delia sat by the fire. Chairs together, their shoulders touching, Ruth unfolded the barest fragments of the journey. Knowing Delia, she'd drag out details piece by piece through the winter.

"In your own good time," Delia said, and nudged Ruth. Again she flinched.

"I didn't mean to—"

"No, that's not it." With all the hard news, why was it difficult to tell the good? "My tender breasts, leftovers from fever, or so I thought."

Delia lifted one eyebrow. "Oh?"

"I haven't told anyone, but I think Gert has guessed. Something in the way she offers me milk." Ruth's cheeks pinked. "I wish Aaron had known."

❧

Delia settled in the way she'd settled at Horst's after his wife died. In Gert's garden, they all worked together harvesting, then stewing, pickling, and sealing their winter sustenance in jars bound for the cellar.

"We have a full house again," Gert said one evening as they sat for supper. "And a little one to come." She had tears in her eyes.

"A blessing," Abe agreed, and all five of them bowed their heads. The blessings were many, and Ruth was grateful, a family life she hadn't anticipated. A solace she didn't want to disturb with what boiled below her dry-eyed calm.

By late November, the garden beds mulched and covered for winter, sheep in from distant pastures, Ruth wandered far from the house. Her only time to be alone.

Gert was right. She would come to bear her grief. Holding it off only deepened the rage and did no good for anyone. And thus the time came.

Deep in the forest of cold-bitten trees, she took stock of their naked state. She shivered with them, glad Esther stayed warm in the house. The trees freed her to tip back her head, open her mouth, and feel the burn of pent-up tears.

❧

Through the winter, as Ruth knew would happen, Delia pulled the story from her. It came out like a long white tapeworm pulled from the nose of a dwindling calf. Delia wouldn't let it crawl back in, and with the advent of buds on the trees, Ruth came to the semblance of a self she barely knew. No more trembling in the wind.

In their midst, dressed in black, Delia served as a reminder of decisions to come. They talked of New Eden. Of Horst. Of Dan'l. Of return.

"But how?" Ruth said. "I couldn't sit in church with my hands folded in my lap. I couldn't listen to Horst enforcing our old fears." She leaned forward in her chair. "He doesn't know English, not like you and I know Gert and Abe. Does Horst even know God?"

"He knows his own mind and the ways that kept us for generations," Delia said. "He believes fervently. I can say that much."

"Dan'l too. But he expects the obedient person I was. That person died on the fire."

❧

*March 1869*

*Dearest Dan'l,*

*You are more than generous asking me into your home to live with you in the comfort of your beliefs. I know you would protect me and support me. You would lead me where you think I ought to go. But I am not a horse to be led.*

*I truly wish I could accept but in the end you would resent thoughts I couldn't wash from my face and I would resent the curbing you would deem necessary. For these reasons Esther and I will not be returning with Delia come spring.*

*I will miss the surety and peace of the Fold. I will miss your loving approval and hope you can understand I love you still. May you forgive me and let me live in your heart though not in your house.*

*Your loving and regretful sister,*
*Ruth*

❧

As spring advanced, a letter came from Horst.

Delia folded the paper. "I can't go now," she said. "Not till after the baby. Horst can dust his own lintels."

Trees on the farm blushed green, and Jordon came to build lambing pens. Abe couldn't bear to let the sheep go. He turned them over to Jordon along with the fields.

The man worked beside Esther, Ruth, and Delia turning the garden. He came in the house and oversaw the seedlings started on the windowsills—tomatoes, peppers, broccoli.

Ruth took no notice until early one Saturday he stopped his cart in the dooryard, untucked long legs, and hopped down. He took off his hat and tipped his smooth face to the sun. Clean clothes and combed hair set this day apart from others.

The house door slammed and Esther ran out. When he spied her, the quiet lines around his mouth broke to a wide smile. "Hellooo, Chickie Pie." He knelt and gave her a quick squeeze before she pulled him toward the barn.

"Piglet's in the pen," she said. Piglet, her very own sow. Abe promised after Dan'l had left. Big to begin with, now the pig weighed six times as much as Esther, the massive pink head at the level of her chest.

Jordon nodded hello to Ruth on her way to dump a bucket of slops. He took the brim of his hat in his teeth and swung Esther up to his shoulders. She gave a shriek from her high perch and looked down at Ruth.

"I'm bigger than you," she crowed.

He removed the hat from his mouth, smoothed his hair, and said, "I told her we'd give Piglet a bath before the show in Moline."

At the pigpen, Ruth dumped her bucket. Jordon lowered Esther to the ground and admired her sow with grave sincerity, then gathered a pail, water, and brush. Together they scrubbed the pig's massive back, cleaned her ears, and oiled the spread of her cloven hooves. Esther and Jordon's serious talk of animal habits, their care and feeding, floated after Ruth as she continued to the barn.

Later that evening, Delia said, "He has a way with Esther."

"Yes, she's taken to him." Ruth's voice drifted as if talking to herself. "If he had a beard, he'd look like Aaron."

Delia guided Ruth away from the others. "And what about you?" Not a hint of her usual playfulness.

"What about me?" said Ruth.

Delia didn't lift an eyebrow. "You and . . . ?"

Ruth shook her head. "He's Esther's friend."

&

Ruth's feelings for Jordon came with unexpected joy and startling pain. Straight shouldered, he walked with her slowly in the budding hedgerows. She wanted him to slip his hand in hers, and when he did, the absence of a stunted finger against her palm tore her heart.

She pulled her hand from his and sewed herself closed with bristling stitches. The threat of tears made her turn from his attentions.

All the while he worked beside her, pressing her with questions. And when she couldn't answer, he continued as if she had. One by one, he tried to snip her bristles, even showing off his farm to Esther. A visit just down the road, with Ruth and Delia along for the ride.

They drove in the curved lane through a swale of greening fields. The four of them walked from the dooryard around the orchard, through the well-tended barn, and out to the garden. He showed them where the tomatoes would go, the lettuce, squash, beets, and carrots.

Esther crinkled her brow. "Where's Frau Jordon?" she asked. She looked toward the clapboard house.

"I have no wife," he said. "She's in heaven."

"Like Papa and the boys?" Esther took his hand, her eyes on his. "Are your littles there too?"

"We weren't blessed with children." He picked her up. Her legs circled his waist, and he plucked a piece of hay from her hair.

"You'll need help with your garden." She touched a finger to the tip of his nose. "You need . . ."

Delia drew a long breath and wandered toward the barn. Ruth followed. She took her hand, wishing Delia didn't have to endure the conversation.

"Where could I find such a person?" she heard Jordon say as he jiggled Esther onto his hip.

"I wonder." Esther hummed. "Maybe Mama knows."

Delia and Ruth in great concentration watched a swallow build its nest on the beam of the barn's open shed.

Late April, and the baby came as if it couldn't wait to see the light of day. Ruth, with none of the fear on the trail, held Delia's hand through the pains. At the end, Delia had only to catch the infant as he dropped.

Free and kicking, the boy lay on Ruth's belly. Tears slid down her cheeks, while Delia sat on the bedside, her face suffused with light and a streak of worry. "Aren't you happy?" she said.

Ruth smoothed a line on Delia's forehead. "More than I can say." And Ruth was, but she couldn't bring the words, how this precious child carried the visage of Daniel, his dark hair, and Matthew's down-covered body. This beautiful new boy had Joseph's long toes, and when she put him to her breast he suckled eager as Maus, a blister rising on his lip. Ruth brushed at her tears.

"You're missing them," Delia said. Of course, she would know without words.

She knew Ruth's silences. She knew the dark places pulling at her. Ruth had told her how her littles called in the night, how she would reach for them, and for Aaron, the wagon bearing them into an ever-diminishing distance.

From the bedroom window, she took in Abe's red barn, the fields Jordon planted, one sprouting corn, acres of hay, the fenced horses, cows, pigs, sheep, and Jordon with the plow in a patch of newly turned earth.

He'd offered to be a loving father to the baby and Esther, no less than Aaron, and he promised he'd be their fortress. Did Ruth want a fortress? The safety had an appeal. But the confinement?

The thought sat like a weight on her chest.

The baby cried, and a soft knock came at the bedroom door. The latch clacked and Esther poked in her head. "May I see?"

Ruth waved *Come*, and Esther sat on the bed next to Delia.

"Tante," she said. "He has a tail like Maus." She traced a circle on the baby's belly.

"You had one too," Delia said. "I remember when you were small." She tickled Esther's belly. Esther snuggled under her arm and looked into her wistful face. "Does this mean you have to leave?"

The question, so easily asked by Esther, had been on Ruth's mind. The answer fraught with prickly questions.

Delia glanced at Ruth. The moment stretched, before Delia's eyes went to the window. That moment filled with hope and love and want, all built from a lifetime of mutual devotion.

"Maybe not," Ruth said. "We'll have to see."

❧

Weeks later, a letter arrived from Dan'l. Ruth retreated to her bedroom, closed the door, and sat on the bed. Her fingers trembled as she lifted the flap. She unfolded the paper, her mouth dry.

> *June*
>
> *Ruth—*
>
> *I write at great risk for Horst has declared you shunned.*

Ruth covered her mouth with her hand and closed her eyes. Of course he had. What had she expected? She'd given Horst no choice.

> *You must know I am beside myself to think you will not return. But yes you are in my heart always a knot I cannot untie.*

Her eyes stung. A stain spread on the page. She hadn't wanted to hurt him.

> *I pray you will reconsider. At least think of Delia. It seems the English infect her too.*

English? Or Ruth herself? Was this fair to Delia?

*Please keep in mind if you truly repent Horst will lift*
*the shun on both of you and our lives will unfold in grace.*
   *My prayers are with you*
   *Daniel*

The infant grew robust, his head sturdy on his neck, and one afternoon after the midday meal, Ruth laid him swaddled in his cradle on the porch. Gert and Abe watched, unable to stop their doting smiles, while Esther and Delia made the most of a warming sun. Ruth joined them tending to the garden's pervasive nettles, rampant after a few days left on their own.

A wren sang its long song from a peaked house nailed to the porch. From the barn a striped cat ambled among them, winding between their legs and purring. Esther patted the smooth fur from head to the tip of its raised tail before setting to with the weeds.

Delia followed suit and, squatting, ran her hands into the midst of the nettles. "Ach." She flailed. "They sting."

"In your mouth," Ruth said. "Spittle, quick."

She gathered her skirts and bent beside Delia. "Better?"

Delia nodded. Around a mouthful of fingers, she said, "What are they?"

"You've never pulled nettles?" Ruth parted the weeds with her flowered sleeve and worked her way to the base of a stalk.

"Esther, you watch too." Grasping carefully, she pulled along the knap of the needle-like hairs and the roots came up.

Stalk after stalk, with Delia and Esther's help, Ruth cleared the patch, exposing a group of self-seeding carrots. The sprigs, feathery and defiant, poked green through the fresh, dark earth.

# An
# Unseemly
# Wife

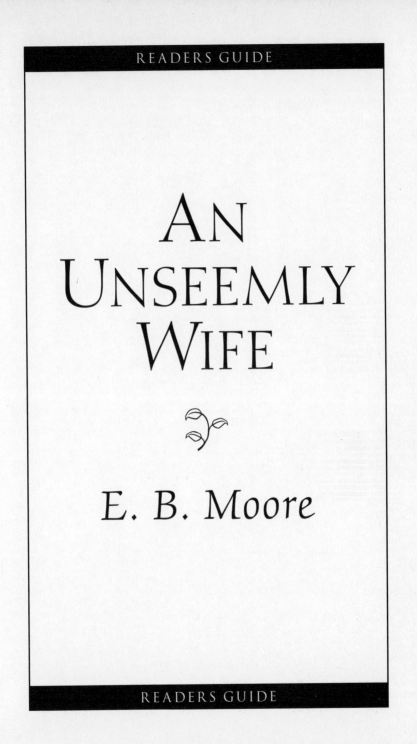

# E. B. Moore

# A CONVERSATION
# WITH E. B. MOORE

Q. *How did you come up with the idea for* An Unseemly Wife?

A. My mother set a fire under me. She reveled in her family's Plain roots and never tired of touting the strength it took for her mother and grandmother to survive their aborted trip west, the foundation of *An Unseemly Wife*. She even had a scale model of their Conestoga wagon in the living room. If a brain tumor hadn't taken her memory, she might have written the book herself, but somehow her interest never faded. Every day she'd look at the Conestoga model and say, "Tell the wagon." I would, and every day my kids would groan, "Oh, please, not the wagon of death again." For me, this brought home how easily family stories get lost, and I had to be sure this one didn't, if only for my own kids.

Q. *What kind of research did you have to do?*

A. I went beyond rummaging the Internet. I read journals of women pioneers, histories of the Amish, and followed pieces of Ruth's route. A friend and I started in Lancaster, Pennsylvania, and ate our way across the county, with me (not my friend) delighted to imbibe pickled meats, headcheese, and scrapple. We both liked every kind of pie from whoopie to shoofly, all those specialties a part of my childhood I now crave and rarely eat.

*Q. Ruth is a complicated character living a life far different from your own. Did you find her hard to write?*

A. Ruth's life in New Eden resembled my early years farming in Pennsylvania, though I grew up Quaker, not Amish. I loved being transported back to a stone house, barns, and fields, and could imagine what she might be feeling as her husband forced her to leave. Getting into her skin for the rest of the trip proved a more daunting process. Some days, looking up after hours of work, I'd be amazed and grateful to find myself in Cambridge, where I cooked on a gas stove, slept in a bed, and could hold my children close.

*Q. What do you hope readers take away from this book?*

A. I hope they can submerge themselves in Ruth's life enough to feel her love and the conflict it generated, and know what it's like to judge and be judged for the slimmest of reasons.

Q. *Who are your favorite authors and did any one of them influence you in writing this book?*

A. Everything I read influences me. However, my favorites, the ones I read and reread, whole and in part, are Geraldine Brooks, *March*; Michelle Hoover, *The Quickening*; Marilynne Robinson, *Housekeeping* and *Gilead*; Wallace Stegner, *Angle of Repose*; and John Steinbeck, *The Grapes of Wrath*.

Q. *What do you like best about being a writer?*

A. Writing is a constantly unfolding puzzle as wide as the Great Plains, yet it fits into snippets between subway transfers and shortens the wait in a doctor's office. It has given me a supportive community of friends and colleagues I treasure, and fills my insomnia with accomplishment even if I delete most of it the next day. Also, it's a godsend for my neighbors—no more interminable hours of hammering sheet bronze to satisfy my need to create. And that's what writing is: a need.

Q. *Do you have a set writing routine?*

A. Early morning works best for my writing. Luckily I wake up around five a.m., giving me a good stretch of time before lunch. Of course, that is when contractors like to arrive (the other part of my working life), and it's the least crowded time for grocery shopping, so it takes effort to guard those hours.

Q. *What's the best piece of advice you've ever gotten about writing?*

A. It's a muscle: use it or lose it. That means every day, if only for five minutes.

Q. *Are you working on a new novel?*

A. Yes, my second novel is loosely based on my grandfather's life. The story follows Joshua, an Amish boy who, during a fire, escapes from his secretly abusive father. Alone and burned, he struggles to find his way in the outside world, among the dreaded English. Meanwhile his mother, Miriam, mourns his presumed death and cobbles together a life hollowed by his absence. She works to maintain the rhythms of their Plain farm and to understand her husband's reticence about the facts of the fire. Determined, she extracts his secrets sliver by sliver until the day a grown-up Joshua reappears at their door and tests the foundation of all the family holds dear.

# QUESTIONS
# FOR DISCUSSION

1. In what ways is Ruth an "unseemly wife"? Do you think her answers would be the same as yours or different?

2. What were your first impressions of Ruth and Aaron? Were they positive or negative? Did they change over time?

3. Although Aaron's actions ultimately lead to tragedy, do you think he was justified or unjustified in his determination to go west?

4. Ruth, Sadie, and Hortence represent three very different backgrounds and competing notions of right and wrong. Is one of them the most "wrong" or most "right," or do all have equally valid reasons for how they behave?

5. Do Ruth and Aaron have a good marriage? How would you compare their relationship to marriages you're familiar with today?

6. Have you ever gone along with something for the sake of a relationship? Was it for the best or was it a mistake?

7. In many ways, the settling of the frontier changed the United States from a society based on community to a society based on the nuclear family. What have been some of the consequences of this change?

8. How does the author use animals to clarify the attitudes of people who care for them?

9. How does Ruth's relationship with God change over time? Is it a loss or a gain?

10. What do you think Ruth does next, after the book comes to a close?

**E. B. Moore** grew up in New Hope, Pennsylvania, living in a fieldstone house on a Noah's ark farm, the red barn stabling many animals two by two, along with a herd of Cheviot sheep. After a career as a metal sculptor, she returned to an early interest in writing poetry. Her chapbook of poems, *New Eden, A Legacy* (Finishing Line Press, 2009), was the foundation for her novel, *An Unseemly Wife*, both based on family stories from her Amish roots in Lancaster. Ms. Moore received full fellowships to the Vermont Studio Center and Yaddo. She is the mother of three and the grandmother of five, and she lives in Cambridge, Massachusetts.